Throw Me A Bone

Jenni Bradley

ISBN:0996683828
ISBN-13:9780996683821

DEDICATION

For my incredible brother, who drives me absolutely crazy and is a royal pain in my butt. I couldn't have handpicked a better brother. Thank you for always having my back. Most importantly, for not letting me take life too seriously!

CONTENTS

ACKNOWLEDGMENTS

Thank you to all of my family and friends who continuously encourage me to do what I love. A huge thank-you to all of my beta readers: my mom, Kim H., Kelly W., Jenn M., Erin F., Liz L., Chad W., Iris S., Bill S., and Melissa L. A special thank-you to Kim H., for making sure I take the time to keep writing. This book wouldn't be as entertaining without all of your input. Thank you to my editor, Faith Williams, for making this book a smoother read. Thank you to the Killion Group for formatting, designing the cover, and helping to publish it properly.

I'd like to thank all of my readers for taking the time to read, send me feedback, and post reviews. Without you, they are just words on a page. Thank you very much for being an essential part of my journey.

CHAPTER 1

I carefully avoided all of the city grates that were strategically placed in my path. Stepping on one would certainly lead to my untimely death. *Who really wants to die that way?* It would be totally embarrassing, especially when it could be avoided. Hell, I was wearing a skirt. Can you imagine if, at the end of my fall, my skirt ended up above my waist, exposing my granny underwear? I wasn't even wearing my sexy panties. To be honest, I never wore them. No reason to—not even a prospect on the horizon. Luck seemed to avoid me at all costs. As I was about to step around the grate, a weasel of a man plowed into my side. My balance isn't that great on the best of days, so you can imagine what happened next.

To my utter dismay, I squealed as the heel of my favorite Manolo pump hit the grate. My momentum did not stop upon impact. Oh no, my body decided that it did not need that particular appendage. Instead, it continued its forward motion. I was pretty attached to my foot, as is anyone. Not wanting to be left behind, my foot decided to thwart my body's attempt to leave it and yanked me viciously backward.

I fumbled around like a beached whale, trying to persuade my heel to detach itself from its imprisonment. *Why I didn't just remove my foot from the pump is beyond my intellect.* In my defense, I was a frog's hair away from requiring a straitjacket and a padded room. My body lounged on the entire grate, which could possibly buckle at any moment, and my hand entangled itself in someone's previously chewed piece of gum. My OCD kicked in high gear and then as quickly switched into overdrive.

Fortunately for me, masculine hands reached down, grabbed underneath my armpits, and yanked me to safety. Unfortunately, in the rescue attempt the heel of my pump broke free from the rest of the shoe. It tumbled into the dark abyss, never to be seen again. A lone tear ran down my cheek as I said a silent prayer to the shoe gods. They would take care of my beloved pump. I vowed to never ever walk that close to a grate again.

I had forgotten that I still clung to my hero while I performed the short eulogy. He used his fingers to try to dislodge my imbedded fingernails from his arms. Realizing that I was making a fool of myself, I quickly disengaged my talons.

"Thank you for saving my life. I am really sorry about digging my nails into your arms. That was pretty rude of me," I regurgitated as I looked up at my hero.

"My pleasure. I am glad that you are okay." He coughed, trying to disguise his amusement.

And yet I continued to grope around like a moron, trying to right my disheveled clothing. "Would you like to get some coffee, on me?" I looked up, horrified. *I can't believe that had just come out of my mouth.* It was a fine time to lose all of that college education. His eyes twinkled and the skin around them creased as he tried to hide another smile.

"I mean, I would like to buy you a coffee," I sputtered out.

"I am sorry but I can't, as much as I would like to."

I must have looked as though he just kicked my beloved dog because he dug out his wallet and handed me a stark white card with bold black lettering.

"I am running late but here is my card. Give me a call and we can meet up later in the week."

I smiled at his retreating back and then slapped my hand on my forehead for being a nitwit. He was a true gentleman, only being polite. I'm fairly certain that men like that don't go for women like me. I mean, come on; a handsome man does not seek out the girl next-door type, even if I portrayed a damsel in distress. I was definitely not the long-legged, stick-thin model type that I'm sure he only dates. Hanging my head dejectedly, I mentally berated myself and walked unevenly home.

I walked in the apartment, absolutely famished. I threw my purse on the counter and watched the contents spill out as my aim missed its intended mark. "REALLY!" I shouted to no one in particular, seeing as I lived alone. I could have picked up the mess later but my irrational tendencies overrode my procrastination propensities. It took me ten minutes because I had to reorganize the damn thing. *Curse you, OCD!* I'm totally self-diagnosed. It's not as if I have to complete a task five or six times before I can let it go. It's more like the insane urge to be overly redundant with some aspects of my life.

For example: I will write out a grocery list. Then I will rewrite it, according to the aisle of produce or product closest to the entry door, and ending with the last item closest to the checkout lane. Of course, the list cannot have a crossed-out item before you get to the store. Once again, rewriting the list without errors. Another example: I wash my hands every time I put a new piece of bacon on the skillet. Place raw bacon on to skillet, wash hands, place cooked pieces on to plate, and repeat until all bacon is cooked. You get the idea. Some might call that crazy with a high probability of needing a shrink in the near future. I call it nasty bacterial eradication.

I can be a little eccentric to those who don't know me personally. Okay, if I'm honest, my family is the one who saddled me with that heart-warming moniker. When they introduce me to someone new it's always: this is our daughter Harlow; she is the eccentric one in the family. Of course my brother, Cash, was the charismatic one. I believe the reason I turned out this way was because I had to look after Cash even though he is older by two years. My mother deemed me his keeper after I displayed a natural propensity to abide by her rules and, of course, my excellent tattling skills. As I got older, my maturity level spiked way beyond Cash, further handcuffing me to him.

Enough of my family dynamics; I needed substance. My belly was on the verge of eating itself. I was that hungry. I stared at the contents of my fridge. Nothing but some foul-smelling deli meat. I couldn't even tell what it had been originally. I chanced the freezer. *Ah ha!* One package of zebra cakes left. *Oh happy day!* Trust me, frozen zebra cakes are delicious. They really don't freeze at all. It keeps the miniature cakes from crumbling when you bite into them.

I went to stuff the last zebra cake in my mouth, when my apartment door flung open. I flinched and dropped the cake on the floor. *Son of a bitch!* Tears automatically sprang to my eyes.

I turned and glared. "Damn it, Cash. You scared me to death. Look what you made me do. I really wanted that fucking cake. Now I have to throw it away. What a flipping waste," I whined.

4

"There is a thing called the five-second rule, ya know," he smarted back.

"There is no such thing. Haven't you seen the show where it totally debunked that particular myth? There are germs that immediately attach themselves once it hits the floor. As much as I wanted that, I'd rather not have the flaming flux because of some stupid microscopic germs that latched on to my icing-clad cake."

"Well, you are in luck. I come bearing Jets pizza." A slice of the most delicious piece of pizza materialized in front of my nose. Literally, getting sauce on the tip of it.

"Really? Did you have to do that? You could've just handed it to me, on a plate no less. You didn't have to shove it in my face." I sighed dramatically.

"Damn, sis. Why don't you look into having that stick removed?"

Well, that just pissed me off more. I didn't have a stick stuck anywhere. What I had was a pain in the rear who thought he was hilarious. I took a deep breath in until my lungs grew full with air. Slowly I let it out until my lungs gasped for more air. It wasn't until then that I could utter a word to him. Needing another minute to collect myself, I got up and retrieved the paper plates and napkins. I threw him his, knowing he'd never use it. One could always hope, though.

"I had a shit day. Some douche knocked me over onto a grate. My favorite high heel got stuck and I fell down. A super sexy guy helped me up and then I fumbled all over myself. I looked and sounded like a total jackass," I blurted quickly.

He burst into a fit of laughter. I personally did not find

it all that funny. However, the longer I watched his theatrics, the more comical it became and I laughed along with him. "Only you, sis—only you."

"Tell me about it!"

We commenced to eat in silence. The one thing that my brother and I took seriously was our food. We never made idle conversation while we ate. *What's the point?*

"How is the new design coming?" I asked.

"I haven't even thought about it."

"What the fuck? You know we have to put the new catalogue out next week. We need to put the new designs on the cover."

"No biggie. I'll get it done in time."

It amazed me that the two of us got along at all, let alone partnered a successful business.

When my brother came to me with his crazy business idea, I laugh-snorted in his face. Looking back on that, it probably wasn't the nicest way to tell him that his idea held no merit and was fanciful thinking at best. Being the pestering self that he is, he finally wore me down. That was five short years ago. We are finally to the point where we operated in the black and were able to pay ourselves a modest salary. Thankfully we were financially stable. The business kept growing despite my doubts. His nonchalant attitude drove me nuts. I seemed to be the only one perpetually uptight about keeping the business successful.

Cash had wanted to name the business Hotdoggers. I adamantly raised both of my hands and vetoed the idea. We finally agreed on Firedog Bling Inc. Trust me when I say that coming up with the name for our business was not easy. We argued about it for weeks. Once we settled on the final name, I quickly registered it to ensure that no one else had it or would use it. Plus, Cash might change his mind again. Essentially, we make high-end dog collars. Cash designs the collars and I fit them to the clients' dogs, among a plethora of other duties.

I know what you are thinking. How does this business make any money? Well, Cash is a true artist and makes one-of-a-kind collars that hold up for a long time. We are strategically placed in a high-end district, where a lot of people have money to burn on frivolous trinkets. I am not bashing our clientele by any means; without them, we don't exist. We take orders online and we will ship anywhere in the world. Every six months, we send out a catalogue of new collars to help with the advertising. Word of mouth brings in about seventy-five percent of our business. Cash also traveled to certain conventions and dog shows to sell the collars and drum up business. I handle the day-to-day boring office issues and the occasional fittings, basically everything else but designing the collars and making them.

I must have been a bad hostess because the next thing I knew my brother gave me a noogie and walked out the door. Ah, the great wonders of having a sibling. Well, good riddance, I say. I had better things to do anyway, like get my comfy pajamas on and go to bed.

CHAPTER 2

I always set my alarm a half hour ahead of when I really wanted to get up. This gave me plenty of time to punch the snooze button a multitude of times before I actually got out of bed. Mornings were not kind to me. I don't wake up with a smile on my face, ready to greet the day. I personally curse the suns cheery hello rays, streaming through my blinds. It's a good thing it takes me all of twenty minutes to get ready and run out the door. Otherwise, I'd have to change the store hours.

I grabbed an iced caramel latte with Splenda and no whipped cream because that is what makes me smile and cope with the wee morning hours. I also ordered a bacon and egg bagel—hold the bacon—for Cash. Yeah, I don't get it either. Why not just order a bagel with egg and forgo the whole bacon thing? If for some reason I didn't order it exactly that way, he would know and throw the whole thing away, uneaten. He is exceptionally weird. Yet, I became known as the eccentric one. Regardless, if that is what it took to bribe my brother into designing something spectacular, then I would order it that way every time.

I walked in the back door of the shop, fully expecting to see my brother in full creation mode. Instead, all that greeted me was his empty desk. Frustration clouded my vision and boiled my blood as I set his bagel in the fridge. What I should've done was left it on his desk as a big fuck-you. Knowing full well that by the time he arrived it would officially be in the food poison range.

I checked the appointment book to see whether any clients were due to get fitted or to talk with Cash on a particular design. We had three appointments scheduled later this afternoon. This would give me plenty of time to fill any online orders from the previous night before the appointments arrived. I liked to get those done and shipped out as quickly as I could. We didn't employ anyone else except for during the holidays. That's when our online orders picked up drastically and I needed the help to fulfill them all in a timely manner.

Mornings were usually slow. The socialites were too busy scarfing down mimosa's or whatever they did with their robotic friends for breakfast. We did most of our walk-in business between lunch and closing. I texted the asshat to see whether he would show up today but I got no response back. I hated to have to harp on him but he drove me to extreme measures sometimes. No wonder he referred to me as Mom's clone.

Our first fitting of the day was from one of our regular clients. She ordered a new collar every month. They were always custom made. She never chose the few collars that we kept in stock. The ones that she had designed were very elaborate and expensive. She liked a lot of Swarovski crystals. It was a good thing that her dog was a miniature poodle with a tiny neck. The collars only ran her around four hundred dollars a month. That amount for her was like my pocket change collecting in a dish. I do have to say that the collars were beautiful. She had exquisite taste.

I greeted Sasha and her companion Lady. They say dogs emulate part of their owner's personality. Sasha and Lady didn't fit that mold. Sasha could have made Forbes richest people list. She came from old money but never looked her nose down on anyone—a rarity within her social class. For that alone, I treasured her short visits. She was sweet and quiet, whereas Lady barked relentlessly and has been known to bite on occasion.

You would think that the dog would be used to the store by now. She ran straight for the plush English Mastiff that modeled one of my favorite collars—Cash had made it for his late dog, Rhino—and barked at it the whole time. By the time they left, I felt ready to start stocking electric shock collars. I enjoyed talking to Sasha. She was very nice and a pleasure to speak with. However, her dog made me want to speed her along as quickly as I could. Maybe next time she would leave Lady home. That was wishful thinking on my part because Lady went everywhere with Sasha.

By the time the third client walked in, my headache had made my eyes twitch as though I had developed some weird nervous tic.

"Hello. I am Harlow. Welcome to Firedog Bling." I walked around the counter, my hand extended. "You must be Victoria."

The tall, elegant woman looked at my hand as if I had recently stepped out of the restroom and didn't wash my hands. Of course, if she knew me, she would find that thought absurd.

One of my biggest pet peeves was when people use the restroom and then walk out without washing their hands. *Disgusting*! Just knowing that people do that makes my choice of carrying hand sanitizer, or three, around with me a wise decision. I dropped my hand and bent to talk to the chocolate Labradoodle. I scratched the dog's head in greeting. Her tail thumped as she wagged it up and down. I could feel the soft breeze of air upon my face the harder she wagged. She had successfully upstaged her owner's lack of manners.

Finally, the waif-like creature spoke. "I am here to speak with Cash about Fifis' collar."

"Of course. Let me go in the back and see if he is available." I turned away and headed to the back room and rolled my eyes the entire thirty feet. It was worth the extra pain shooting through my head. *Fifi? Who in their right mind would name their dog Fifi?* It was so cliché.

Of course, I knew Cash wouldn't be in yet and probably spaced the appointment. *Damn him.* I would have to pull his portfolio and speak with the stunning monster—I mean, client. A split second after I opened the desk drawer, the man of the hour waltzed through.

"So glad you could grace us with your presence."

"You betcha, fuckface."

"You kiss your mother with that dirty mouth?"

"Sure do. I learned from the best."

"As much as I would like to continue this heartfelt welcome, you have a peach of a client waiting for you."

I sat in his chair, not bothering to return to the front. Cash could handle her. I didn't want to see the flirtation between the two of them. He would charm her like he usually does. She would trip all over her feet trying to entice Cash into a romantic rendezvous. *Gag me.*

I've seen it a million times. It's a miracle that we retained the clients after he had his fun with some of them. I couldn't even get a date while the master had hordes of women coming and going from his place. Come to think of it, that was why he was probably late getting to work. *Lucky bastard!*

Fixing the dry spell I had going on quickly moved to the top of my list of things to do. The dry spell most certainly had nothing to do with the fact that I was picky. *Was it too much to ask for decent looks, a job, and one who didn't live at home with his mom?* See, my standards were not that high. Which brought to mind the gorgeous brown-eyed specimen who took the time to help a poor girl in need. A man who looked that good probably had already been taken off the market. Not that something as trivial as a girlfriend would stop me from calling him next week.

I securely stowed his business card in the inside zipper pocket of my purse so I wouldn't lose it. I chomped at the bit to dig it out. I snatched my hand away from the purse as if it had burned me.

"What are you doing?"

"Nothing. Why?" I stared at him like a deer caught in headlights. I was never good at lying. Plus, my brother could read me like an open book. Nothing got past him.

"You look like you got caught trying to sneak a cookie out of the jar. That's why."

"Did you get the digits from Victoria while you were going over the details of the dog collar?" My voice dripped with sarcasm.

"Nah. She really isn't my type."

"What? You have a type?" I couldn't believe it. My brother shagged pretty much anything with a pulse. I'm surprised that Victoria was excluded from the revolving door.

"Yes, I have a type. Most of the time all I require is for them to be single but this particular person is no lady." He shrugged and walked toward me.

He tipped the back of the chair forward, throwing me to the floor with a loud thump. He continued to laugh as I gave him the most evil look I owned. He was so frightened that he used his gigantic feet to slide me farther out of his way. I stood up and slapped him on the back of the head on my way back to the front of the store. I was so mad that I could have spit nails. I even forgot to ask him what he meant by his last comment.

The phone rang just as I got ready to lock up for the night.

"Firedog Bling, how may I help you?" I managed to answer in my chipper phone voice.

"I need to speak to Cash," the feminine caller demanded.

Well, if I knew where His Majesty was, I would give him the phone. That's what I wanted to say but what I regurgitated came out entirely different. "I'm sorry but Cash is unavailable at the moment. Can I take a message and have him get back to you as soon as he can?"

"Just tell him to go ahead and start the pattern."

"I will. And your name is?" I asked sweetly.

"Victoria."

"Thank you. I will let him know," I said to the dial tone. *Wow, the nerve of some people.* Us meager servants would never measure up.

I sent a text to Cash, letting him know that the devil incarnate wished to start the design process of the collar. His lack of a response told me his level of excitement about the new job. Taking this project meant that he would meet with her several more times before the actual collar was made. He would need her approval on the final draft before he began to make it. This ensured that the client was one hundred percent satisfied. We did not want returns on custom-made pieces. They were much harder to resell.

I trudged home, dreading tomorrow. Sundays were reserved for family dinner at my parents' house. I loved my parents. However, I didn't feel like answering a bunch of questions from my mother on my lack of husband material. Cash never had to endure her meddling. He stuck with my dad and the sports channel. I managed to get bamboozled into cleaning up and doing the dishes. Usually the mundane task held some quality merits. The simple task allowed me to just be. No thinking required. It was the final blow from my mother that made it unpleasant.

She made sure to advise me on how to become a domestic goddess. That's about the time that I made my excuses to leave before she turned to the art of seduction to snare a man. I sighed heavily and sent a quick prayer to the big guy to suddenly strike my bowels with a bout of diarrhea, so I had an excuse to stay home.

Unfortunately, no sign of the slightest stomach

cramp reared its ugly head. A perfection of health claimed residence. That didn't stop me from calling my mother and telling her that I would be a little late and to go ahead and start dinner without me.

"Do you have a date? Is that why you are going to be a little late? Don't worry about it, honey; just bring him along. We would love to meet the man who asked you out."

"Mom." I drawled out. "I don't have a date, just some work things that need to be finished before Monday morning," I lied. It was easier to fib when not in their presence.

"You can finish them on Monday. It will still be there tomorrow. Don't be late. See you tonight. Love you," she purred, effectively cutting off any rebuttal.

Fanfuckingtastic! I couldn't even excuse myself properly. *How the hell does she do that?* She was such a talented conniver. Herein lies the proof as to where Cash got his mad skills.

I strolled into my old home about forty minutes late, feeling guilty for my white lie and tardiness. Acid burned in my throat. I took my shoes off, walked on the plastic runners that protected her precious carpet, and headed to the dining room. I hated those damn things. They made it really hard to sneak out at night or back in. They were like a damn watchdog, alerting the whole house of your arrival and departure.

Those runners had gotten me into trouble more times than I could count. That is, unless you were more determined and used your bedroom window to climb in and out of. Not that I did any of those things but my brother had it down to an art. Not really; my mother was extremely safety conscious and had fire ladders in every room upstairs. He would just pull up the window, anchor the ladder on the sill, and out he'd go. I unfortunately sucked at lying and sneaking out of the house. Guilt consumed me for even thinking about it when I was younger. I had an excessive dose of respect for my parents. I wouldn't be able to look them in the eye the next morning. Sure as the sun rises, it gave me away every time. I'll have to remember to add that to my resume if our business ever failed.

I bypassed the dining room because my family's loud voices came from the kitchen. I walked in, expecting everyone to be halfway done with dinner. To my surprise, they were just sitting down to eat. *Great; even my planned lateness didn't work out for me.*

"Come on, Harlow. Quit sulking and sit down. It's time to eat," my mother chided.

"Cash, you hungry? Looks like there isn't going to be enough for the rest of us." He had filled his plate a mile high.

"You know, if you don't have anything nice to say, then don't say anything at all."

"Sorry, Mom." I sat at the table with my eyes downcast like a thoroughly scolded toddler.

Did I mention that I hated family dinners? Cash took that moment to kick my shin under the table. I raised my hand and pinched my pointer finger and thumb together repeatedly. It looked as if I were popping his head between them. Childish yes, but highly therapeutic. I suggest you try it.

"Can't you two be nice to each other for one night?

It's amazing that you are able to work together without running it into the ground."

"Now, Maggie, leave them alone so that we can eat," my dad said in a loving tone.

"You're right, dear. Let's eat." Mom clapped her hands together.

My mom was an incredible cook. The food adorned the table with its bounty. I may have walked out with a tension headache but my belly reserved the rights for being fully satisfied. Thankfully, Cash did me a solid tonight and kept my mother's attention on him. Dad was never one to say much, so I didn't have to talk about my lack of romantic options or how my ovaries were going to shrivel up and die soon. I get it. She wanted to be a grandmother in the worst way. I would remain a disappointment in that area for the foreseeable future.

"Good-night, dear." She hugged me and then yelled for Cash to help her with the dishes. I quickly scooted over to my dad and hugged him good-bye. I laughed until tears ran down my face as I scooted to my car and headed home. *Oh, I would pay for that.* Cash would make sure of it but it was so worth it.

CHAPTER 3

I spent most of the week filling online orders and setting up appointments for Cash. He was still missing in action but I knew it was his way of getting back at me for making him do the dishes. This didn't hurt me in the least. The place ran quieter, not to mention smoother, when he was out playing the martyr. By Friday, the store had become blessedly free of clients. I finally had a moment to breathe.

I picked up my purse for the millionth time this week. This time, I unzipped the protective pocket and snatched up the card quickly before I chickened out. I wanted to call first thing Monday but somehow managed to restrain myself. Cash had finally shown his face today but had gone home early. Go figure. That meant he wouldn't be around to mess with me while I made the call. I picked up the card gingerly, as though it were made of ash. If I fingered it too much, it would crumble and float in the stale air of the shop like tiny dust particles. It's not as if I really needed the card. All of his information had been stored in my long-term memory bank. It read Cole Devlin. That's all the information besides a phone number listed on the card. I know, mysterious. I wonder what he did and who he was.

I dialed the number and chewed on my fingernail as it rang. I squealed and hit the End button. I couldn't call him. I would inevitably make an ass out of myself. *Oh hey, this is Harlow. I'm the girl who fell onto the grate and couldn't get back up without your help.* I slapped my forehead. *Get your shit together, girl. It's only coffee and he probably is dating someone really hot. He is not interested in you romantically.*

With nothing to lose, my fingers punched in the number again. I chewed on my nonexistent fingernail once more as the phone continuously rang. His voicemail popped up and I debated on leaving him a message but gave in at the last second.

"Hey, Cole. This is Harlow. You helped me up after I had fallen on a grate last week. The invitation for coffee still stands. If not, I simply wanted to say thank-you again for helping me. I really appreciated it. Umm. Okay. This is Harlow again and here is my cell phone number if you want coffee." I rattled off my number.

I finally got my blubbering under control and ended the call. Gosh, what a bumbling idiot. What a complete and total disaster. I needed tips on how to ask a guy out without sounding as though I had diarrhea of the mouth.

I had gawked at my phone, willing it to ring, for so long that my eyes crossed and the screen blurred. Finally, I had to walk away from it. I grabbed the glass cleaner from the bottom shelf of the counter. Then I snagged the paper towels and proceeded to clean the nose prints on the glass. I cleaned that and then the counter, and swept the rug. By the time I finished, I only had an hour left before closing.

As the minutes ticked by, so did the sliver of hope that Cole would call back. While my giddy mood plummeted, the phone buzzed.

I jumped, startled with the loud ringing in the quiet shop. "Hello?"

chance to come in and get one for Juno."

"Well, Cash has already left for the day. Why don't you look through his portfolio while I get the appointment book?" I ran to the back and grabbed his book. While she looked through it, I took down her name and phone number. She made a tentative appointment for the following week.

While she occupied herself with Cash's portfolio, I took the liberty to play with Juno. I loved this breed so much. They were big ol' slobbery lapdogs with such sweet dispositions. I sat on the floor and she laid her head on my lap with her tongue hanging out the side. She exposed her belly and I couldn't resist petting and fawning all over her. I had rubbed my face all over her as she squirmed to get closer. She made me miss Rhino terribly. A few tears escaped. I swiped them away as Cole walked through the door. By God, that man was even better looking than I remembered.

Both Juno and I perked our heads up and slobbered all over each other as he came closer. If I had a tail, it would wag just as wildly as Juno's was. Cole sat next to me and that traitor of a dog switched to his lap.

"Traitor," I wasn't above calling her out on her deception.

He laughed. "Are you ready to go?"

"Just about. Give me a minute." I stood and brushed off the dog hair from my pants.

"Excuse me, Miss. I didn't catch your name."

"Peyton."

"Thank you. What do you think of Cash's designs?"

"I think I am really going to like meeting him. I'll get out of your hair. Thanks and I'll see you next week." She walked out the door.

"I'm sorry about that—last-minute customer. We do a lot of business with her aunt and I didn't want to push her out the door." I shrugged.

"I'm not in any hurry. I'm a sucker for dogs. I couldn't help but want to join in on your fun."

Oh my goodness, was he flirting with me? Nah, it's totally my imagination. I kept quiet and quickly ran through my closing duties. I grabbed my purse and locked up. We walked in comfortable silence toward Gilroy's.

We snagged the last table in a corner at the back of the bar. Cole pulled out a chair for me to sit. *Wow, chivalry is not dead!*

"Thank you," I pronounced, not hiding my surprise.

"My pleasure."

I set my purse on the floor in front of my feet as I scooted the chair in. The waitress came over and asked what we wanted to drink. Being the snobby beer drinker that I am, I asked for Pabst Blue Ribbon on tap. Cole raised his eyebrows and ordered himself one.

"Pabst, huh?" he questioned.

"Yep, nothing but the best, baby."

He laughed. "I thought that I was the only one who genuinely loved it."

"Nope. You'll have to add another fan to your inner circle."

"It's pretty selective. I'm not sure you belong yet."

"Well, I'm fairly confident that I'll pass all of your selective tests."

"I don't know. They are pretty tough." He chuckled charmingly.

Before I could respond, our drinks were set in front of us. It was nice to be able to banter with a hot guy. Being myself became easier, especially knowing that I wasn't a contestant competing to be his girlfriend. I didn't know for sure whether he dated someone or not. I took the liberty to believe that he was.

"Would you like to order anything from the kitchen?" The waitress stood close to Cole and fluttered her lashes.

I looked at Cole and shrugged.

"Why don't you give us a couple of menus and we will take a peek." He winked at her.

I held in my snort at his blatant flirtations. She blushed and sauntered off to heed his wishes.

"Wow! Do all women jump to do your bidding?"

"That has yet to be seen," he said cheekily.

I rolled my eyes. I'm sure they all did. I know that I fumbled all over myself when I first met him. They had good reason to. He was delicious. I had to check a couple of times to make sure I wasn't drooling. I licked my lips as though he were the main course. His deep baritone voice smoothed the rough planes of his chiseled bone structure. The intensity of his gaze could make an angel step over the line. Depending on the context, his eyes ranged from cold and penetrating to sweet comfort. He was quite the conundrum. I could literally sit here and watch him all night him and never see the same characteristic twice. I thought about all of this as I blankly stared at the menu.

"Have you decided on what you wanted to eat?"

"What? Oh, yes, um…" I quickly scanned the appetizer section. "Fried pickles."

"It took you that long to decide on fried pickles?" He arched his brow inquisitively.

"When you're hungry, everything looks good. It makes choosing just one item really difficult. What did you decide on?"

"I originally decided on a burger and fries until you took forever and I second-guessed myself! Now I'm going with loaded potato skins and boneless buffalo wings."

"Oh, that sounds better than fried pickles! I'll share if you share," I pleaded with him.

"Maybe, if you're good."

"No worries there." I smiled triumphantly.

We talked about everything and then some. It amazed me how quick-witted and delightful he actually was. He was the exact opposite of what I thought. When our meal came, we ceased all talking and got down to business. I started to get a little uncomfortable about midway through our eclectic meal. Every time I looked up, his eyes bore into me. I wiped my mouth.

"Do I have something in my teeth?" I smiled really obnoxiously, showing him all of my pearly whites.

"No. But there is something wrong with your face?" He seemed a little disturbed.

"What? Do I have airplanes in the hanger or food on my face? Just tell me. I'm not going to be embarrassed. Plus I suck at the guessing game."

"Okay." He elongated the word, reminding me that I asked for his honest answer. "Your lips are swollen, as well as your cheeks. Your face looks like a ripe tomato."

It had to be serious because he looked so concerned. I quickly excused myself and went to the bathroom. *What the hell was going on?* I couldn't feel anything out of the ordinary as I had sat there eating.

I pushed open the door and abrasively pushed past a lady trying to exit. She whipped her head around and gave me a snarky look. Ignoring her, I peered into the mirror and squinted, afraid of what I would find. *Shit. Shitty, shit.* Cole had been kind. My face looked as though I had gone three rounds in a cage match. I was the prizefighter lying knocked out on the canvas floor. What the heck did I get into to create such a disturbing sight? *OH MY WORD!* I rubbed my face all over the mastiff at the store. *How could I do that?* I am allergic to dogs. Yeah, and I still work with them. As long as I wash my hands and don't touch my face then I am fine. *I am so stupid.* What a way to ruin a second impression. I sighed heavily, squared my shoulders, and pushed the defeatist attitude out of the way. *Oh well, nothing I could do about it now. What's done is done.*

I walked back to the table, conscious of the other patrons gawking at my disfigured face. I had to get out of here immediately.

"I'm sorry, Cole. I need to get home and get some allergy medicine." I managed to get most of that out with only a minor lisp.

"I'll walk you back to the store or I can take you home. My office isn't that far from there." He signaled the waitress for the check.

"Really, I'm fine. I promise I can walk to my car and get home without you having to go out of your way." I made a grab for the check but he was lightning fast.

Maybe due to my eyes being on the verge of swelling shut, I moved at a snail's pace. Everything looked half its size.

"I've got it this time. Next time it's your treat. I am going to take you home. You can't even see properly, let alone drive."

"Thank you." Relief saturated my body.

I could have argued but there really was no point. Hated to admit it, but I needed his help. He wrapped his arm around my elbow, much like a concerned gentlemen. It became a necessary evil. I couldn't see very well and had already stumbled into another table. I wasn't hurt, not that anyone asked because the patrons were too busy wiping the wetness from their drinks being knocked in their laps. No sight needed for me to cringe at the sound of their squeals of surprise and of disgust. I threw out my apologies but never slowed down. Nevertheless, it was nice of him to take care of me. Cole managed to surprise me again by opening up the car door for me. He took my hand and gently guided me in to the comfortably cushioned leather.

With my excellent directions, he guided us to the right door. I fished out my keys and handed them to him. I'd rather take my chances sleeping outside than fight with the key. He steered me to the couch, told me to sit, and went to retrieve my medicine. I could hear him rifle through the cabinets until he found what I needed. Thank goodness for small miracles.

I took a big slobbery gulp. "Phank chew. Chew swaved me from cawwing my bwopher."

He looked at me quizzically for a minute as he cocked his head to the side like an adorable puppy. Then he burst out laughing. I sat there silently while he got himself back under control.

"I'm not sure I understood all of what you said. It was pretty muffled, but you're welcome."

I snorted unsure, what my mouth would do if I tried to laugh. I'm sure it was a pretty hilarious sight from his end. If I had to make the embarrassing call to Cash, he wouldn't have stopped laughing the whole time. He would have thrown it in my face every chance he got.

He didn't say anything else as he got up. I thought he had left. A pang of disappointment shot through my heart. Within seconds, he strolled back and placed a cold bottle of water next to me. Then he plopped down so close that he tossed my body into his. He chuckled as he pushed me back into place. I laughed despite myself and a dollop of slobber rolled down my chin. I quickly swiped it away with the sleeve of my shirt. *How gross.* I don't know why he decided to keep me company but I'm glad he did.

One minute I had been engrossed in some show about a vigilante and the next minute I rubbed my eyes to the morning light. I sat up, trying to work out the kinks the couch had gifted to my body. I looked over at the sleeping body curled up on the opposite side of the couch. *Holy rice crispy treats!* Cole had stayed the night. I slipped into the bathroom and brushed the fur off my teeth. Feeling much better, I chanced a look at my face. Everything looked back to normal. My sorry imitation of Angelina Jolie's signature lips were back to their normal boring self. *Crap! What time was it?* I had to be at work today. Flipping my wrist over, I looked at my watch and freaked a little bit. I had thirty minutes before I needed to open up the store.

I quickly peeked in on Cole. He remained asleep, so I frantically rushed into the shower. I haphazardly threw on some clothing and went out to wake Cole. He no longer lounged on the couch.

"In here," he called out.

"Morning. Thank you for staying with me. You didn't have to do that but I really appreciate it."

"No problem. I thought about going home but the amount of drool hanging out of your mouth kind of concerned me. So, I decided to crash in case you needed me," he said as straight-faced as he could. The smirk he held back made his lips twitch.

"I was a pretty gruesome sight. I can't believe I let my guard down like that. I love dogs. Not being able to snuggle up to one bums me out. My face swelling up like a potato on steroids usually reminds me that it's not worth giving in to the yearning. For a little while at least." I smiled at him and continued. "As much as I would love to hang with you, I have to get to work. So you've got to go."

"Wow! I'm shocked that after what we shared last night you are kicking me out."

"You knew the score," I smarted as I pushed him toward the door. "Thank you again for saving me for the second time. You are my hero."

I stood up on my toes and kissed his cheek. "Seriously, thank you. I'm not usually such a hot mess. Being near you could be dangerous to my health."

"You're lucky I was there both times to save you. I'm good for your health. You might want to keep me around just in case." We both laughed.

"I had fun, even when your face transformed into something from a horror flick. Let's have a redo."

"I'd like that."

"I'll give you a call later," he promised. He gave me a kiss on my forehead and walked out the door.

Fuck, I didn't have my car. Just as I opened the text box, Cole opened up the door again.

"Did you forget something?"

"Yep. Come on, hot potato. I'll take you to work."

I beamed and followed him out the door.

Work was a bust. It had been raining since we opened. I could have closed the store, seeing as not one customer walked through the door. Cash stopped in to make an appearance and then left again. It pissed me off the way he came and went as he pleased. Last time I checked, the business had both of our names on it. He could put in more hours. If he were a nice brother, he would give me a break from opening and closing every fucking day.

It got old and grated on my nerves. Oh, but he was the artiste, according to him. His talent couldn't be rushed nor could he find inspiration sitting at his desk all day. What a total crock of bullshit. Next time he came in, he would get an earful.

CHAPTER 4

I grabbed my vibrating phone before my mother could stick her nose to the screen or God forbid, answer it. I'm not sure what possessed me to leave it on the table in plain sight. She was notorious for butting in on your business.

"You know I don't like you talking on the phone while at the dinner table. It's rude and disrespectful to the rest of us," my mother dutifully reminded me.

"Of course, Mom. Please excuse me. I need to take this call," I replied mockingly and hastily moved from the room.

"Did I catch you at a bad time?" Cole considerately asked.

"Nope. Once again you have impeccable timing."

"Fighting with grates or petting dogs?"

"Neither. More like a nagging mother," I answered truthfully.

"Ah, I see. I'm being used again. I'm starting to feel unloved."

I could hear the amusement in his voice. Which made my heart palpitate a little. *Oh, please don't let me crush on him.* He was a really great guy and I don't want to ruin it by imagining the wedding march and a white picket fence. Minus the dogs and children running around. I'm not ready for all of that self-inflicted craziness.

"You poor thing. I'd hate for you to feel unloved. Want to hang out?"

"You read my mind. I'll meet you at your place in an hour. Will that give you enough time to make your excuses? I know how much fun you seem to be having."

"Plenty. I do hate to break it to them that I have a problem with an order that I have to fix immediately."

"See you soon."

"Bye."

Cash came into the room, whistling with his hands jammed into his pockets. I knew what he was doing. I stood my ground and waited him out. The silence droned on as we faced each other as if we were back in the lawless Wild West. We were about to have a shoot-off. *Who would be the quicker draw?*

"What's the problem at work?" He feigned interest extremely well.

"Nothing I can't handle. Wouldn't want you to worry your pretty little head. Then again, you wouldn't because you don't give a rat's ass." I guess I was still pissed off because I was no longer playing around with him.

"Ah, fuckface is mad. That's so cute. Who's the guy?" he asked with an evil smile.

"There is no guy and quit changing the subject. I am taking Monday off and you will be working the front, as well as any designs. I am tired of having to run the business side of things and you only showing up when you have appointments. Sometimes not even then." I pointed my finger into his chest repeatedly. My finger bent back at the first knuckle with each increased pressure. I let out a huge breath as the weight lifted off my chest.

He slapped my hand away. "I thought you liked how we ran the shop. I didn't realize how much of a pansy you had become. All work and no play made Harlow a bitch," he spat.

I could see the muscles working in his jaw as he ground his teeth. His hands now clenched at his side. Watching him get angry allowed me to let go of some of the resentment that I harbored toward him. He reminded me of a honey badger ready to kill its prey. It was borderline comical. This totally indicated that I had been right. He had been slacking. He also cared about the shop just as much as I did.

"Glad I finally got a reaction from you. I was beginning to wonder if you even gave a shit anymore. I like working together, Cash, but sometimes I feel like I'm the only one putting forth the effort." I slowly crept toward him and gave him a playful slap on his cheek. "I love you, big brother. We need to start working jointly. We need to be able to blend our duties collectively so we are both involved." I turned around one more time. "You are partly right. All work and no play has made me a bitch."

His body coiled with anger. He tightened his hands into fists as I walked away from him. He would need time to let the information sink into his thick skull. I hated fighting with him but sometimes he needed a swift kick or slap to remove his head from his ass.

He had the tendency to get wrapped up in his world and forget about those around him. I wish I were more like him in that respect. We really did balance one each other out most of the time. I was envious of the way he was able to follow his own rules, while I followed everyone else's, letting my needs come second. Now, I felt better knowing that I was steering toward the right road for a change. It only took one night with Cole to realize I missed having friends and a life. My small world had become too automatic. Work and home: that was all my pathetic life had encompassed. Living the boring life of an old spinster had rapidly lost its allure. Creating a life would deter me from hoarding cats in the future.

True to his word, Cole showed up within the hour, bearing ice cream and a movie. I grabbed the hardware for Cole. He scooped out the ice cream while I popped in the movie. The night was low-key and just what I needed. The flick was a comedy that didn't require any deep thought to watch, so we were able to make idle conversation when we wanted. Mostly we enjoyed being in each other's company. I stifled a yawn as the credits rolled.

"I've kept you up too late. Her Majesty needs her beauty sleep," he uttered sarcastically.

"I'm sorry. It's been a long week."

"I'm taking a half day Friday. Why don't we get lunch and play hooky the rest of the day?"

"A very good plan. How about I let you know if I

can swing it? I am taking tomorrow off so I'm not sure I can arrange a half day too."

He hung his head and pouted. That had to be one of the sexiest looks I've seen in a long time. It seemed crazy that hurting his feelings would turn me on. If he continued to pout like that, I would have to continue to teasingly hurt his feelings. The slight curve of his lip reminded me that he was joking around so I didn't feel bad. The contours of his face were sharp so when he pouted it made him appear gentle. He reminded me of the stuffed animals you'd win at the fair. They were stiff and unyielding on the outside but you fell in love with them anyway.

I laughed and swatted his arm. "Come on—out you go. I need my rest."

"Fine. I'll go." He looked forlorn.

I walked him to the door. He bent down and placed a kiss on my cheek. My cheek tingled from the quick touch of his lips. This man wreaked havoc on my hormones. For the most part, they settled in the friend zone but every once in a while they spiked instantaneously to slutty mode. Something in my gut told me not to pursue anything more than friendship with him. He promised me nothing but a broken heart. I'd just let things play out as they were supposed to. For once I would not jump the gun. I was content to just be his friend for now. Hell, this was all probably in my head. He couldn't possibly think of us as anything more than platonic.

I woke up in a slight panic thinking I had slept through the alarm. It wasn't until I made a mad dash to start the shower that I remembered I had the day off.

Never even bothered to set the alarm last night. I squelched the urge to call and check on Cash. I trusted that he went in early enough to open on time. I ate a quick breakfast and went to get ready to do nothing. Then, like most of my plans, they changed. Instead of doing nothing, I put together my range bag.

Cole had called and said he was playing hooky and wanted a sidekick. He didn't have any plans made so I figured going to the range would be good enough. I don't know what most people do with their free time but I liked to go shoot. I owned a nice .45 Sig. My hands were not delicate and feminine. They were rough-skinned and on the large side, which allowed the pistol to fit nicely in my grip, almost like a second skin.

***

I used to be frightened even looking at a gun. My brother taught me to overcome my fears by teaching me how to shoot. The first time we went, I was a hot mess. My hands shook fiercely, sweat beaded along my skin, and then I almost passed out. All of that happened before I even picked up his pistol.

The range we went to was located in a basement of sorts, with only three lanes. The lights overhead provided only enough light to see down the lane. The rest of the room was dimly lit. Unlike most basements, this one boiled you with the type of body heat that could only be produced from adrenaline. A guy dressed in a camouflage shirt and tight-fitting jeans took up the lane next to us. Every time he shot, my body jolted.

We put in our earplugs as soon as we stepped into the room but you still heard the pop. It was unnerving to say the least.

Cash shot first while I stood behind him and off to the side so I could watch. Ever have a hot shell fly back at you and catch in the front of your V-neck shirt? Well, let's just say that the twins were not happy at the intrusion. I bounced around behind my brother with one hand through the bottom and the other down the collar. I tried to disengage the hot metal from my bra. I'm sure the owner watching my theatrics through the cameras had a good laugh. *Mental note: no chest-exposing shirts and maybe some long sleeves.*

At that time, I didn't own a handgun so he let me shoot his. He can be really nice when he wants to. Guys have a hard time sharing their toys. At least my brother does. I assumed that driving his car and shooting his gun are considered off-limits most of the time. I'm still not allowed to drive his truck. Shock registered upon my face when he handed over one of his prized possessions.

Cash showed me how to stand properly, with feet shoulder width apart and knees slightly bent. He reminded me that this stance was only for target shooting. Home defense was totally different. I always thought point and shoot. Totally not true. I won't bore you with those lessons. After I accidently waved the gun at him in my excitement, he repeatedly told me, "NEVER EVER point a loaded gun at someone." I bit my tongue, on the verge of reminding him that I had already unloaded the clip. One other important rule was to NEVER EVER have my finger on the trigger unless I planned to shoot. *Jeez, there were so many rules.* He didn't waste any time on pleasantries with those two important rules. *Who would be when you are pointing a potentially loaded pistol at them!* After having shot all day at paper bull's-eyes and gory zombie targets, I became hooked.

It was the most liberating and rewarding day. It's hard to describe all of the emotions that run through your body and mind when you first step into your lane and prepare to shoot. I like to take my time, loading my clip while I take deep breaths to help calm the adrenaline. It still takes me awhile to settle down and let my muscle memory take over. It's an extreme stress reliever as well as empowering.

Because I liked shooting so much, he took me to go pick out my own handgun. He fought fiercely for the 9mm because he is so fond of his. However, I fell in love with the Sig. The moment I wrapped my hand around the grip, I knew I had to have it. The .45 isn't that ideal for target shooting because the bullets are expensive but I don't care. Cash and I still go to the range and occasionally take some defensive shooting classes for fun.

CHAPTER 5

I felt kind of guilty going to the range with Cole instead of Cash. It was our thing. No outsiders had ever been invited along with us. Cash wasn't going to be there, so he wouldn't be upset with me for allowing Cole to crash. I parked next to Cole. I gathered my bag and stepped out of the car.

"You ready to do this?" I said as a way of greeting.

"Yep. Surprised that you suggested the range. Is this your first time?"

"Nope, this isn't my first rodeo. What about you?"

"I'm about to get my cherry popped."

I laughed so hard that tears ran down my face and I started hacking. I didn't stop until I pulled open the doors to the store.

I had extra earplugs in my bag. The only thing we had to purchase was extra ammo. I didn't bring enough for the both of us. We paid for our targets and ammo. Then I told him to put his earplugs in as I donned my purple and black earmuffs. We opened the doors and walked to our lane. In the mornings they weren't busy so we could've had two lanes side by side. We decided on one lane and took turns.

The next two hours flew by. We blasted through all

of our targets. Cole saved the ones that he shot at, which enamored me more. Hell, if I had a particularly good day I would keep them. He turned out to be a natural and didn't exhibit the same fears that I had.

"That was fun as hell! I'm so glad you suggested this," he shouted.

I laughed at him. We still had our earpieces in. I took mine off because the other lanes were unoccupied.

"Yeah, I come out here as much as I can. It builds up a good appetite." I rubbed my belly in case he missed the first obvious clue.

"How can you eat after that? I need to get rid of all this adrenaline. I can't eat right now."

"Then go run around the building a couple of times or I can go by myself." I smiled at him.

His excitement reminded me of a little boy trying to get a glimpse of Santa Claus coming down the chimney on Christmas Eve.

He literally took off running around the building. I put my bag in my car and waited for his silly ass to finish his laps. *Who does that?* Apparently Cole does. There was much more to him than meets the eye.

He had good form, too. The only way you'd catch me running was if someone chased me or if I heard the ice cream truck. I loathed sweating, so any form of exercise was out of the question. That's probably why I held onto a few—okay, more like

twenty——extra pounds. After his jog, we decided on Mexican. *Yum, salsa and chips—yes, please.*

As I dug into my chips and salsa, Cash decided to ring me. He has the worst timing. I really didn't want to answer but he might have a problem. Against my better judgment, I picked up the call.

"What's up, Nancy?"

"Are you having a good time on your nonscheduled day off?"

"Why, yes, I am. How's work?" I said, making sure to gloat a little.

"Fabulous. You missed the she-devil. She told me to tell you hello."

"I bet she did. Are you going to tell me why you called or are you bored?"

"I've actually been pretty busy. It's slow right now so I figured I'd bother you."

"I'm so glad you called to chitchat but I'm pretty busy right now so I'll talk to you later."

"R-i-g-h-t." He drawled the word out.

"Seriously, I'm having lunch with a friend so I'll see you tomorrow at work. Love—you bye."

"Love ya—bye."

"Sorry about that. My brother was bored so he figured he would harass me," I explained as I shut the phone off.

"Your brother's name is Nancy?"

"Among other things!" I chuckled. "No, his real

name is Cash but I usually call him a bunch of derogatory names before I use his birth name. His given name usually signifies how pissed off I am at him."

He looked at me oddly so I felt I needed to explain myself.

"Cash is older than me by two years, so we are really close. My mom said that we should have been twins. We are and have always been inseparable. We both own Firedog Bling. Our relationship seems odd to other people. It's not the typical brother-sister fighting. We show our affection by picking on each other. It's never done maliciously, mostly, in jest. When we do fight, that's usually when we talk normally." I huffed out a breath in frustration. "I'm not explaining this very well."

"I think I understand but will probably have to witness it firsthand."

"Okay, your turn. I've talked enough about myself."

"I'm fairly boring. I have a sister, who can be quite a pretentious ass at times. We are not as close as you and your brother are. There are times I don't even like being in the same room as her. We basically stay out of each other's life except on holidays. She is nothing like the rest of the family. Quite the opposite, in fact."

I rested my chin on my hands as he continued his story.

"We grew up poor with a single mom. I've stayed true to my roots for the most part, even though I can afford plenty of nice things. I own my own advertising company and have made a name for myself. The company does extremely well." He broke for a drink of his pop. "Does that satisfy your curiosity?"

The twinkle in his eye distracted me. *God, he was super sexy.*

I smiled. "Not even close, but it will do for now." I sucked in a breath, not wanting to admit this but the word vomit spewed forth. "You are different than what I previously thought."

"How so?" he asked in a serious tone.

"Well, when I first met you, you were very polite but standoffish. I figured you had given me your card in hopes that I wouldn't call you. At first, I hesitated to call but then I decided I needed to thank you for helping me. When we went for drinks, you turned out to be more open and funny than I imagined." I couldn't believe that I had said all of that to him.

"Then, when I had that allergic reaction, you held in your laughter until I was on the mend and you stayed. I mean, we are practically strangers and you go above and beyond what any sane person would've done. I'm impressed and glad that you are my friend. The type I haven't had in a long time and one I didn't know I needed."

He was quiet for a minute. I had started to rethink the whole word vomit thing.

"You aren't what I expected either."

"How so?" I parroted him.

"I had watched you on that grate, freaking out, and I thought, *she needs help.* The psychiatrist kind, if you know what I mean. I honestly didn't want to get caught up in whatever world you lived in."

I busted out laughing because I knew how true that statement was.

He snickered. "When I helped you up, you had this look like a deer has when it's in the road and your car is running seventy miles an hour toward it. You simply froze up with a death grip on my arms and spaced out."

I interrupted him. "I had to pay my respects to the shoe gods."

"Exactly! I reiterate my earlier statement. You need mental help." He chuckled and shook his head. "Then you looked up at me with your large doe eyes and seemed sincerely grateful that I actually felt like a superhero. Which is strange because I really didn't do anything heroic. Nevertheless, you were so genuine that you intrigued me. Especially when you mentioned getting a coffee on you."

He looked out of the corner of his eye, as though he were replaying that day. "I was running late to a meeting so I couldn't give in to my curiosity. That's why I handed you my card with the hopes of you calling." He took a moment to gather his thoughts before he continued. "It actually surprised me that we had made such a good connection. There is something about you, Harlow, that makes me really smile. I think it's because I feel like I can be myself when I am around you. I don't have many people in my life where I can simply be me. It's refreshing and slightly addictive."

I smiled, genuinely touched with his admission. I placed a hand over his. "The one thing about me that is constant is that I don't judge. Yes, I will get mad and can dislike many things that you do; however, you are who you are. I can either take you that way or not at all. I am not one to try to change you or mold you to fit in my life. You either do or you don't. It's that simple."

Cole squeezed my hand in a gesture of thanks. "Thanks for letting me play hooky with you. I had an incredible time. I may have to go pistol shopping."

"You must—it's quite the experience."

"If you can get free Friday, shoot me a text and we will do just that!"

"I will try to make that happen," I said excitedly.

I would actually look forward to that. Some women like to shop for new clothes, makeup, shoes, etc. I like to shop for new handguns and antibacterial sanitizer. I know; it's disturbing. We left the restaurant and headed our separate ways. For a split second, I thought about stopping in at the shop to chat with my brother but home sounded much better. He would inadvertently skip out on me and I'd end up working. *Not going to happen today!*

Taking a whole day off work felt exciting in the beginning but now I sat here, twiddling my thumbs. Well, the first half turned out pretty great. The latter half, I spent channel surfing, cleaning, and attempting to read a book. On the verge of pulling my hair out, I grabbed my purse and headed for the door. I swung into Jets, ordered two pies and headed to my brother's for dinner. Boredom and a peace offering were two of the best combinations. My brother would definitely appreciate my thoughtfulness. Especially when I brought his favorite barbeque chicken pizza.

It tastes nasty and smells like sweaty gym socks. I like plain old traditional pepperoni and cheese. I don't understand why anyone would want to bastardize pizza. It's the same with cheesecake. Just make a damn New York style with cherry topping. I had to rein in the thoughts; otherwise, I would seriously have an argument with myself. Which could possibly land me in the loony bin if anyone overheard.

I knocked on the door, unlike my brother, who always barged in unannounced. It didn't bother me. The likelihood of him interrupting something was like finding a pot of gold at the end of a rainbow. Though, the chance of walking in on him and his flavor of the week was like finding a Starbucks on every other city block. *Hello—it's a sight that could never be unseen.* I don't want those images floating through my brain. For heaven's sake, just thinking about it called the nasty images to my mind. I had just stopped dry heaving when the door flew open.

"Hey, jackass! You brought dinner." He grabbed the pizzas and shut the door in my face.

What a dickhead.

"Don't worry. I'll let myself in," I mumbled.

"That's what you should've done in the first place. I don't know why you bother knocking."

"Last time I didn't knock, I got an eyeful. I don't want a repeat," I said dramatically.

It's like waking up in the middle of the night to go get a drink of water and running into your dad walking around the house in his birthday suit. You learn to never get out of bed until your bladder is screaming and your mouth is as dry as the Sahara. Those kinds of images hang around for life. It's truly perturbing.

"You brought my favorite pizza. What do you want?" he asked skeptically.

"Nothing. Can't I do something nice for you without catching shit?"

"What are you planning on doing that will have me bailing you out?"

"Seriously? I can't believe you'd think that."

He donkey laughed at me and shrugged. His laughter was contagious. Before I knew it, we were both buckled over and gasping for air.

We chowed down like we were survivor winners off the reality show. "So, what did the she-devil have to say?" I said with a mouthful of pizza.

"She didn't like my design. So we spent an hour going over what she wanted on the collar. Which happened to be the same shit she had given me the first time we met. The design I created encompassed everything that she wanted."

"So what was her beef with the sketch?"

"Not enough fucking bling! Really? I did it to her specifications even though I knew it would turn out hideous. It still wasn't enough." He rolled his eyes toward the ceiling. "I told her I'd redraw it with the new information and give her a call in a couple of days. When she walked out the door, I tore up the first sketch, lit it on fire, and flipped her the bird."

I laughed so hard tears streamed down my face and my cheeks hurt. "You did not."

"Fine, I didn't light it on fire but I most certainly did the other two." He grinned. "I was professional until she left, then I let the f-bombs fly!"

"I'd have paid to see that show."

"Would have been worth the money. You could've watched it live and for free if you'd have come to work. But nooo, you had to take a day off to decompose."

"It's decompress, you moron." I shook my head at his sarcastic comments. At least he wasn't mad that I had taken the day off. It came as a relief. I hated when he was mad at me. Hence the pizza!

"Which reminds me, I am taking a half day this Friday," I rushed out. I couldn't look him in the eye. I felt guilty for even saying it out loud. I knew I deserved it and shouldn't be asking for permission, even though I told him what I was doing. After a minute, the silence got to me. I chanced a look. He smirked at me. *Oh shit.* That meant he would take a week off just to spite me.

"You earned it. What are you going to do?" He sported a shit ass-eating grin.

"Going to meet up with a friend and go shopping." I was purposely, vague. I didn't know what Cash was up to but I'm sure it's bound to be no good.

His face morphed with disgust. "Yeah, well, have fun with all of that."

I mentally patted myself on the back for the sweetest half-truth I've ever managed to pull off with a straight face and steady voice. I had to leave. Otherwise I would spill the truth. I wasn't ready for the dose of ribbing that he would dish out so I swatted him on the back of the head as I moved toward the door. "Later."

"Buh-bye," he called out.

CHAPTER 6

My cell phone annoyingly alerted me that I had an incoming text. I put the car back in park. There was no way I would chance my life because of a text. I could think of a million other ways to die that would be infinitely better than from reading a text. For example, having a heart attack after a potent orgasm. Now *that* would be the way to go. Hell, even getting struck by lightning would be tolerable.

I wouldn't be able to save it until I got home either. The damn alert would keep chiming and reminding me that I had a text. This would bug me until I opened it and read the damn thing. To save myself the anxiety, I sat in the parking lot and opened it up.

I literally bounced up and down in my seat when I saw it had come from Cole. If someone looked at me through my car window, I probably looked as if I were about to piss my pants. I was also that girl who just dug her phone out of her bra. Don't judge! It's a really convenient place to keep it.

Ice cream?

I laughed out loud. He has got to be the strangest man I've ever met. Scratch that—my brother took first place. Cole came in a close second. My belly was stretched to the max with all that pizza. *What the fuck! I'm going for ice cream!*

I'm down. Where do you want to meet?

I stared at the screen, willing for a quick reply. This is taking forever. *Was he texting a book?*

Pick you up at your place in 20

That's it! He must touch type. *Shit!* I had to get home fast. I had to change my shirt; it had pizza grease on it from my fingers. I couldn't wait for Cash to conjure up a napkin so I just used my shirt. I aim to only please myself! I didn't plan to run for Miss America or anything. I had to reply so I could get the hell out of here.

I'll be waiting

I sped all the way home. It only took me half the time. I try to obey all traffic laws but this situation called for some minor rule violations. Quick wardrobe change—check; teeth brushed—check. I rushed out of the bathroom to answer the door. I took a quick count of ten to steady my breathing. I was marginally winded from my sprint.

I opened up the door to the best eye candy a girl could wish for. He made me hungry—and not for ice cream. I plastered on my best welcome smile, needing to camouflage the flash of desire before he saw it.

"Hi." Yep, I was a little tongue-tied. I couldn't manage anything more than that.

He still wore a suit from work. The charcoal-gray material fit him perfectly in all the right places. I couldn't help my gaze from roaming up and down.

He smiled knowingly and cleared his throat. "You ready for some of the best ice cream in the world?"

He so busted me.

"Yes, sir. Lead the way." I saluted and followed him to his car.

We stepped back in time as soon as our feet crossed the threshold. The ice cream parlor was decked out in 1950 retro style. The floor was decorated with black and white checked laminate. Red covered barstools were haphazardly placed along the mint-green colored bar. Red vinyl booths lined the walls and small checkered tables were placed randomly in the middle.

Memorabilia adorned the walls. Pictures of Grace Kelly, Marilyn Monroe, Elvis, Dean Martin, and many more hung in miniature collages. Each picture was autographed. They even had a replica of an old-fashioned ice cream sign with twenty-five cents printed along the bottom. My eyes landed on the jukebox in the back. I immediately left Cole at the counter as I headed over. I had to see whether it was authentic. *Wow, it's the real deal.* Cole came up behind me as I admired the beautiful machine.

"It's an AMI J Jukebox made in 1957. It plays seven-inch vinyl records." I sighed longingly. "Just look at the large swooping glass cover. You can see the record being selected and played." I ran my fingers along the electronic buttons wistfully.

I felt his hands slide up my back and grip my shoulders, kneading them softly. I leaned into his chest, fully aware of my muscles loosening. I took my time relishing in the strength that had enveloped me as he wrapped his arms around my middle. The gesture felt intimate, as if he belonged to me.

"It's really sexy when you go all nerdy on me." His

the twilight zone. Things were going too well today to suggest otherwise. Cash decided to take an early quit once we figured out the layout for the magazine. I put the finishing touches on it when Victoria graced the store with her presence.

"Good afternoon, Victoria. How are you doing today?" I asked in an overly chipper voice.

"Fine, thanks. Is Cash available?" she asked in a hoity tone.

Keeping the smile plastered on my face proved more difficult than I thought. "No. I am sorry but he had an appointment he had to go to and is out for the rest of the day. Can I help you with anything?"

"I didn't care for the last sketch. So I drew up my own. I will leave it for you to give to him. Make sure that he gets it. I will expect his call tomorrow."

She turned on her Valentino heels and sauntered out of the store. She managed to throw the sketch at me before she walked through the door. Too bad there was no breeze to carry it out the door after her. I may have disliked her immensely but she sure had great taste in heels.

I bent down to retrieve the drawing. I wadded it up into a tiny ball and grabbed the garbage can. *Shit!* I couldn't throw it away. I unrolled the wad of paper and pressed out as many of the wrinkles as I could. I went to the back and placed it in his appointment book. *For someone who probably went through cotillion, she lacked social manners.*

I always thought high society preached good manners in every situation. She probably flunked that portion of the etiquette class. I bet she had the pinkie finger placed at the proper ninety-degree angle, or whatever, while drinking tea down perfectly. Slurping would not be a byproduct from her delicate sip. She was the only client of ours that I thought ill of. She had the worst personality ever. There were mean people and then there were sadistic haters.

She fell in the second category. Sadistic haters were people I categorized as having no heart. They thrived on being cruel. They did for themselves and only themselves. It didn't matter who they trampled on to get what they wanted. They were the type to let the world know just how wrong you were and how right they are.

Pleasing clients was our number-one priority. However, there are some you want to send on down the road. The sale was not worth the hassle and time spent trying to make them happy. I guess Cash wanted this sale because he hadn't sent her packing yet. Oh well, it's his rodeo. I just filter through the horseshit.

Hey Cash, Cruella De Vil stopped in. Drew up her own sketch for you. Will you be in tomorrow to speak with her? She will be expecting your call.

Cash immediately texted back.

FUCK THAT BULLSHIT! I'll be in.

While I was in a texting mood, i.e., bored out of my mind, I decided to shoot Cole one as well.

Hey Rockstar, you still going pistol shopping Friday?

I moved to put my phone away, figuring that it would take him awhile to get back to me. It vibrated in my hand before I could place it in my pocket.

Sure am. You taking a half day?

I grinned as my fingers flew over the letters.

Just for you. Figured I owed you one.

I enjoyed our banter. Talking to him in any fashion had the tendency to brighten my day.

That doesn't even cover the suit but it's a start. Call me later.

Oh, I most definitely would. I wouldn't miss the chance to hear his voice. I treaded in deep water here, not sure my legs could withstand the required energy needed to wade through the friend zone. I might have to go against all of my insecurities and make a move. To hell with it: even if nothing came of it, I'd kiss those gorgeous lips.

CHAPTER 7

I ordered Cash his special breakfast and my coffee on my way to work. Cash needed the incentive to get past the brutal slap Victoria served up yesterday. His mood would be foul. Good thing my sneakers had a thick sole. Tiptoeing over eggshells all day tended to get a little messy without the proper footwear. Oh, how I wished today were Friday. Working with him would sure be a pleasant picnic. *Not*! Speaking of which, Mr. Sunshine walked in.

"Hey, brother. Got your breakfast. It's on the desk."

He never responded. He stalked heavily to his desk. His massive body flopped into his chair. He unwrapped his sandwich and chomped his food as though his teeth were a meat grinder. It was best to leave the beast alone. Didn't want to poke him if I didn't have to.

I walked out front, flipped the open sign on, and unlocked the door. The phone rang shrilly, breaking the wonderfully silent morning.

"Thank you for calling Firedog Bling. This is Harlow. How may I help you?"

"Is Cash in?"

"Hold please and I will transfer you."

I put her on hold and I yelled to Cash. "Hey, Cash,

Lucifer is on hold for you."

I heard him grunt a response as he picked up the line. I chuckled to myself as I went about my morning duties.

The bell above the door rang and I looked up to see who walked through the door. I gave a big toothy grin as I recognized Peyton and Juno. Of course, I had to greet Juno first with one of our finest dog treats in hand.

"Hello, Peyton. It's good to see you again. Are you here to meet with Cash?"

"Yes. He said he could meet with me this morning."

"Great. I know he will be excited to start on a new project. I'll go in the back and get him."

"Thank you."

I walked quickly toward the back, listening to make sure that he wasn't swearing up a storm from talking with Victoria. I didn't hear anything so I felt it safe to open up the door.

"Cash, your appointment is here. Peyton is her name and Juno is her gorgeous mastiff."

He blew out a deep breath as he stood and smoothed out his shirt. I'm not sure why he does that but it's his way of composing himself. Some people take deep breaths or count to ten. Every time, Cash smoothed out the nonexistent wrinkles of his shirt. I kept the information of her being a beautiful woman to myself. She was stunning and a perfect match for him. She would brighten up his day for sure. I planned to eavesdrop throughout the entire conversation. I wanted to see his reaction as well as his slutty interactions. It would be better than any daytime soap opera.

In the front corner of the store sat a scarred antique wooden table with bench seats. I lined the benches with heavily padded, bright-colored cushions. One side had turquoise and the other bench sported a vibrant orchid purple. They may not be Cash's taste but they brightened up the store and cheered up the customers. Especially considering most of our clientele happened to be women. Everything else was done in a creamy ivory. The only other colors were from the gems on the collars that we carried. We had decided to paint the walls in a creamy ivory color to make the crystals pop on collars. When the sunlight hit them just right, they created a multitude of tiny prisms along the walls.

Cash and Peyton sat on the same side of the bench, speaking softly and their heads bent close together. It looked quite intimate and secretive. I hated to eavesdrop but I couldn't help myself. The overwhelming urge had my feet moving silently toward them. I sat on the floor next to Juno. I made sure not to get my face too close to her soft fur.

"Do you want a particular design or are you looking for something simple?"

"Well, I don't want a ton of crystals. I just want something simple but tasteful. Does that make any sense?"

He laughed. "Perfect sense."

I looked up just in time to see them stare at each other. I coughed to hide my chuckle. They seemed to come out of their daze when they heard me.

Cash turned to sneer. "Don't you have something to do besides pester us?"

"Nope—just giving Juno some attention. Got a problem with that, brother?"

"Yes. You are interrupting our meeting. I would hate for Peyton to be wasting her time," he said testily.

"Harlow, you are not wasting my time. Juno adores you. You are not interrupting either." Then she looked at Cash with a menacing look." Cash, don't be so rude to your sister. Your family is all that you have. One day when she isn't here, God forbid, you will be sorry about being harsh with her." She turned toward me and winked.

It was difficult to keep a straight face when she so eloquently put him in his place. She had a sarcastic side that made her even more adorable. Cash looked thoroughly reprimanded. He even sported a nice frown. Then Peyton and I burst out laughing.

"Oh, you got jokes."

"Oh, lighten up, big brother. You have to admit she got you good!"

He narrowed his eyes. "Just for that little stunt, I'm going to have to refer you to someone else. I'm sorry if I wasted your time this morning." His tone was all business.

He shut his portfolio and got up. "It was a pleasure meeting you, Peyton."

Peyton's beautiful stunned face quickly morphed back into elegance. She sat ramrod straight on the bench as her mouth formed a tight smile. Even I couldn't believe his behavior. Cash had managed to become a bigger asshole than I thought possible. He used to be able to take a joke. Hell, he loved pulling pranks on people. I should—know I got the brunt of them.

He turned on his heel and took a step toward the back Peyton found her voice. "Yes, of course. I apologize for my rude behavior." She angled her body toward me. "It was a pleasure to meet you, Harlow." She got up to leave.

Cash turned back around. "Cuz I'm the best there is!" He busted out laughing. He laughed so hard that he snorted and coughed. He bent over at the waist, trying to catch his breath. "Now that's how to pull a joke. Please sit back down, Peyton, and we can finish with your ideas." He barely got that out due to his own hilarity.

Peyton and I followed his movements, wide-eyed.

He sat back down next to Peyton. "Now where were we?"

She slapped him upside the head. "You are an ass."

"Yes, I am. You have to admit that I got you pretty good." He grinned as though he had won the lottery while he rubbed the spot where Peyton had hit him. "That's what you get for trying to pull a joke on me."

"Yeah, and paybacks are a bitch," she replied menacingly.

I watched them flirt back and forth for a couple of minutes before I went and did some actual work. My neck hurt from twisting it back and forth from their volley. I do declare that Cash met his match in every way. She could give just as well as she took. She was graceful, smart, and beyond beautiful. Most of all, she seemed down-to-earth and had a quirky sense of humor. I might just add her to the family myself. If I only swung that way! *Hell, I'd make an exception for her.* She was a breath of fresh air that our family needed. Let's hope that Cash didn't screw this up.

Peyton and Cash talked well through lunch. When she finally left, I proceeded to harass the shit out of him.

"When's the wedding?"

"Cute, real cute."

"What? Ya'll were huddled over in the corner forever. You have never had an appointment last three hours before. Come on—did you at least get the digits?"

"Not telling, but we are going out to dinner this weekend."

"You mean hooking up this weekend. Do I need to open on Saturday so you can sleep in and play happy household?"

"Nope, fuckface. I will be in Saturday morning to open; you can come in later."

"Oh, so, it's just a booty call Friday night then."

"Don't talk about her like that. It's just dinner," he spat over his shoulder as he slammed the back door.

I smiled to myself. *He defended her. Incredible! He must really like her.* Oh, how the mighty player fell hard. I couldn't wait to see how this would unfold. I needed to keep Peyton around if she made him this happy. Hell, I couldn't remember a time where he willingly opened and I got to stay in bed. I probably shouldn't keep badgering him or he'd change his mind.

I walked into the back to see whether he was still here. Good; he hadn't left yet but he was about to.

"How did your conversation with Victoria go?"

"She is a piece of work and that is saying it lightly. I have never worked with somebody like her. I don't want to ever again that's for sure." He groaned and rubbed his hands over his face. "I looked at her kindergarten sketch and it's close to what I had previously drawn up. Instead of getting pissed off at her, I told her that we would use the crude drawing. I will make the collar from my last sketch and tell her that it was her design we used. That should make her happy. I'd really like to drop her as a client but with all that gaudy bling thrown in, it will bring us a hefty sale."

"Sounds like a good plan. How long do you think we will have to put up with her?"

"Not much longer, I hope. She wants another face-to-face before I start. I agreed to next week. Once that is done, then I can start on the collar. Maybe another month or two tops."

"All right. I can handle that."

"Let's hope we both can."

I had a bunch of orders come in after lunch. I was so busy cataloging the sales and making sure that the custom orders were all in one pile that I didn't hear the door chime.

"Are you busy or just looking busy?"

I smiled at hearing my favorite sexy voice. I looked up and into those deep chocolate pools. "Trying to look busy. Is it working?"

"Sure is. Do you think that you will take a dinner break?"

"Depends on the dinner offer."

"Well, supposing that you do, I was thinking takeout, your place, and a movie."

"It's a deal if you get Uncle Chen's and bring a romantic comedy to watch."

"Is it a deal-breaker if it's not Uncle Chen's?"

"If you have a place better than that, we still have a deal."

He beamed. "See you after work." Then he walked behind the counter and kissed my cheek.

Holy hot tomalley—can you say swoon worthy! I had to fan myself once he left. I hope he wasn't that friendly with his other female friends. I'd like to think that I was special. Usually when you made plans, work would run at a turtle's pace but for once it flew by. Before I knew it, I was dashing home to wait for Cole.

CHAPTER 8

Cole waited outside my door with takeout bags filling his large hands and a movie tucked under each armpit. Now, that was a sight I could get used to. He leaned leisurely against the doorframe, as though he did it every day. His broad shoulder tilted slightly higher than the one up against the door. His long lean legs crossed at the ankle. A sly smirk played along his generous lips as a mischievous twinkle turned his chocolaty eyes to a deep mahogany.

"You beat me home."

"You should just give me a key so I can let myself in next time."

"You are putting a lot of faith into a next time." I laughed.

"It's a pretty safe bet," he said with a gleam in his eye.

I quirked up an eyebrow at him as I unlocked the door. I took the bags from him and set them on the counter.

"I wasn't sure what you liked so I got a little bit of everything."

My stomach growled at that exact moment. "There isn't a Chinese dish that I don't like. Why don't you get

"You may continue, peasant."

He chuckled silently but his body shook loudly with it. I smiled to myself as my eyes once again closed. It was freeing to know that I felt utterly comfortable with him. I said what I wanted, even if I gave myself away. Usually I lied and said something felt good when all I wanted was for them to remove themselves from my personal space. Maybe that's why I'm still single in my thirties. Being near Cole felt as natural and easy as breathing. He felt right.

My thoughts completely shut off when his other hand had inched my shirt up underneath my breasts. His strong fingers were now splayed over my bare stomach. I had a muffin top. My stomach was not toned. It was kind of squishy, like a bowl of Jell-o. I'm usually confident in my own skin. However, when he touched the supple flesh, I squirmed slightly, hoping that he wasn't turned off by it.

He ran his fingers languidly up my stomach over my fleshy ribs, to the underside of my breasts. He skimmed the material but never ventured any higher. I sucked in a breath and arched my back, pushing my breasts out, completely turned on.

"Does this turn my master on?" his deep, husky voice questioned.

I couldn't speak; all I could do was nod my head in answer. His other hand left my hair and pushed underneath my shoulders. I slowly eased up and swirled around to face him. His hand went behind my head, coaxing me closer. My mouth closed over his waiting lips. The kiss was gentle and sweet. He took his time exploring, as I did the same. Our tongues danced to the tune of a slow waltz.

When he finally eased back, I sighed in satisfaction. *God, that man could kiss.* His tongue and lips were felt in every crevice of my body even though they only mated with my mouth.

I licked my lips. "You are a very skilled kisser."

"I aim to please. You are not half bad yourself but I think you need a little bit more practice."

I looked at my watch sarcastically. "I'm free for a couple more minutes."

We ended up making out like two teenagers for hours. Neither of us pressed for more. I was reluctant to stop but his phone rang and interrupted us. I got up from the couch so that I wouldn't be tempted to listen in on his conversation. I wanted to but it seemed pretty rude to do so. I glanced over at him and he seemed irritated. He ended the call and stood.

"I'm sorry but I have to get going."

"No worries. It's getting late anyway and I have to work in the morning. Thank you for dinner."

"It was my pleasure." He kissed me one last time and walked out the door.

I leaned up against the door and exhaled. Whoever said that PG was overrated never experienced Cole. I ran to retrieve my cell phone as it chimed.

I'm sorry for running out on you. Sweet dreams, Harlow.

Holy cow, this guy made me giddy. It would be

unfortunate for me to walk around with a perma grin. It would ruin my reputation. I quickly typed back.

Don't apologize. I'm not upset. Thank you for tonight. I had a lovely time. Good-night, Cole.

Just when I thought it was safe to set my phone back down, another text came through.

Not upset and just a lovely time. I must be losing my touch. It should've been, oh my God, tonight was amazing. I'm so pissed that you had to leave. I'm going to have to put it on hand throw to alleviate all of the desire coursing through my body.

I laughed so hard at the text that my cheeks hurt. I'd fix his ass, right now.

You're a fucking bastard for leaving me all hot and bothered. Now I'm going to have to just imagine that it's your hand pleasuring me instead of my own. YOU OWE ME!

I figured that we would go back and forth for a while, so I just crawled into bed and got comfortable. My eyelids were heavy and closing of their own accord. I held onto the phone in a tight grip as though it were my lifeline.

Holy shit, Harlow, that was a major turn-on. Just picturing you pleasuring yourself is sexy. Knowing that you are thinking of me has got me hard as hell.

I smiled at his reply. My nether region pulsated. I would have to put it on hand throw after all.

Now we're even!

I didn't wait for his reply. I slipped under the covers and pulled his face to mind. As his image became sharper, my hands roamed all over my body. I touched my breasts and massaged my nipples to hardened peaks. My chest rose and fell with my heavy breathing. Just as my fingers headed south, the phone rang. I ignored it but whoever it was kept psycho calling me. My sexual rush faded.

"What?" I demanded.

"Did I interrupt you, Harlow?" he seductively teased, his voice husky, just as affected as I was.

"Yes, you did." I sounded more breathless than angry.

I wasn't ashamed to admit that I had been pleasuring myself. He already knew. My irritation had me snapping at him for interrupting me.

The phone line crackled with heated silence. His heavy breathing sounded a beacon that shot straight to my clit.

"Are you home?" I asked seductively. A wanton woman poked through my voice.

"Sitting in my driveway," he breathed out heavily.

"Are you hard, Cole?"

"Yes, baby, only for you."

"Unzip your pants and pull your cock out. Put me on speaker so I can hear you," I commanded.

"Okay. You do the same. I want to be able to hear you."

I lay back on the bed, switched to speaker mode, and set the phone on my pillow. "Wrap your hand around the base of your cock. Are you imagining my hand around your swollen dick?"

"Fuck! Yes, baby, I can feel you."

"I'm slowly twisting and pumping my hand up and down as I take you in my mouth. Licking and sucking your thick cock."

"Yes," he ground out. "Slide your finger along those perfectly wet folds as though it were my tongue, licking you from your glistening center to your hard clit." His breath hitched. "Do you feel me, baby, tasting your sweet pussy?"

"Hmm. Feels so good," I purred.

"That's it. Now insert your finger in that tight pussy," he demanded.

"Shit." That's all that would come out as the pleasure mounted. I could feel his fingers and tongue playing my body as though he knew it intimately.

We directed each other in a blind symphony. The only thing that could be heard was our moans of pleasure, each of us lost to our own imagination.

"Cole, I'm going to come," I practically shouted.

"That's it, baby. Let me hear you come. I'm right behind you."

I let out a passionate cry as my orgasm tore through my body. My breathing calmed as I heard Cole growl with his own ecstasy. We both stayed quiet, gathering our thoughts.

"That was intense. It was as though you were right here with me."

"I didn't expect it to be such a turn-on for me. Holy hell, Harlow, you are so vocal," he said, bewildered.

"That was a first for me. I've never had phone sex and it was incredible." I laughed. "I always pictured it like 'oh yeah, baby, that's it—talk dirty to me.' While rolling my eyes the whole time, like a big porno cliché."

"I've done it once and it was just like you said. I wasn't turned on in the least but with you it felt as though you were touching me and whispering naughty things in my ear." He chuckled out loud. "I can't believe I just did that in my car. I'm sure the neighbors are wondering about the noises and why I sat here for so long."

"To hell with them. I'm glad that we did that. Now I can go to sleep fully satisfied."

"Me too. Good-night, Harlow. Sweet dreams."

"Good-night, Cole."

CHAPTER 9

I waltzed into work, happy as a pig in shit. Probably not the best analogy but I couldn't come up with anything else at the moment. I had been sexually satisfied—yes, by my own hand, but that hardly matters. I've pleasured myself plenty of times before. Having Cole whisper naughty things to me felt as though it were his hands playing my body. Nothing was going to bring my mood down today. I flipped the open sign and logged on to the computer to look at the orders. I hummed to myself when the door chimed.

Well, shit—there goes my fucking mood. Flushed right down the shitter. *What the fuck was she doing here*? She didn't have an appointment until next week. I did not want to deal with her this early in the morning.

"Hello, Victoria. What a nice surprise. Can I help you with anything?"

"Is Cash in?"

"No. He is not. He should be in later. Is there anything that I can help you with?" I said, trying my best to appease her.

"If you could help me then I would be asking to speak with you and not Cash." She dug her imaginary claws in cruelly.

"Of course. Would you like to wait or would you

like me to have him call you as soon as he gets in?" I tried to remain pleasant but I hung on by a thread.

"I don't know how you manage to run a business when your designer is never in. That is the problem with the lead time on the collars. He cannot possibly make them in a reasonable amount of time when he is never here. I should take my business elsewhere." She stomped out of the door. Her exit looked more like a three-year-old's tantrum than a well-mannered elitist's departure.

Well, good fucking riddance. We don't need your business. Of course, I said all of this quite loudly to the empty storefront. I wanted to gouge her eyes out and punch her in her throat. I'm normally not an aggressive person. I preferred to stay clear of most confrontations. There were occasions that I just couldn't let things slide. Victoria quickly became one of those occasions. Cash better finish that damn collar and quickly before I kicked her stuck-up ass.

I rang Cash. "Hey slacker! Get your ass to work and pronto before I punch your client in the baby maker! I'd be happy to make sure that she couldn't procreate and release the little devil spawns into society."

"Let me guess—Victoria came by looking for me."

"Yeah, that bitch did. She even said that it's no wonder you couldn't make collars any faster when you don't come to work." I took a deep breath. "How do you like that, big brother? She not once but twice dissed you and your product. Do you still want to continue with this or can we dump her ass?"

"No. We will see this out and then never work with her again. I have invested a lot of time with her and I have already started working on the collar. The crystals came in the other day." He tried to hide his irritation. "I'll be in within the next fifteen minutes. Don't worry, little sister. I'll put some of the other projects on hold to finish hers up."

"Just make sure that the ones you put on hold are not our best clients. Don't forget we have a bunch of online orders that need to go out by next week."

"I'll get them done. You might need to pinch-hit for a couple of them."

"Not a problem. When you come in, we can go over the ones that are relatively simple and I'll take those. I know I can accomplish them with minimal help."

"See you in a few."

I stewed for a bit longer as I paced the empty store. I needed to calm down before anyone else came in or I was going to go postal. I decided to give Cole a buzz. He seemed to have a knack for making me forget about the little things that bothered me.

"Hey, beautiful. I was just thinking about you."

"Hi there, stud. Whacha you doing?"

"Working. But since you called, I'm going to take a little break."

I could hear him step out of a meeting or something because the background noise grew quiet. "I didn't interrupt anything important, did I?"

"Nope, it's nothing pressing. How is your morning going?"

"It was great until one of our clients walked in and

stirred up a bunch of shit. I didn't call to whine. I just wanted to say hi. Hi."

"It might help you release some of that anger if you talk about it. Get it all off your chest."

"Hmm… Get it all off my chest, huh?" I teased.

"You are evading but I don't mind talking about your chest. I have a feeling that you have the most beautiful breasts ever created. It will be a hardship to look, taste, and tease them. But somebody has to do it."

"Yes, I'm sure that it will be a hardship for you and dreadful for me to experience."

His guttural laugh lifted my mood instantaneously.

"Thanks, Cole. I am feeling much better and a little horny."

"My goodness, Harlow. Do you always say what you are thinking?" He sounded shocked.

"Not always but around you I can't seem to censor what comes out of my mouth."

"Maybe I just need to keep your mouth busy in the future. Seriously, though, I love that you are this open. It takes the guesswork and games out of the picture. It's very refreshing and probably why I am so attracted to you."

"Good to know."

"See you tomorrow. Do you want me to pick you up?"

"Sounds good to me. Thanks again, Cole."

"Anytime."

Cash strolled in as I hung up. He didn't look pissed off or annoyed at all. Maybe I was the only one Victoria could get a rise out of. I swore I would no longer let her bother me anymore. Just let her snooty behavior roll off my back like water off a duck.

"Morning, Cash. What brings you into work so early?"

"Ha, ha, ha, little sister, very funny." He grabbed me in a headlock and gave me the worst noogie ever. Still trapped within his clutches, I came back with, "I hate you. You are the worst brother ever!"

"Love you too, sis. Come on. Let's go over these orders and then I'll call the Princess of darkness."

"She makes the Devil look like an angel."

We went through all the orders and determined that I would take about half of them to work on. The other half Cash could knock out within a week's time.

I let out a pent-up breath. "Thank goodness we went through these and split them up. I started to stress out, having to put them all on your plate."

"Honestly, Harlow, there is no reason why you can't work on some of the collars yourself. You can always run them by me when you are done or have a question. It's not like you have to stay glued to the front and number side of the business. Plus, the collars from online are mainly ordered from our catalogue. All you have to do is follow the picture."

"Really? Thanks, Cash. I would like that."

"I will also start picking up some of your duties as well so that this is more of a partnership. Fifty-fifty is the way it is supposed to be. I am sorry for taking advantage of you and all that you do."

"I appreciate it and am very glad that you are seeing the business differently. But why the sudden apology?"

"The day you took off work and I covered—well, it made me realize that you need more in your life besides this place. Seeing your friends is what you need. You have been happier these past few weeks and I like seeing you happy."

I giggled at the *friends* remark. If Cash knew that it was Cole, he would not be so willing to let me enjoy life a little more. He would keep me under lock and key until he was one hundred percent sure that Cole was a decent guy. Cash was very protective of me. It really ruined my social life in high school. Needless to say, I didn't have many dates. The boys were scared of Cash. The ones who dared to test the limits soon fell to his mercy. Now he's more like an annoying fly buzzing around your face.

I figured now was as good of a time as any to start some of those online orders. We couldn't afford to get backlogged. I yelled into the back for Cash to get his ass out to the front because high society's favorite member headed straight for the store.

"Hello, Victoria. Are you ready to finalize the sketch so that I can get started?" Cash asked politely.

"Yes. Let's get started."

They walked over to the table and began the tedious process. I could still hear what they were talking about but I chose to ignore them altogether. He was using his fake phone voice, which grated on my nerves.

I went into the back to gather up the materials I needed for my first collar. Jubilation skipped through my body at the task that lay before me. I scanned sharp eyes over at Cash and Victoria. They seemed to be getting along, so I went back to the counter and laid out my things. I picked up the order sheet and selected the collar from the catalogue. This one didn't seem too bad. The design was fairly simple and didn't need a lot of stones. I forgot the nameplate. It needed to be engraved and placed on first before I began the stonework.

You would think that making these collars would be simple but there is a lot of prep work involved. Without the prep work, then you have the potential to screw up the whole layout of the stones. The stones were what cost the most. You definitely did not want to waste them. They were no longer usable if you took them off repeatedly; you ended up eating that cost. Too many of those mistakes and you lose money.

I chanced a brief look over at them. It looked as though the meeting of the minds was coming to a close. The sooner she left the store, the better. I know I would breathe easier when she departed. I'm glad that no other customer came in. I couldn't be certain that her mouth would run them off or not. Seventy-five percent of our business came from word of mouth. One sketchy or rude remark had the potential to severely cut into our profits.

"Alright. I'm going to get started on this collar."

"You mean she signed off on the design!" I hopped up and down and clapped my hands as though I were a cheerleader at a pep rally.

"Yep. Got her to sign the paper and everything," he gloated, waving the paper with her signature in my face. I snatched it and quickly filed it so it didn't get lost. It was our only insurance in case the client decided that we didn't adhere to the actual design. Thus far we have never had to use one.

I lost myself in the collar, so absorbed in it that I was caught by surprise that it had grown dark outside. A quick check of my wristwatch confirmed that it was already closing time. I flipped the sign and locked up. I was ready to go home. Yet, the urge to finish the collar superseded my desire to head out. I literally couldn't put it away unfinished. If I did, my brain would start its incessant nagging.

It closely resembled a veteran smoker laying their pack down for the final time. The obsessive mind verbiage is enough to make you immediately pick up a pack after an hour. I worked feverishly until I had glued the last stone. I held up the collar. Amazed and proud of myself, I stuck out my chest like a champion. *It looked fabulous!* The colorful stones surrounded the titanium nameplate perfectly. They trailed halfway down each side of the collar. *Ta-da! I am finished. Oh yeah, oh yeah,* I chanted as I danced horrendously around.

My phone chirped in mid dance. *Holy shit, it was ten o'clock already!*

Are you naked?

What a loveable pervert!

Unfortunately for you, I'm not. Still at the shop, finishing up an order.

I packed up the leftover supplies and cleaned up my

mess.

Late night for you. Have you eaten?

Being busy in the creative zone, I hadn't stopped to eat anything all day.

Nope. Figured I'd just pop some popcorn when I got home. Are you still at work or home?

At work tying up some loose ends so that I can skip out tomorrow. You want to grab something to eat?

Sounds like a great offer but I'm going to decline tonight.

Fine! Be that way. I'll just go home with a hangry belly! Are we still on for tomorrow?

I would have loved to meet up with Cole but I would see him soon enough.

Absolutely we are on for tomorrow. You are a big boy. I'm sure you'll figure something out.

I'll see you around noon.

I'll be ready.

My spike of adrenaline quickly waned. My neck hurt from bending over the collar all day and my belly growled. I wanted to head straight home and put on my pajamas. I heard a knock at the front door of the shop. *Who the hell would be knocking this late at night?* I grabbed an umbrella some customer had left behind and went to open up the door. A girl can never be too careful. Not sure what I would do with it, but anything can be used as a weapon!

"Cole?" A huge breath of relief exited my lungs. "What are you doing here?"

"I was texting you on my way over, hoping you'd want to get a bite. Even though you blew me off, I took the chance on you still being here. I wanted to see you for a minute."

"Come in." I locked the door behind him.

"Are you expecting rain?" He raised his eyebrows in question.

"Nope—more like trouble."

He openly donkey laughed at me. "Really?"

"Hey, it can make a good weapon. Would you like for me to try it on you?"

He held up his hands in defeat while still laughing. "No—I give. Please don't hurt me with your flimsy umbrella."

For good measure, I walked around him and whacked the back of his ass with it.

"Ouch, that kind of hurt!"

Now that was funny. I busted out laughing as I put the umbrella back in the lost and found box.

"You liked it and you know it. I know you're kind of kinky like that!"

"You think you know me so well."

"Yep. I sure do."

He rounded the corner so fast I didn't even see him coming until he grabbed me and spun me into his chest. I let out a high-pitched squeal of delight. At least I thought I did, but I'm not sure. He surprised the hell out of me. Next thing I knew, his lips were devouring mine. His hands ran down my backside and rested on my ass. He gently squeezed and then smacked my ass playfully.

"Next time, I will have to bend you over my knee for that little trick you played on me."

"I'd like to see you catch me first," I flirted.

"You don't have a chance of getting away from me." He smiled and let me go. "Well, Miss Harlow, it is time for me to go. I just wanted a good-night kiss from those sweet lips of yours."

Dang. Just when I got all hot and bothered. "I'm happy to oblige anytime."

He gave me a quick peck one last time. "Make sure you lock up after I leave. I don't want some poor innocent Samaritan getting beaten with an umbrella."

"Hey, if you are trying to walk through the door after hours you deserve to get hit."

"See you tomorrow."

"Night, Cole." I smiled, totally geeked out by the way that he made me feel special.

CHAPTER 10

The motivation to get out of bed for work was alarmingly absent. As much as I wanted to, I couldn't leave Cash hanging. It's not a long drive into work but this morning, every circus monkey was out. The drive was agonizingly slow. By the time I got to work, my road rage personality had reared its ugly head. In my defense, I had only flipped off three people and honked my horn once. I mean, come on; when the light turns green, you go. You don't hang out until it turns yellow.

For the love of Pete, never ride your brakes. When you do, I have the tendency to think that there is a bunch of traffic ahead. Or, you might be getting ready to turn. Not spend the next four miles grinding your gears with no one in front of you! *Ugh!*

I stepped out of the car just as Cash's blacked-out Chevy truck pulled in. He drove a sweet ride. Made me want to trade my gas-efficient Cavalier in for something cooler.

"Fancy meeting you here! What are you doing here so early? I thought I'd open and you were coming in later."

"Figured you could ignore me and pretend that I was still at home. I wanted to come in and get some uninterrupted work in on the collar before you left."

"Do you want me to open Saturday just in case you

have a late evening with Peyton?" I asked seriously. All joking aside, I really wanted him to enjoy his evening with her.

"Nah. Like I said, it's only dinner. I am not planning on an after-hours nightcap."

Wow, if Cash had uttered that a month ago. I would have thought he was being sarcastic. He seemed to actually respect Peyton and would behave like a nobleman. I silently chuckled, thinking it ironic that he would court her before taking her to bed. That was so not his typical style. Truth be told, I was proud of him. That particular bit of highly valued intel would never pass through my lips. He had a big enough head as it was.

"Cash, before you start, will you take a quick look at the collar that I finished? Please make sure it's exactly what the customer ordered and I will ship it out today."

"Sure, no problem. Bring it in and set it on my desk."

I made sure I did that before I even opened up the store. I was proud of my craftsmanship. *Would putting this collar in a shadow box be too weird?*

"Harlow," Cash shouted.

The deep baritone of his voice sliced through the quietness of the shop, startling me. "What's up?"

"The collar looks great. I don't see a flaw anywhere. Good job. You can send that out."

I practically glowed from his compliment. "Thanks, Cash. I will."

The morning flew by. Another collar took shape. My

skills were on the upswing. I stuck my head in the back. "I'm heading out. Do you need anything before I go?"

"Nope. Have a good time."

"I want details tomorrow when I come in."

"You know I'll need your opinion on how it went. You'll get the 411."

"Love ya—bye."

"Love ya, too."

I sailed out the door eager to get home. I quickly checked the balance in my checking account. The urge to splurge on a new piece hit me square in the face. *Score!* Being frugal had its merits. I signed off just in time for Cole to knock on the door.

"Hey, stud. Come here and give your woman a kiss." I grabbed a fistful of his shirt and yanked him toward me.

"Mmm. Now that's a welcome I could get used to." He grinned sexily. "Would you like to go get some lunch first or afterward?" He wriggled his eyebrows. "Or we can skip it all?"

I chuckled. "Come on, smooth talker. You know how serious I am about my food and guns."

He winked. "Then let's head out. I'll have to ravish you another time."

I stopped dead in my tracks and contemplated my next move: On the one hand, Cole's skilled hands and mouth doing dirty things with my body. Or on the other hand, we got to put holes in shit.

I shook my head and laughed. "You're so cute. But I want food, range, and then your sexy body. All in that order."

"Well then, your chariot awaits."

He swept his hand out in an after-you gesture. I sauntered down to his car with him nipping at my heels.

We went to a little hole-in-the-wall Mexican joint. It was the best authentic cuisine that I've ever had the pleasure of tasting. I had the urge to unbutton my jeans but decided that I needed to maintain some decorum.

"I ate too much. I'm about to burst!" I groaned.

"It was really good," he mumbled as he wiped his mouth with the napkin.

"We are both members of the clean plate club. That should hold us off for a couple of hours."

"I should think so." Cole paid the tab and we hightailed it to my favorite gun store.

Excitement bubbled through me at the mere thought of seeing Marge. She had to be about fifty-five but she looked older than that. Her skin was leathery and permanently tanned from hours of being outside. Myriad wrinkles hung on her boney figure. She had a deep, raspy voice from smoking most of her life.

For as long as I've known her, Marge owned the small shop. She was colorful and didn't sugarcoat anything. She always carried her 9mm clipped to her belt. She made no attempt to conceal it. No one dared mess with her. She was a true badass in every sense. She smoked, drank, swore, and could outshoot any man or woman. I was convinced that she was Annie Oakley reincarnated.

"Hi, Marge. How are you doing today?"

"I'm hanging in there. The good Lord blessed me with another day. I can't complain about nuthin'." She winked.

"Oh, I'm sure you could."

"I could talk your ear off but it ain't gonna change nothing so why fucking bother."

I grinned at our usual conversation. When I asked her how she was doing these were the exact answers every time.

"I want you to meet my friend, Cole. He is in the market for a pistol. Seeing as it's his first one, I wanted you to have the honors."

"Well, shit, that just brings a tear to my eye." She pretended to sniffle and wipe away a lone tear. Then she looked at Cole critically. "You gonna respect this new piece of yours? Or are you one of those types that is gonna blab all over the county that you're a badass?" She took a deep, rattling breath. "Cuz if you think you're tough, I ain't selling you no pistol."

Cole, taken back from her bluntness, cleared his throat. "No, Ma'am. I will be very respectful. I do not need to be a badass. Harlow already calls me Nancy so I won't be going around town pretending to be John Wayne."

"Good answer, son."

Cole lifted his eyebrow at me and I just shrugged in answer. Marge moved on down the display and stopped at the far corner. We followed. Curiosity pulled at me. *What handgun would she pull out?* Cole followed, too stunned not to. She had a knack for picking out the best fit for her customers. She was the one who pulled out the Sig for me to try. It was the first piece and only piece that she selected for me that day. How she knew exactly what would fit most naturally still impressed me. She had also selected my brother's piece. I never questioned her choices again. Her accuracy spoke loud enough.

She laid out the cloth mat on the countertop. Then she pulled out the sleekest piece I had ever seen. She checked the chamber and the clip, making sure they were empty before she set it upon the protective cover. I sucked in a breath. I stared down at the .45 Kimber Ultra Carry. It was compact and stainless steel. I went to reach out to touch it, but she slapped my hand away.

"I don't think so, missy. This is for Cole."

He stared at it for a moment, almost afraid to pick it up.

"Go ahead, son. It ain't gonna bite you," she hacked out.

He tentatively picked up the piece and pointed it toward the back of the store away from us. It looked petite in his large hands. *It would look much better in mine!*

"How does that feel?" Marge asked.

"It feels comfortable. Almost as if it were meant for my hands alone." His eyes sparkled with excitement.

She smiled knowingly. "Thought it might. Why don't you grab yourself some plugs and a box of ammo and go shoot a few rounds."

He looked like a kid in a candy store without parents. He grabbed what he needed and went through the range doors.

I really wanted to go but this was for him, not me. I stayed behind and talked with Marge.

"You are sweet on that boy."

I blushed. "That obvious, huh?"

"Only cuz I know you, girl. He is a handsome devil. You make sure you tread lightly with that one. He has the makings of a real heartbreaker."

"It's hard to take it slow. He makes it so easy to fall in love with him." I sighed dreamily with my confession.

"I know. Just promise me to go in with your eyes wide open."

This was a strange conversation for the both of us. So I made sure to swear that I would. "I promise."

"Good. Now that that's settled, I want to show you something that just came in the other day. I held it in the back hoping you would be in soon."

My excitement bubbled over. I couldn't wait to see what she would bring out. She carried out the carry case and set it on the counter. My body hummed with excitement as she unlocked the case. She opened the case agonizingly, slow as though the world's top secrets were carefully nestled inside. I gasped. She laughed at the way my eyes brightened and ballooned up as large as saucers.

"Wow, Marge. She is pretty."

"Ain't she?"

I pulled the pistol out and admired the two-tone colors on the grip and the stainless-steel barrel. It was a Sig Sauer 1911 style but smaller. It was similar to the Kimber Ultra Carry that Cole was shooting. This handgun would be more comfortable to carry than my traditional .45 at home. I had seen this same handgun in a magazine the other day. I thought it sleek on the pages but up close it deemed itself more worthy.

She pulled out a target and plugs for me and pointed to the lane next to Cole. She didn't have to tell me twice. I practically skipped through the door.

We shot our pieces respectfully until all of the ammo was spent. We came out with gigantic smiles permanently etched onto our faces. Marge, the All-Seeing-Eye, knew we would be.

"I take it you enjoyed the pistols," she simply stated with a little *I told you so mixed in.*

"Hell yeah!" we both chimed.

We all cackled. I shut my mouth and let Cole go first.

"I loved it. It feels like a natural extension of my hand."

"Do you want to see any other pistols?" Marge questioned.

"No, I'm sold. I want this one."

"What about you, missy?"

"Are you really asking me that silly question?"

"Nope. I knew you wanted it as soon as you got a look at it." She smiled as she rang us up.

CHAPTER 11

We said our good-byes, with a promise to come back soon.

"She kind of scares me."

"When I first met her, she really intimidated me. Give it time; she'll grow on you. I love her and her ballsy ways. Mind you, I wouldn't mess with her either."

"Like poking a rattler!"

"Exactly like that. She strikes fast and is deadly."

"What do you say to some dinner?"

He had switched the subject so fast that I had to give my brain a minute to catch up.

"I say definitely. I can't believe that it's that late already."

"Time flies when you're having fun." He winked at me.

The final decision was greasy steak subs and a vat of thick-cut fries. Quick and easy takeout. We sat in front of the TV and gobbled our dinner in comfortable silence. I leaned back against the couch, disgustingly full.

"I need to quit eating like that. Ugh. I feel gross and

yet it tasted so good." I rubbed my protruding belly.

"So ice cream is out of the question."

"Seriously?" I looked at him as if he were crazy. *Where the hell would he put it?* I couldn't even think about eating another thing right now.

"No. Now that I think about it, you would make a better dessert."

Yes, please! Desire built low in my belly. He pulled me underneath his warm body. He possessively claimed my mouth. Our tongues mated with languid strokes. We took the time to learn each other. He moved along my jaw, showering me with sweet tenderness. I drank it all in as my pleasure radiated throughout my body. Blood pounded in my brain, leapt from my heart, and made my legs clamp tight, fighting the aching need that clenched my sex. He nestled between my thighs, adding the much-needed pressure against my clit. I moaned in ecstasy as his mouth traveled along the tender flesh of my neck.

His hot breath fanned my already heated skin. "You have too many clothes on."

He slipped his clever hands under my top and swiftly brought it over my head. He balled up the material and tossed it across the room. On his knees, he raked his eyes boldly over me. A rush of nerves settled in the pit of my stomach, overriding my desire. I moved my arms over my bared stomach, trying to cover myself. I was helpless to halt my embarrassment. He removed my arms and gently placed them at my sides. Without haste, his fingers unclasped my bra and pulled it down my arms, freeing my swollen breasts. I turned my head to the side, unable to witness his scrutiny.

"Look at me," he commanded.

I turned my head slowly and met his gaze. My heart lurched and my pulse pounded at the smoldering flame that I saw in his eyes.

He yanked my hand over his bulging crotch. "This is what your body does to me. You are so fucking beautiful that I ache for you all the time."

I closed my eyes and breathed in his carnal words, allowing them to wash away any remaining insecurities. My lips broke into a wide, open smile. "Show me."

His fiery palm reached inside my waistband, pulled my pants down my legs and chucked them. I lay completely open to him. His gaze roamed from my eyes, down and over my breasts, making me feverish. In one swift motion, he jumped off the couch and shed his clothing.

He opened my thighs as far as they would go. "Beautifully wet and all mine."

I squirmed under his bold gaze, driving my need into a frenzy of lust. He leaned over me and sensually fused his lips with mine. I wrapped my arms around his sides, running my fingernails up and down the length of his back. His lips and teeth grazed down my neck to my overly sensitive breasts. I moaned as his tongue swirled around the hardened peak while his hand massaged and kneaded the other. He switched, lavishing them with equal attention. The tip of his cock teased my entrance. My pussy begged to be filled.

"Fuck me, Cole. I need to feel you inside me," I pleaded as I moved my hips up and down, allowing the tip of his cock to slide through my drenched folds.

"Jesus. Baby, if you keep that up, I'm going to come," he growled.

I wound my legs around his hips, pushing him tighter to me. He eased his thick girth inside, allowing my center to accommodate him. The slight twinge of pain quickly turned into pleasure. I pushed up my hips to allow him to go deeper. Each of us panted as our release built. He placed his palm between our bodies, circling my clit with his thumb as he pumped in and out of me, harder and harder.

"Fuck, Harlow—I'm not going to last. You feel so good." He groaned.

My muscles contracted, pulling at his cock, demanding his release. I screamed out his name as stars exploded behind my eyelids.

"Oh, fuck," he hissed as he spilled his hot seed inside my welcoming pussy.

He tenderly kissed my forehead as he slid out of me and maneuvered behind me, spooning. We lay exhausted on the couch. As the sweat cooled my skin, I shivered. Cole pulled the afghan over our entwined bodies. I burrowed up against his chest as he cocooned me in his solid arms. Sometime during the night, we ended up in my bed. Not a minute was wasted.

I woke up and stretched my sore muscles. I couldn't remember a time that I was this sore and enjoyed every minute of it. Cole had a stamina that I wasn't sure I could keep up with but I'd sure as hell try. I grinned as I thought back to last night. I rolled over, hoping to wrap my body around his. My hand met with a cold pillow and a note. My smile quickly faded. *A fucking note! Really?* He could've at least woken me up to tell me good-bye. *Just read the note before you determine that he is a douche bag and that you're an idiot.*

You looked so beautiful sleeping that I didn't have the heart to wake you. Please forgive me for leaving without saying a word. Call me later.

All right, I have to admit that the note was sweet and he wasn't a total douche bag. However, the verdict was still out on whether or not I'm an idiot. I couldn't lounge in bed all day. I had to get the dish on Cash's night.

I dashed into the store as if there were a fire encroaching on my heels. I was out of breath from my twenty-foot sprint. My newly sore muscles screamed in agony, reminding me of last night's sexual escapades. *I'm so out of shape.* I flung open the door with so much force that it promptly smacked back into my face. *Shit, that hurt.*

"You are an idiot! Do you need the details that badly?" He raised his eyebrows as he snickered.

"Yes—yes I do," I replied, still panting.

"Well, I'm not giving them to you."

"What?" I grabbed a fistful of his hair and tipped his head back. "Speak now or you're going to have a nasty bald spot."

He no longer looked smug. His whole body convulsed as he roared with laughter. Granted it was funny. As if I could even hurt him. He was six three and built like a linebacker. I didn't stand a chance against him. I was five seven, so height wasn't the issue. It was my lack of muscles and coordination that would be my downfall. Tripping over my own feet was a common occurrence.

He twisted his body to dislodge my hand, grabbed my waist, and flipped me upside down as though I were a measly feed bag. I squealed in fear. He had been known to do this and drop me without guilt.

"I give, fucker! Put me down. Uncle! Uncle!" I screamed.

He was still busting a gut with laughter. How he was able to maintain his hold through his maniacal laughter puzzled me and yet I was beyond grateful. We looked up when we heard someone clear their throat.

He quickly bent me in half and allowed my feet to touch the floor before he let me go.

Peyton's eyes narrowed as a brilliant-white toothy grin took over her features. "Am I interrupting your family bonding time?"

"You just saved Harlow from an ass whooping," he smugly replied.

"Whatever. I so had you. As a matter of fact, dear brother, I believe I see a small bald spot on the back of your head." Then I ran to the front and left the two of them in the back. I would owe that girl for saving my ass.

Cash popped his head through the door. "Peyton and I are getting ready to head out. Are you good?"

"Yep. Have a good time."

I waved them a bon voyage and got back to work on my collars. My butt started to go numb sitting on the stool at the counter. I picked up all of the stuff and carried it to the benches in the corner. It was much roomier over here. I spread out and went back to work. I was thankful for our slow days. Even more grateful for our high-dollar collars and online orders that kept us afloat on days like today. I looked up and saw Sasha and Lady getting ready to come into the store. I quickly cleared the table and turned on the coffee pot.

"Good afternoon. Sasha." I welcomed her into the store. "Care to have a cup of coffee with me? I was just about to take a break," I lied sincerely.

"That sounds wonderful, dear. Thank you."

"Please come and sit down. I'll get a bone for Lady."

I swiped two coffee cups from the back and went to pour our coffee. I placed Sasha's coffee in front of her and bent down to give Lady her bone. The little yapper about took my fingers off. I yanked them back quickly before she took a chunk of skin with her piranha-like choppers.

I took a seat opposite from her. "What brings you in today?"

"Peyton said that she was headed over here to meet with Cash, and I figured I'd meet her here. I wanted to see the design that he is working on. I guess I just missed her. Is Cash in the back?"

I looked at her, trying to figure out what to say when I caught the amusement in her eyes.

"You just missed them. They went to lunch." I winked.

"Cash is a nice young man. A little rough around the edges, but charming and good for my niece."

I giggled at her remark. If she only knew how charming Cash could be. "I'd say that Peyton is good for Cash. He needs a woman who will stand up to him."

"I'm glad that I sent her his way then. I knew they would hit it off once they met. I talked about him all the time but she has a tendency to dismiss me. I showed her the last collar that he made. Once she saw it, I knew she would have to have one for Juno." She slapped her hand on the table, startling Lady and me. "Took her sweet time coming in here, though. I almost gave up on the whole idea."

"She will be mad when she finds out you were meddling," I announced, trying to hold back my laughter.

"You better not tell her anything. You are not too old for me to throw over my knee."

"Oh, I wouldn't dream of it." I shook my head and chuckled.

I spent the rest of the afternoon talking with Sasha. She was a wonderful woman. Meeting people like Sasha was one of my favorite perks from working in the store. It's nice to know that some of our regulars were as familiar as family. I always cherished these times. *Where else could I work at a place I loved, sipping coffee with a customer who I adored?*

Sasha promised to feed me details and I swore to do the same. Of course, I would make sure mine were of the PG nature. Not filled with the vulgarities that came out of Cash's mouth. I made Sasha agree to come back in and have coffee with me again soon. I suppose that I just created my own little knitting circle of gossip! Well, a partial circle at least.

I left Cole a voicemail before I started back on the collars again. I would get so wrapped up in them that I would forget to call. I stretched my neck and rolled my shoulders. I had been working in the same position for so long that my back and neck began to bother me. I finally put the finished collars on Cash's desk and put the unfinished ones in a box underneath the counter. I'd tackle those next week. Now that I helped Cash with some of the orders, we were well ahead of the game. I could walk out of here with a clean conscience. No lingering nagging thoughts.

As soon as my tired ass hit the couch, I was sound asleep. I woke up, trying to turn the TV off because whatever show was on was loud as hell. I grabbed the remote and hit the power button. Only it didn't shut off; it turned on. *What in tarnation was that banging noise?* As my senses began to fire coherently, I realized that someone was knocking on the door. *Jeez.* Whoever kept knocking would be sent on the yellow bus straight to hell. I stumbled to the door and looked through the peephole.

I opened the door. "What the fuck, Cole? Are you trying to wake up the neighborhood?" I snarled. I quickly glanced at the time on the microwave. "Cole, what are you doing here? It's two in the morning."

"I know it's late and I'm sorry for waking you up. I had to see you. I didn't get a chance to call you back today. I felt shitty for having to leave without saying good-bye this morning." He looked at me with puppy dog eyes. "Can I please come in?"

Shit! Is that all that he had to do for me to cave? His thick eyelashes batted. *Boy, was I in deep trouble.* I opened up the door and let him in. In the back of my mind, I knew exactly what this visit was. It wasn't because he felt guilty. Let's call a spade a spade—or in my case, a booty call. I picked up the line and answered. I shucked my clothing as I walked to my room. Might as well give him my expectations for the evening. He would put out considering he had the audacity to wake me up. I'm sure it would be a real hardship for him.

I didn't get more than two steps inside the room when I heard a low growl. The vibrations slammed viciously through me and pulsed their way to my clit. Liquid heat pooled between my legs. He wound a hand in my hair, tugging slightly. I moaned with the possessive contact. My body shuddered as his free hand reached around and tweaked my hardened nipple.

I arched my back into his smooth chest, pushing my nipple deeper between his fingertips. He continued the sweet torture as his other hand tilted my head to the side to bare my slender neck. I was completely at his mercy when his mouth descended on my sensitive pulse point. The strong harness of his lips sent new spirals of ecstasy through me.

"Need you so bad," I whimpered.

His mouth never broke contact as his lips seared a path down my neck and shoulder.

"I've been hard all day, thinking about your tight pussy," he groaned out.

His hand caressed the flesh from my breasts down to my stomach and cupped my swollen sex. I bucked wildly into his hand from the exquisite pressure. I craved the release that only he could give me. His thick finger slid between my slick folds and into my warm center.

"Oh," was the only sound I made.

"So fucking wet. All mine," he possessively snarled in my ear, sending sparks straight to my core.

I ground my ass against his erection when he added another finger, stretching me. His fingers curled inside, hitting my g-spot as his thumb lazily circled my clit.

"That's it, baby—fuck my fingers until you come."

"Fuck, Cole," I screamed as my orgasm blazed fiercely, scorching my insides.

His fingers never slowed; they continued to pump in and out as my climax subsided. My breaths came out hot and heavy. My body shuddered anew as he continued his divine torture, building a new wave of heat.

"Cole," I pleaded, needing so much more.

He slipped his fingers from my pussy and led us to the bed. I climbed up with my back facing his chest.

"On your knees, baby. I want your sweet ass in the air as I fuck you from behind."

I moaned at his crass words as they tossed more fuel onto my already burning flesh. His dirty talk sent a bout of heated desire directly to my pussy, making it pulse feverishly with need. I felt the dip of the mattress when he climbed up behind me. Anticipation hummed through my blood. My body coiled tightly and my core opened for him.

His fingers grazed the back of my thighs sensually,

making my body jolt from the unexpected tingles. He moved up my thighs and over my ass. His palms massaged gently at first. The pressure increased and drove me wild with want. When I thought that I could no longer take anymore teasing, he drove his cock into me.

"Ah!" Pleasure ricocheted through me.

"God, you feel fucking fantastic. So wet and needy."

He thrust hard and deep, building an inferno deep within. My pussy contracted around his cock, squeezing as my orgasm built.

"Oh, God, baby. That's it—come all over my cock." His arousal was evident in his hoarse voice.

He moved his hand to my mound and slid his index finger through my swollen lips, seeking my pleasure zone. He made short circles around my bundle of nerves. He moved his other hand over my ass, stroking each cheek. Then he placed his thumb and circled my rosette. I bit my lip and arched my neck, tossing my head back as I became inundated with responsiveness. I've never had my anus played with and it felt dirty and yet phenomenal. My body was in sensory overload as he played with my clit, pounded into my center, and circled my virgin hole.

I dug my fingers into the sheet and screamed his name as my body shattered into a million pieces. My pussy convulsed, milking his cock as he thrust into me one last time. He groaned my name as his essence coated my inner walls. Gently slipping out of me, Cole rolled to the side and pulled me to him. We lay there, entwined together and lost in our release. He kissed the back of my neck and snuggled tighter. I smiled sedately and fell fast asleep.

I woke up the next morning, expecting another note. To my surprise, he lay with his back to me, snoring softly. I openly admired his athletic body. He had strong arms, a chiseled stomach, and muscular thighs. He had a gorgeous runner's body as well as the stamina. I soaked in as much of him as I could before the urge to run my hands over him took over. Not even two seconds later, that was exactly what I did.

"What are your plans for today?" Cole asked me over breakfast.

"Going to my parent's for dinner tonight is the only thing that I have to do." I smirked. "Would you like to come? It might be a good time for you to meet them."

His hand froze midway from the plate to his mouth. The gap between his lips could have been mistaken for a black hole.

Before he keeled over from panic, I reassured him. "Lighten up, Cole. I'm just kidding."

"I'm sorry, Harlow. That probably wasn't the best way to handle your question."

I laughed so hard that egg popped out of my mouth. Thank goodness it popped out instead of lodging down my throat. *Death from choking on an egg—that'd be my luck!*

"Seriously, Cole. I was only playing around."

He loosened up but not entirely. His body remained coiled tightly as he shifted the remainder of his breakfast around his plate. I hated to see our carefree morning ruined because of my mouth. I tried my hardest to heed Marge's words. I also understood that my feelings for him were much stronger than his were for me. It wasn't as if I were a bombshell of the month.

However, the more I looked at his distressed face, the more pissed I got. *Was meeting my family that terrifying?* They were hard to handle and I was born into it. More than likely, the thought of a committed relationship petrified him. Just because we had a mind-blowing night didn't mean that I wanted to marry him and have his babies. For fuck's sake, give me some credit. I wasn't one of those clingy, obsessive girls.

A sharp stab of pain went right through my chest. All I wanted was an exclusive relationship. That didn't mean he had to meet my parents today or a month from now. *Fuck!*

"Look, Cole, I'm sorry for what I said. Obviously it upset you. I am not asking you to come and meet my parents as my boyfriend or at all." I took a mental count of five and a couple of deep breaths to try to subdue my anger. I was about to unleash a side of me that would make Satan sit back in his throne and cower. "We had a fun night. Let's leave it at that."

His body uncoiled even more as I took his plate to the sink. I didn't even bother rinsing it out. "If you don't mind, I have to go talk to my brother about work."

He finally looked at me. "Are you kicking me out?"

He tried to lighten the mood but I honestly couldn't fake any enthusiasm. I wanted him to leave. He got what he had come for. My heart sank in my chest with a heavy dose of reality. This would have been so much easier if he would have left me floundering on that fucking city grate. I would have never known what I was missing. With my back turned, I placed my hands on the sink and took another deep breath and plastered a smile on my face.

"Sure am. I'm a busy gal." I went for upbeat but it fell flat, even to my ears.

I grabbed his hand and pulled him toward the door. I let him kiss me good-bye. He may have thought that he could continue to use me as a booty call but I was too old for that shit.

"Thanks for a wonderful day and evening. I am truly sorry for the way that I acted earlier. You caught me by surprise. Give me a call when you get home tonight."

I smiled and said nothing. I wouldn't call him, even if he paid me to. I shut the door behind me and locked it. I washed the damn dishes before I went to my room and had a mini meltdown. *I couldn't even fathom crying with dirty dishes in the sink!* It would totally ruin my well-deserved pity party.

CHAPTER 12

I finally dragged my ass into the shower. No amount of makeup would conceal my red, puffy eyes. It didn't matter because I didn't own any. I would blame it all on my allergies. *No sweat!* My family wouldn't know the difference.

I strolled through the door, as happy and carefree as I could muster. The house was louder than normal. *Did she invite the whole neighborhood?* I turned the corner and about pissed myself. There on my brother's lap, was Peyton! I blinked a couple of times to make sure that my eyes weren't playing tricks on me. Nope; she remained seated on his lap.

"Hey, Harlow. Long time no see!" Peyton chirped happily.

Oh whatever! Damn happy couples make me want to gag. My brother peered around Peyton. A silly grin adorned his ugly mug. I hated him right then. It felt as though he were rubbing his good fortune in my face. *Asshole!*

"Hi, Peyton!" I said, overly bright. Cash's eyebrows drew slightly closer at my inflection. *Better tone it down or he would start to ask questions.* "I'm surprised to see you here. Is Cash blackmailing you?"

She laughed sweetly, like church bells ringing for

church service. "Of course not. He asked me to come. I am an angel with no closet full of dark secrets."

"Really? You have nothing hidden at all?"

I wasn't being facetious either. Hell, everyone had at least one skeleton hidden in his or her personal closet. No one was that saintly. I had plenty and I lived a relatively boring life. She smiled back so innocently that I almost missed the mischievousness swirling around her hazel eyes.

I burst out laughing as I walked into the kitchen to see whether Mom needed any help. I walked up behind her and enveloped her in a tight hug. She gently placed her hands over my arms, giving me some much-needed warmth. She knowingly turned around and wrapped me in to a tight bear hug of an embrace.

My mother was not a petite woman. She had height and broad shoulders. She teetered on the more masculine side with her frame and yet maintained pure femininity. I felt like a child again, needing her solid embrace to make the world right again. My mother could annoy me to death sometimes but I still needed her to ease my heartache. The way she loved bordered on smothering. For tonight I cherished it.

"Why don't you set the table for me, darling?" She held me at arm's length and scrutinized my face. I inwardly cringed, thinking she might start in on me about needing a good man and some babies. Instead, she surprised me by pushing me lightly toward the dining room.

Cash snuck up behind me and pinched my side.

"You are such a juvenile! I almost dropped the

plates!" I huffed, thrusting half of the plates for him to dispense. He took it in stride and set half the table as I gawked at him.

"What? Can't I help my sister out?"

I quickly rebounded. "What do you want? I know you don't do anything for free."

"Nothing. You look miserable. I wanted to help you out. Looks like your allergies are messing with you again."

"Umm. Yeah," I stumbled out. "I have a killer headache. Thanks, Cash." I ducked my head at the little white lie that seamlessly rolled off my tongue.

We all sat around the table in comfortable silence, shoveling food in our mouths as if we hadn't eaten in months. Once we finished our meal, a barrage of voices talked over one another. The laughter and squabbles managed to lift my spirits. My mother fawned all over Peyton, probably envisioning a church and a baptism within the year. Which left me talking to my dad.

I hardly ever had the chance to engage in a lengthy conversation with him. My dad was a quiet man. When he chose to speak, it could be blunt or filled with sarcasm. My dad and mom made a good pair, even if it seemed odd. He was private and reserved; she was outspoken and theatrical. Dad was observant and laid-back. Mom was more reckless and spontaneous. They were complete opposites but complemented each other perfectly.

It had been awhile since I left my childhood home feeling blessed and happy. I had a wonderful family who loved all of my idiosyncrasies. If I could only find a guy who shared that belief, I would be complete. I thought I had—or at least a prospect.

I walked into my apartment, melancholy at the prospect of being alone. I walked a fine line, heading toward feeling sorry for myself. I had a hard time grasping the depth of my sadness. It was as if Cole and I had a long relationship. I had only just met him and we were not even technically dating. A knock at my door had me abandoning my morose thoughts.

I opened the door to find Cole on the other side. My treacherous body hummed with desire at the sight of him. I kept my features as neutral as I could. I was still peeved at him. I didn't want him to know how much he affected me. He pushed through the door as if he were invited. He stalked me until my back hit against the counter. He restrained my hands behind my back after I tried to push him away. The sensation was simultaneously unnerving and erotic.

"I'm sorry for behaving like an asshole." He kissed along my neck. "Let me make it up to you."

I continued to thaw as he nipped and licked down my neck. My body betrayed my thoughts of playing it cool. He used one hand to hold my hands behind my back and he used the other one to unbutton my blouse. He glided the cups of my bra down to set my breasts free and used his teeth to graze each nipple. His wondrous mouth made me forget why I was angry. All I could think about was moving this party to my bedroom.

"It better be so good that I black out," I barely managed to get out.

He scooped me up as though I weighed nothing.

"I'll make you come so many times that you'll be begging me to stop."

"Promises, promises."

He set me on the bed tenderly. My heart ratcheted at the gentle gesture. I scooted up toward the headboard, watching his every move as he shed his clothing. He was a sight to behold. My eyes raked over his sinewy muscles down to the prominent V shape that was like a treasure map, leading me right toward his thick erection. My nipples hardened to sharp points and I sucked in a breath as he stood at the side of the bed.

He scaled the bed stealthily, as though he were a hunter going in for the kill. His eyes never left my body as he inched closer. My nerves held stationary, anxiously awaiting his touch. He settled between my legs, unbuttoning my jeans, and yanked them off. He slipped his fingers in the waistband of my panties and shredded the lacy material as he tore them from my body. My pussy constricted and my body vibrated with carnal need. His possessiveness drove my desire to a frenzied level. I wanted to attack him with my hands and lips but the power swirling in his chocolate depths had me submitting willingly.

His hands pushed my thighs out as far as they would go, opening me fully up to him. I trembled from desire and vulnerability. I had never felt this exposed and yet this turned on. He shoved me past all of the insecurities that I owned, forcing me to break down the walls that I had carefully constructed over the years. He slipped his tongue past his lush lips and licked up my thigh, toward my overheated core. My legs trembled at the amatory sensation. I threaded my fingers through his soft hair and stroked his scalp in tune with the way that his tongue laved my outer lips.

My nails dug into the taut skin of his scalp the more he demanded from my body. He was asking for more than a physical release. He was trying to own my soul. His warm breath fanned the flames that licked along my skin, breaking me down, swirl by swirl. He increased the pressure and speed of his tongue, making me dizzy. My hips rotated to the beat of his tongue, chasing the high of my orgasmic addiction. With one last languid lick, I toppled over the summit and soared between the valleys of pleasure.

"Open your eyes, baby. I want you to watch me while I take what's mine." His gravelly voice scraped along my puckered flesh.

He bent his head and scraped his teeth over my nipple and then the other, before he slammed into my tight channel. I arched my back as his cock filled me to the core.

"I love the way you fuck me," I cried out.

"Jesus, your pussy feels so good," he growled through clenched teeth.

He was the epitome of every one of my fantasies. He consumed my body, taking what he needed, only to give it all back with a rush of pleasure that had the potential to break me apart and at the same time mend all the pieces together to make me whole again. He slipped his thumb over my clit and circled the hypersensitive nerves. My inner walls clenched around his cock as my orgasm clawed its way through my body. I cried out his name as my body imploded with passion. He drove into me one last time as his body trembled with his release.

I whimpered as he slipped out of me. The loss was almost heartbreaking. He touched my lips gently with his before rolling to his side and pulling me into his chest. He placed a delicate kiss to my shoulder as I snuggled deeper into him.

"Holy shit, Cole! Where the hell did you learn to do those things? Wait. Never mind—I don't want to know."

His throaty laughter vibrated down my neck as we snuggled together. "I'll never tell. It keeps getting better and better. I can't seem to get enough of you. I'm afraid you are my drug. Is there a prevention line or addicts class devoted to your exes?"

I giggled. "Yep. I'll give you their card when I'm through with you."

Without mercy, he tickled me ruthlessly. As quickly as it began, he abruptly stopped and he pulled me over on top of him. He pushed my hair out of my eyes and kissed me sensually. My body began to burn as I felt him stirring beneath me.

"You are so beautiful, Harlow." Then he pushed inside me and all talk ceased.

* * *

I woke up the next morning thoroughly ravished. I smiled, ready to give Cole a wake-up present. Once again his side was empty. I flopped on my back and sighed in frustration. I went into the bathroom to get ready for work and on the mirror written in toothpaste:

Good Morning Beautiful.

My heart leapt into my throat. I wasn't used to

thoughtful gestures from guys. He made it hard for future guys to live up to. With my mood lifted, I hummed badly through the rest of my morning routine.

I walked into work with a silly ass grin still stuck on my face. I tried to remove it but it just wouldn't go away. If I were honest, I rather liked it there.

"Harlow, did you run over Victoria this morning?"

"What? I just bumped her—no real damage done."

"That doesn't explain your dopey grin then."

Oh shit! There's no way I would get out of this alive. "I slept really well."

"You think I'm going to believe that crock of bullshit?" His brows quirked upward as he connected the dots. "Oh, fuck me, you got laid!"

"No I didn't. Can't I just be in a good mood?" My eyes darted everywhere but at Cash.

"Yes, but you have that just got fucked well look. Who is he? You might as well fess up. You know I'll hound you until you give me his name."

I smiled. "Maybe. Maybe not."

I managed to escape Cash for most of the day. Then Cole came into the shop.

"Welcome to Firedog Bling. How can I help you?" Cash addressed Cole.

"I'm here to take the lovely Harlow to lunch—that is, if she can be spared for an hour."

I quickly grabbed my purse and headed toward the door. "Bye, Cash. See you later." I grabbed Cole's suit jacket and pulled him out the door. I didn't care whether I wrinkled his expensive suit. Cash's maniacal laughter rang loudly, assaulting my ears.

He chuckled. "What was that about? Are you that eager to be alone with me?"

"No. I mean, yes." I stopped dragging him long enough to give him a scorching kiss.

"Wow. I should steal you away more often."

I grinned. "Yes, you should. Now, let's go eat. I'm starving."

It was a short walk to my favorite sandwich shop. They had the best smoked ham with melted Swiss cheese that I was dying to have. The meat and cheese is piled so high that you couldn't eat it all but I tried every time. Cole ordered their Rueben. It's pretty good but the ham was even better. I laughed so hard when he tried to bite into his sandwich without cutting it. The sandwich was wider than his mouth. When he pulled it away, there were dressing marks left on each side of his mouth.

"You saving that for later?" I laughed.

He seductively licked the corners of his mouth. My sandwich was now forgotten as I openly ogled him.

"I might just do that if you keep looking at me like that."

I shrugged. "Can't help it. Makes me think of other things."

"Unfortunately, we don't have time for those things at the moment. I do want to talk to you about something. Are you busy tonight?"

"I'm not busy right now. Let's hear it."

"Nope. Later." He grinned wickedly.

I pestered him all throughout lunch and on the walk back to work. I tried all the tricks I knew to get him to tell me but he didn't budge at all. *Damn stubborn fool.* He opened the door for me to go through. With all of my attention focused on our talk tonight, I had forgotten that Cash still manned the front. There he sat, in all his conceited glory. *Fuck, here it comes—wait for it, and bam!*

"Well hello there. Did ya'll have a good lunch?"

"The food's excellent but the company was even better." Cole extended his hand toward my brother. "I'm Cole. It's nice to meet you. You must be Cash."

"In the flesh. I'm sorry; Harlow failed to mention you to me," he said rudely. He lifted his eyebrow as he looked at me.

"Don't be rude, Cash."

"I'm just stating the facts. Are you Harlow's boyfriend?"

There was a moment of tense silence. I opened my mouth to step in.

"Yes. I am." Cole took my hand and gave me a toe-curling kiss. As he sauntered out the door, he called back, "See ya round, Nancy."

I busted out laughing. I was still laughing until I turned around and got a good look at Cash. I immediately shut my mouth and backed slowly toward the door. The veins in his neck bulged to the surface like vipers. His face turned beet red. His head slowly morphed into a cartoon screaming whistle, billowing smoke. If I were smarter, I would have run. A sense of déjà vu froze my limbs in place.

***

When we were little, my brother and I had started fighting and to this day I can't remember what started it. It was all minor name-calling in the beginning. He sat down in the recliner after he had called me a cunt. I hate the *C* word and as he said, it I became enraged. I stalked right up to him and slapped him across the face. It wasn't a regular quick slap either. It was a slow motion from the bottom of the cheek to the top of the temple swipe.

Once I realized my mistake, I took off like a bat out of hell. I managed to run into the kitchen and inadvertently backed myself into a corner. Next thing I knew, my arms instinctively covered my face and I curled into a fetal position as shoes were being launched, ramming into my body. I'm not sure how long I lay there curled into a ball but it was long after the rain of shoes had quit.

***

Finally, stepping out of my head, I got my ass in gear. I wasn't sure what he would do but I knew that a physical beating wasn't totally out of the question. I ran out the door and hid at the coffee shop down the block. I'd give him a couple of hours to cool down before I went back. I drank my latte and had a muffin. I wasn't hungry, merely bored. Only an hour had passed. I couldn't prolong the inevitable. I slowly trudged back to the shop to take my punishment.

CHAPTER 13

Cash started in as soon as my foot crossed the threshold.

"You know, dear sister of mine, you will pay for your little boyfriend's dig."

I guess he hadn't calmed down that much. A rosy dusting still colored his cheeks. A slight tic around his jawline formed as he mashed his teeth together. At least his ears no longer looked purple.

"Yes, I'm sure that I will. It's not my fault he overheard me calling you Nancy. If it makes you feel any better, I gave him the same nickname!" I walked deeper into the store, feeling confident. "You know, if you would have been nicer to him, he wouldn't have had to throw that snide remark at you. If you would just think before you speak, you could have had the upper hand. But n-o-o—you just couldn't resist, could you." I continued to poke the bear in the chest. "For once, Cash, would you please act like an adult? I didn't grill Peyton, did I? I sure as hell didn't. I let you figure your relationships out on your own. Now you better give me the same respect."

He started to speak but I poked him one more time for good measure.

"The next time Cole comes around, you better be

fucking civil and if you're not, so help me God, I will tell Peyton about your music box collection."

His eyes got as big as saucers. "You wouldn't dare."

I laughed sadistically at him. "Oh yes, my dear brother, I would." I needed a dramatic exit.

I threw my purse around my shoulder, stuck my chin in the air, and exited the building. I would not stick around and duke it out with him. I had better things to do with my time.

I whipped into the grocery store parking lot, making sure I was as far away from the entrance as possible. The farther I parked, the fewer dings I got in my car. Plus all of the great health benefits from walking a few extra steps. Not that exercise is a high priority of mine, but a little goes a long way.

I hated to shop at the grocery store when my stomach rumbled. Every aisle tantalized my hunger. It all looked good. I couldn't make a rational dinner decision if my life depended on it. Pasta sounded appetizing but boring. Hamburgers became an option but tasted better grilled. That wasn't happening either. I didn't own a grill.

Aha, light bulb moment: tacos. They were easy to make, flavorful, and everyone enjoyed them. Now the bigger question was soft shell, hard shell, or on a salad? To be on the safe side, I would get the package that contained both soft and hard shells. I grabbed the shredded lettuce and the rest of the fixings. I wouldn't waste my time fixing a taco salad. What's the point when you could put some roughage in the shell? It was a win-win situation.

Cole knocked just as the meat started to sizzle. He had impeccable timing. I gave him a quick chaste kiss and went right back to the browning meat. Along the counter, I set out the shredded cheese, sour cream, a can of diced tomatoes with chilies, and a mild premade salsa. I liked salsa, just not on my tacos. Salsa lessened the seasoning of the meat. I liked the kick that the can of tomatoes with chilies donned. It contained the right amount of heat.

Cole grabbed the paper plates and napkins. Within minutes, we were dishing up our dinner. I'm glad I grabbed the box with both kinds of shells because Cole had dished up both types. I only ate the hard shells. Something tasted off with store-bought tortillas. They never tasted as good as the ones in the restaurant.

With my mouth full, I asked, "So what did you want to talk about?"

He laughed so hard that bits of taco flew onto my plate. *Nasty!* Thank goodness I was on my last one. There is something so wrong about a wasted taco.

"I wondered how long it would take for you to bring that up."

"Well, I waited all day. You have to give me points for not blowing up your phone with curiosity."

"That I do." He took his last bite and chewed thoughtfully. He took his sweet time and it drove me bonkers.

"How much time can you get off from work?"

"Depends on the month and time of the year. Why?"

"What would you say to a long weekend in Vegas?"

"I'd say hell to the yeah. When do you want to go?"

"This weekend."

"What? You already have tickets and everything?"

"Not yet. I wanted to talk to you first. I have a business meeting there on Friday and Saturday morning. If you wanted to come, I'd extend my trip. We could spend Saturday and Sunday together and fly back Monday night."

"That sounds great. Let me call Cash and run it by him first. I need to make sure that nothing pressing is going on. Can I give you a definite answer tomorrow?"

"Yes. I'll book the flight and hotel as soon as you let me know."

I scraped my chair across the floor and jumped into his lap, lavishing kisses all over him. I had never gone on a weekend trip with any of my boyfriends. This would be an incredible weekend. I hoped that Cash would cover for me. I knew for a fact that the online orders were finished and the ones that were filtering through could be put on hold.

The Antichrist's collar was almost done and I couldn't really help with that anyway. I didn't see any reason I couldn't take a couple of days.

"That was the big talk you wanted to have? I thought for a minute it would be something more involved."

"Like what?"

"Hell, I don't know but you know when someone

says 'we need to talk' or 'I have to ask you for something,' it isn't going to be pleasant."

"What sort of people do you hang around with?"

I lightly punched him in the arm and kissed him again. I kept his mouth plenty busy so he wouldn't make any more sarcastic comments.

The next morning felt surreal. For once Cole didn't disappear before I awoke. We made use of my early alarm clock settings. And then took quick separate showers because we were both running late. One toe-curling kiss later and we were headed in different directions.

I had never shared my space with a man before and I found it pleasant. If I wasn't careful, I could get used to waking up with him every morning and coming home to him at night. He had quickly inserted himself into every aspect of my life. Trying to guard my heart proved extremely difficult. It wouldn't be long before he owned the whole thing.

I felt charitable this morning, so I picked up breakfast for Cash. Let's call it for what it really was: a peace offering with a slight bribe attached. I needed the long weekend to spend with Cole. It would prove to me that we had more than just great sex tying us together.

I threw the bag of food toward Cash, knowing that he would instinctively catch it. He had cat-like reflexes.

"Thanks, I'm starving. I came in early to try to finish up this fucking collar. It's giving me a migraine, it's that bright."

"You need shades just to work on that monstrosity. I

can't believe that you are going to let that thing leave the shop. With your name attached to it, nonetheless."

"I know."

"Hey, Cash? Do you think that you could take care of the shop Friday and Monday?" I held my breath as he looked up at me.

His eyes were cold and hard. "Yeah, sure. No problem. What are you doing that you need both those days?"

"Cole invited me to Vegas. He has a meeting on Friday. After that, just hang the rest of the time."

"Note that I am only doing this for you. I don't like or trust him. Keep your cell phone on at all times. Call or text at least once a day or I'll report you as being kidnapped."

I huffed out a breath. "Are you fucking serious, Cash? Isn't that a little extreme? I am a fucking grown woman. I think I can handle a weekend out of town."

"Those are my conditions. Take it or leave it."

I stomped through the doors. Anger dripped off me as though I had bathed in it. I could scratch his eyes out. *What gave him the right to boss me around?* I wasn't a naïve little girl. I owned half of this business too. If I wanted the fucking time, I'd take it.

I sent a quick text to Cole to let him know that I was good for the weekend. Despite being pissed at Cash, Cole had dramatically lifted my mood. I looked up as Peyton rushed through the doors.

"Where's the fire?"

"Just excited to take Cash off your hands for the rest of the day."

"Thank you! Please don't bring him back until Friday!"

"If I had my way, I'd tie him to my bed and make him my sex slave forever!"

"La, la, la," I sang loudly. I raised my hands and cupped my ears. "Earmuffs," I shouted loudly in her face.

She continued her cackling on her way to snag Cash.

"See you later, Harlow," she cooed.

I heard a bunch of slurping sounds and then the door being slammed behind them. *So gross!* Those two were sickening to watch. My brother went from hardcore badass to wet noodle the minute Peyton came around. Secretly, I was happy for the two of them. I really hoped that Cash would settle down. When he did, he would finally butt the hell out of my love life. He could also give my mother the grandbabies she wanted so desperately. Then I would be free to live my life without constant harassment from the two of them.

CHAPTER 14

I closed up and headed to my favorite coffee shop. The sun sat low on the horizon. It cast a lavender hue as far as I could see. I smiled, thinking that if the old wives' tale were true, it would be a nice day tomorrow. I decided to go get my favorite latte before I jumped into my car and headed home. The evening air felt warm along my skin, making the short walk pleasant.

A smile appeared upon my lips as I looked at the empty space leading to the register. Most of the patrons probably already abandoned the place for home. I paid for my coffee and turned to head out the door when someone called my name. I cringed when I realized to whom the voice belonged. It sounded like nails across a chalkboard. I wanted to continue on as if I hadn't heard a thing. That is, until I was summoned again.

"Victoria! What a pleasant surprise." I smiled as genuinely as I could. It probably looked more like a sneer but what the fuck did I care.

"Hello, Harlow. What brings you in?"

I held my coffee up in what I hope conveyed an easy response. I mean, we were in a coffee shop, for goodness' sake. *What the fuck did she think I was doing in here—getting my nails done?*

"Getting my caffeine fix before I head home for the

night." I took a deep breath. "How are you doing?"

"Very well, thank you. Meeting up with my fiancé. We are going to look at a couple of venues before he goes out of town on business."

"Well, that is wonderful. I won't keep you. I hope you find a place. Have a good night."

"You as well."

I shook my head as I digested one of the weirdest conversations I've ever encountered. She seemed almost pleasant and nice. However, if you looked long enough, you could see the evil coursing through her veins. It seeped through her pores and lifeless eyes. She was no more interested in my life than I was hers.

I drove home, still in somewhat of a daze. Our conversation threw me for a loop. Something there, bothered me. I couldn't place my finger on it. Being nice to me wasn't in her bag of tricks. She could have easily ignored me and I would have been none the wiser. Heck, I would have rather that little scenario play out than the one that actually occurred. I had to let it go. There was no reason I should be dwelling on someone so insignificant to me.

I picked up my phone when I heard it chirping incessantly.

Thinking of you. Call you later XX

I smiled like an idiot. Cole always had perfect timing. I couldn't wait to tell him the good news. I was more than ready to get the hell out of Dodge. I was going to respond but then thought better of it. He was probably busy and he would call later anyhow.

***

I kept slapping at my alarm to cut off the incessant buzzing but the damn thing wouldn't stop. I finally cracked open an eye and realized that it was still dark out. Groggily, I looked at the time. Realization finally hit me that my alarm wasn't going off but my cell phone. *What the hell?* It was early morning. The damn ringing wouldn't quit.

There better be a damn good reason someone decided to blow my phone up. I hoped it wasn't an emergency but then again if there wasn't, I'd make sure there'd be one in the future. The person on the other end of the line would be hurt in some fashion for waking my tired ass up. I really wasn't a morning person and that was grossly understated.

I threw the covers off with gusto and got out of bed. I stomped into the kitchen where I had left my phone charging.

"Yeah," I huffed out, more than agitated.

"I'm sorry. Did I wake you, beautiful?"

Oh, that sexy baritone voice had my knees quivering. Instantly my hormones kicked into overdrive.

"Yes, you did," I said, all husky. My anger dissolved instantly at his words.

"Are you going to open up or leave me hanging outside your door?"

I thought about it for a split second. I hung up, dashed to the door and threw it open. There was Cole, in all his stunning glory. I jumped into his arms as if it had been a year since I'd seen him. He crossed the threshold swiftly, carrying me as if I weighed nothing. He deposited us in the bedroom. My irritated mood dissipated as quickly as our clothing. He was able to douse the anger with a heavy dose of pleasure.

***

I knocked my alarm off the nightstand, trying to shut the fucking thing up. I had finally fallen asleep an hour ago. I stretched to loosen up my well-used muscles and scrambled out of bed. I rushed into the bathroom to take a cold shower. I jumped around like an idiot as the freezing water pelted my skin. It would be a minor miracle if I didn't break my neck. *I was fully awake now!* I placed a chaste kiss on Cole's cheek and left for work.

Once I got to work, I sent him a quick text to tell him that I would be his traveling companion. I knew he was still sleeping so I didn't bother to wait for a response. He'd call later and let me know of our travel arrangements. I took an extra couple of minutes to daydream about the upcoming weekend before I opened up the store.

I hadn't seen Cash and I expected that. Because he was covering, he took the liberty to spend the last couple of days with Peyton. At least, I think that's what he was doing. I filled a bunch of online orders while the morning was slow. I also scheduled a couple of our clients to come and pick up their collars. I checked my phone and saw that Cash sent me a text.

Call Victoria and schedule a final fitting for next Friday

Oh, thank my lucky stars; he finished the collar. Jubilation had my fingers pushing the buttons in rapid succession.

"Hello, Victoria. This is Harlow from Firedog Bling. I called to let you know that the collar will be done next week. Give me a call back and we will get you on the schedule for next Friday. Thank you and have a great day."

I hung up the phone, squealing and jumping up and down. *We would finally be rid of her!* Curiosity had me wondering how she would act when she came in. *Which face would she be wearing that day?*

After lunch, we had a steady flow of customers. The appointment slots booked full for the next month. We always get an influx of customers this time of the year, close to the holidays. Nevertheless, we have never been booked solid with appointments before. I was overjoyed at how busy we were becoming. I might look for an intern or apprentice to work with Cash on some of these. I'd have to run that idea by him. Having another designer on hand would be helpful. I don't think that we would have to hire them full-time just yet.

Victoria finally called back and scheduled first thing Friday morning. I texted Cash the good news and headed home. I made myself some tuna fish and Ritz crackers. It was a nice, hardy meal. I sat in front of the TV and zoned out. I needed to pack but I just couldn't muster any energy. Cole had kept me up into the wee hours of the morning. I wasn't complaining but my body and mind were exhausted.

I had just finished washing up my dishes when my cell rang. I scampered around, trying to dry my hands before I answered the call.

"Hello," I rushed into the receiver.

"Harlow, love. How are you?"

Great. My mother. I so did not want to talk to her right now.

"I'm good. How are you and Dad?"

"Fantastic. Thank you for asking, dear."

Our conversation had hit a lull. I wasn't sure what she wanted but it was definitely something.

"Mom, I'm really tired. Was there anything that you wanted to discuss with me?" I didn't mean to be a bitch but I was cranky and I wanted to curl up and go to bed.

"Nothing important. I wanted to make sure that you were planning on coming to dinner Sunday."

I huffed out a huge sigh. "Not this time. I am going out of town for the weekend. Sorry, I was going to call you tomorrow and let you know that I wouldn't be there."

"By yourself?"

"No, with a friend. I'll be back on Monday and be at dinner the following weekend."

"Going with some girlfriends or that boyfriend of yours that you have kept a secret?"

Oh, I would kill Cash. He had gotten me back from Cole's dig. *That dirty, rotten motherfucker!* I stomped around the kitchen like a toddler gearing up for a tantrum.

"Hey Mom, Cash is calling in and I need to answer. I love you and will talk to you later." I hung up without hearing her parting words.

I went right to my favorites list and hit Cash's number. While it rang, I made a mental note to delete it from my favorites. He no longer held that honor. The longer it rang, the more I fumed. He purposely ignored my call. He knew that I had probably gotten off the phone with Mom. His stupid voicemail picked up. I hung up and typed him up a nasty little message. Then I deleted it and sent another one instead.

GAME ON FUCKER!

He bested me as sure as fresh dog shit smells on a humid day. This time around, I would beat him at his own game. He always had to one-up me, no matter what we did or where we were. He usually succeeded, too. Not this time. Oh no, it was my turn. He texted back while I mentally psyched myself up for his beatdown.

I ain't no punk, bitch. BRING IT!

I cackled loudly at his fighting words. He knew how to goad me. I would bring it and it would be the last time he screwed with me. *What was I thinking?* It wouldn't be the last time. This would only make him work that much harder the next time. I had challenged him. *Damn it!* I would not back down. It was on.

I mentally kicked around some payback scenarios while I got ready for bed. I was so engrossed that I didn't hear the knocking at the door until it became so loud that I thought the person on the other side would break it down. I ran and opened it before the neighbors put in a noise complaint. Apartment living could be arduous with noisy neighbors. I almost had enough saved to buy a small house. It couldn't come soon enough. Especially considering the foot traffic had increased.

I threw open the door so fast that Cole staggered through. I laughed as he came close to a nose dive but caught himself just in time. He looked up at me menacingly. I took the hint and made a mad dash to the bedroom. He grabbed me around the waist before I had the chance to shut the door and lock him out. I laughed hysterically as he threw me onto the bed. He hovered over me for the longest time. I bit my lip in anticipation.

He lowered his head and nipped along my neck. "You are in so much trouble."

I giggled. "What's my punishment?"

"You'll see." He tore my tank top in two.

I gasped as a surge of pleasure coiled in my belly. Goose bumps fanned across my inflamed skin. He delicately pulled the remaining material from my arms. I was entranced by the way his chocolate eyes blazed and glowed with hunger for me. My body trembled with need the way his gaze traveled over every inch, as though he were committing it to memory.

His tongue jutted out and caressed my swollen nipples, paying equal attention to each. His mouth let go of my hardened peak with a popping sound. He walked us backward until the back of my knees bumped into the frame. His hands painfully teased down the sensitive skin along my rib cage until they landed on my waist. He lifted me up and onto the bed with ease. I scooted to the middle as he climbed his way up. I bit my lower lip, trying to keep my hunger for him at bay.

He nestled between my thighs. The head of his penis sat at the apex of my sex, unmercifully teasing the entrance. I squirmed as his body imprisoned mine in a web of growing arousal. His mouth swooped down and captured mine. I reached between our heaving bodies and gripped the base of his cock, guiding him to me. His tormented groan fueled my desire to catastrophic proportions.

"Need you inside me. Now," I panted.

No longer concerned with what came out of my mouth, I ached for him to fill me. The mere thought of not having him drove me wild. The smoldering heat between our bodies demanded that we join. I cried out as he slammed into me. His intensity was like nothing I've ever experienced before. It burned white-hot in a flash and then smoldered until we both found our release. I curled into him as I succumbed to sleep, a satisfied lover.

CHAPTER 15

I strolled into work feeling thoroughly used. Today was my last day for a while. I couldn't wait to get the heck out of here. A couple of days in Vegas would be exactly what I needed. My silly grin and daydreams kept me busy well into the afternoon.

Cash strolled in with a scowl on his face.

"Did somebody piss in your Lucky Charms this morning?"

His scowl deepened. "Don't start. I've taken a look at our orders and the appointment book. We are getting more business than I can handle and you are going on vacation."

"Put your big boy pants on. Quit whining—it's unbecoming, even for you. You can handle the influx for a couple of days. It won't kill you." I rolled my eyes. "It's only three days and I will be back. Really, Cash, what is the problem?"

He rubbed his hand down his face, irritated. "I just don't like you going away with him. I don't trust him. How long have you known him?"

Jeez, were we really going to get into this? "Since when have you ever cared who I went out with? I am a grown woman and can go away with my boyfriend without anyone's approval." I reined in my anger and chose my words carefully. "Look, Cash. I realize that you are worried about me. This isn't typical behavior for me but I am happy. I want to do this—please be happy for me. This is my chance to find someone who hopefully loves me for me, quirks and all." Nervously, I paced around the room. "I understand that you don't trust him. You hardly know him. I admit that I don't either. That is why this trip is important to me. I promise to check in with you."

I walked over to him and hugged him tight. Cash was my brother and he had always had my back. His methods may be unorthodox but it was who he was. I wouldn't change him for the world. I also knew that if I ever ran in to trouble, he would be the first person to bail me out. "I love you, big brother."

"Ditto, baby sister. I want you to be happy; I swear it. There is just something about him that bothers me. I can't put my finger on it. If you are happy, then I am happy for you. Don't forget to check in or I will be in Vegas to drag you back myself."

"Deal."

I headed home early to get a head start on my packing. I checked and rechecked the weather in Vegas. Even though the weather forecast was warm and clear, I didn't take any chances. I packed a couple of nice dresses in case we went to a show or a nice dinner. I didn't know whether Cole had anything planned or whether we were going to wing it. I made sure to cover all of the bases just in case. I even splurged on some sexy undergarments. Most importantly, all of my bras matched my underwear. Cole didn't seem to mind my mismatched attire. Usually, he was too busy getting me naked to notice if my panties matched or were lacy enough.

For this trip, I decided to spruce it up. My mother

would be so proud. I normally hated to shop but this time around I enjoyed the prospect of seeing the look on Cole's face at my transformation. I laughed to myself; he probably wouldn't even notice. I wouldn't mind spending most of our time in bed, but this being my first visit, I hoped we would take in some of the sights.

Even though I was excited and nervous, as soon as my head hit the pillow I zonked out. I woke up extra early to make sure that I had my boarding pass and everything that I needed packed. I should probably wear something nice on the plane but I wanted to be comfortable too. Cole would probably be wearing something that made him look gorgeous without any effort.

I, on the other hand, couldn't fathom wearing anything other than yoga pants and a t-shirt. Sexy and alluring it wasn't. Comfortable—hell yes, it was. Sitting on a plane for two plus hours with your pants pinching your belly just didn't seem appealing. In such circumstances, I turned to elastic.

Cole knocked on my door right on time. I opened the door and gazed at the sexy man before me. It was too bad we didn't have time for me to ravish him. Instead, I gave him a kiss that promised a good time.

"Good morning, beautiful. I wish we had more time for me to explore your eagerness. Are you ready to go?"

I smiled adoringly at him. I'm sure that all of the love simmering beneath shone through my eyes. I couldn't deny it any longer and yet I wouldn't dare let those words pass my lips. "Absolutely. Let's go."

He grabbed my bag as I locked up and we headed out. The ride to the airport was quiet but comfortable. The dreaded awkward silence was the number-one problem with most of my relationships. I wasn't the best conversationalist. If I didn't have anything to say, then I stayed silent. Some mistook that as being a stuck-up bitch, especially from initial introductions. I really had a hard time making friends. That's probably why I only had a select few—okay, mainly my brother. Oh well, I liked my small circle—less drama that way.

We parked in the long-term parking lot and hopped on the shuttle. The check-in gate didn't have a long line so we only had to get through security. I loathed the security line. I would get selected for the gunpowder residue check. Then I would have to subject myself to the full body scan. Which, by the way, is demeaning. I don't care how "professional" they are. I wonder whether they could tell what kind of bra and panties I wore. *What about my slight muffin top?*

Not to mention I had to take my shoes off to walk through. *Do you know how dirty airport floors are?* I don't either but I can imagine that they are disgusting. Thank God I put on socks before I left. There was nothing more pleasing than a case of athlete's foot on your vacation. I'd rather visit the gynecologist twice in one week, than subject my feet to extreme itchiness.

Once we worked our way through the security line, my stomach growled loudly. Cole just raised his eyebrows at me.

"Can't be helped. I'm starving."

"Then we shall feed you before you keel over from hunger."

"Such a smartass. I won't keel over but I will become a cranky bitch. Your peace of mind and overall health might be in jeopardy if I don't eat. Just saying."

He laughed at me and kissed my forehead. He thought I was joking. I never joked about food. When my stomach wants food, you better believe that I will do whatever it takes to feed the beast. There is no telling what will happen to the people around me if I don't. That's one experiment that I am not willing to try.

On our way to the gate, I spotted a donut shop. I pulled Cole toward the counter. He didn't look too enthusiastic by my breakfast choice. I quickly ordered a vanilla long john, an apple fritter, and an iced coffee before he dragged me away. I looked over at him. "You going to join me in an unhealthy breakfast?"

"Nope." He ordered some egg white wrap with absolutely no flavor and a black coffee. What a boring palate he has.

We sat in silence, eating our sugary goodness (at least mine was) by our gate. After I ate the long john, I felt marginally better. I thought about saving the apple fritter for later but I was still hungry, so I scarfed that down too. I resisted the urge to lick the icing off my fingers. I gave Cole a quick kiss on the cheek and headed toward the restroom to wash my hands. By the time I got back, they were opening the doors to board.

"Will you please try to grab an exit row so we have more leg room?"

"No need, beautiful. We are flying first class."

I stared at him with my mouth slightly open in surprise. "Are you serious?"

"Nothing but the best."

"No shit? I have never flown first class."

"Let's pop that cherry!"

This day just kept getting better and better.

I sat in the roomy, plush leather seat and sighed with content. "I could die a happy woman right now. You know, you have ruined me."

His eyes scanned mine questioningly. "Ruined you? How have I managed to do that?"

"Now that I know the comfortable feel of first class, we will never be able to fly coach again."

"Is that so?"

"Yep. You've created a monster. As long as you know it's entirely your fault. I had high hopes for an exit row."

"Duly noted." He kissed me on the cheek and clicked the buckle around his trim waist. I took my book out and got ready for takeoff.

I took full advantage of the first class accommodations. I reclined my seat without worrying about the person behind me. Getting a stomach full of your tray table is not a pleasant feeling. Yep, that's about all I took advantage of. Baby steps.

CHAPTER 16

My head hung out the window like a dog on its first car ride. I stared in awe at all of the hotels jammed together along the Strip. Each one was unique in their own outlandish themes. We passed the pyramids, Paris, and Hollywood in the span of five minutes. Where else but Vegas could you experience such sights without a passport?

Cole entwined his fingers through mine. "It can be overwhelming the first time."

I laughed. "You think! There is so much stimulation that my brain is overloaded. It's like Disney World for adults!"

We continued to hold hands while we drove into the valet of the Bellagio. I wasn't sure where he had booked our room, but I didn't expect this.

I squeezed Cole's hand. "Wow. Look at that water fountain. That is insane."

"Yes, it is. The spouts are configured to spray the water with the music."

"Are you serious?"

"Yep. It's actually pretty neat to watch at night. It's a must-see before we leave."

I followed Cole into the hotel in a daze. It was overwhelmingly beautiful. From the floor to the ceiling, the intricate details were amazing. They had the most vibrant yellow and red flowers strategically placed around the front desk. I had a hard time taking it all in. Before I could soak it all up, Cole grabbed my hand and dragged me to our room. He whisked me past the bells and whistles of the casino floor before I could sink my heels in and gamble some money away.

"You have seriously ruined me for flying and now hotels. I can never go back to a regular room again. This is gorgeous, Cole. Thank you so much for inviting me."

"You are most welcome. I couldn't imagine being here with anyone else." He pulled me into his arms and kissed me until I blushed. When he pulled away, I attacked him.

I tackled him onto the bed. I tore his pristine buttoned-down shirt that probably cost more than a month's rent on my apartment. Buttons popped, making soft clinking sounds when they landed.

"Fuck, baby. I don't know what has gotten into you but it's hot as hell."

I silenced him with my mouth, using my tongue to softly lick the seam of his lips. He opened and my tongue darted inside to twirl with his. You could hear our teeth clank together as we tried to devour each other.

I ran my hands down his hard pecs, lowering them over his taut abs. They quivered beneath my touch. I thrived from the power I held over him. I swiftly unbuttoned his pants and pushed them down far enough so that I could claim my prize. His cock twitched as I wrapped my hand around the base of his shaft, applying more pressure as I pumped my hand up and down.

"Jesus. You undo me."

I smiled as I rained kisses down his torso until I hit his thick, veiny member. I licked my lips with anticipation; knowing that he came unglued at my touch had me on a full high for what I'd do to him with my mouth. I licked the precum off the tip of his dick as if it were my favorite ice cream. His hips jutted forward, wanting entrance into my wet mouth. I swirled my tongue from the base of his shaft and around the tip before I granted him access. I wrapped my lips around his girth and pulled him in. He groaned in approval, which spurred me on. Having control over his pleasure made me heady with desire. I didn't mind going down on a guy but it had never felt like this. Cole made it seem as though my mouth had special powers and the only one who could drive him wild like this was me. My hand and mouth worked in tandem, driving his pleasure to another level. I sucked him all the way to the back of my throat.

"Get up on that, Harlow. I won't last if you keep your sexy mouth on me," he growled.

I hummed my response. He tossed his head back and hissed. I let his cock slip from my mouth with a popping sound. With one last swipe of my tongue, I climbed up and straddled his hips. I reached between our bodies and guided his cock to my warm center and seated myself. I sat unmoving, relishing in his fullness, enjoying the way that he felt inside me. He felt like home, opening up the door after a long trip. I sighed with completeness.

He reached forward and tweaked my nipples. I tossed my head back and moaned with pleasure. Without thinking, my hips moved, finding their own rhythm and seeking out an exquisite release. I rose up on my knees and slammed back down until my pleasure built so high that I moved erratically. He wrapped his hands around my waist and moved them for me. I was lost in the euphoria that was his body. I teetered on the edge, more ready to fall than ever.

"That's it, baby. Let me watch you make yourself come. You are so beautiful."

I reached between our sweat-slicked bodies and found my bundle of nerves. I circled my clit with my fingers as he moved my hips. My fingers circled the hard nub between my soft petals—once, twice—and I fell over the edge. I cried out as my orgasm tore through my body, shredding every ounce of strength I had. His fingers dug in to my hips; he pumped his hips up savagely as his own release ruptured. I fell on top of him, completely drained. He rolled us on to our sides, gave me a chaste kiss, and got up to get dressed.

I lay on the king-sized bed and watched him dress. His three-piece Armani suit hugged his gorgeous body. I mentally undressed him again.

"Quit looking at me like that, Harlow, or I won't make it to my meeting."

"I can't help it. You're quite the specimen. I could look at you for hours. You could just get back in bed with me."

He finished knotting his tie and turned around; lust shimmered in his eyes. He walked over to me and kissed me longingly. "I won't be long. I'll text you when I'm done. I should be out by dinnertime. We can order in tonight. Make sure you're naked when I get back."

"Yes, sir. See you later."

Once Cole shut the door, I scurried over to my suitcase and retrieved my bathing suit. I would not waste my time sitting in the hotel room waiting for him to come back. This was my mini vacation. I never went anywhere. I would take full advantage of it. God only knew when I would be able to get away again. I put my hair up in a ponytail and double-checked that all body parts were modestly covered. I wasn't a stick thing by any means. I had curves and wasn't confident enough to strut a bikini. However, I rocked a tankini.

I may feel marginally sexy in my bathing suit but not confident enough to parade through the hotel in front of everyone. In reality, no one would be looking at me but I would imagine that they were. I'd probably trip and fall flat on my face, trying to act like I wasn't half naked in front of thousands of strangers.

Satisfied with my attire, I threw on my cover-up. I patted my pocket to make sure that I put the room key in there and then headed out the door. I headed left toward the elevator but ended up in a dead end. *How the hell was I going to find my way downstairs?* This place was too fucking big. After two more wrong turns, I finally found the freaking elevator. I blew out a heavy, frustrated breath as I punched the button for the lobby. I hoped to Hades I could find my way back.

I may have to ask the concierge if they have a map of this place. I now understood the saying, "What happens in Vegas, stays in Vegas." It probably originated from drunken people who ended up doing crazy shit because they couldn't find their way back to their room. Might as well stay out and keep on drinking and gambling!

I blew out an agitated breath. I couldn't find the sign for the pool. Every hotel has markers of some kind. I walked in circle after circle. I could've sworn that I had passed the same slot machines five times. I finally marched to the lobby to ask. I hated not knowing my way around. At any regular hotel, it was easy to find—a pool sign that pointed you in the right direction—but here, oh hell no, it wasn't that simple. The grandiose scale of everything was borderline outlandish.

I headed through the lobby to the concierge desk. I looked up as a bunch of color caught my eye. I stopped dead in my tracks. The largest, most beautiful chandelier hung from the ceiling. People walked all around me as I absorbed the stunning work of art. The vibrant colors and intricate work of the glass sculpture was exquisite. I could have gazed at it all day if I hadn't got a crick in my neck. I gently massaged the muscle as I continued on my mission.

The gentleman who manned the desk was extremely helpful. He kept a straight face and didn't laugh once when I asked him to point me in the general direction of the pool. He was kind enough to find me a personal escort, as well as reserving a lounge for the day. When Stacy, my personal escort, walked me to my cabana, she helpfully informed me that there were five pools at the Bellagio. *What was this place?* We ended up at the Cypress Lounge. I promptly thanked her for taking the time to help me find my way. She left me in the hands of Antonio, my personal host.

Antonio had the most gorgeous caramel skin. No tanning bed could ever make me look that creamy and delicious. He looked as though he were made for pleasing women. I could so get used to having a "pool boy" if he looked like that. I subconsciously licked my lips. *Might just put that on my Christmas list!* I wondered whether asking him to put sunblock on my back was going too far. He probably got asked that multiple times a day.

I inhaled his exotic cologne as he bent down and set a bottle of water on the small table next to me. He caught me sniffing him. He slyly looked at me from the corner of his artic-blue eyes and winked. My cheeks burned hot as coal embers at being caught.

"Can I get you anything else, Mrs. Devlin?" His smile held a hint of flirtation.

"Umm…" I was thrown for a minute at being called Cole's wife. "Yes. I would love a piña colada."

He tipped his head slightly in a nod and away he went.

I lost count of how many of the deliciously sweet coconut drinks I slurped down as I lounged by the pool. Antonio proved stealthy and extremely good at his job because I never saw him again. However, every time I reached for my umbrella drink, it was full.

I must have dozed off because Antonio gently shook my shoulder. "Mrs. Devlin, you should turn over. Otherwise you'll look like a lobster."

I gave him a glassy-eyed look before I realized where I was. "Thank you so much. I appreciate your thoughtfulness." I smiled goofily at him for another awkward moment before I flipped on to my belly.

I lay there for probably another hour before I got up. I had Antonio charge everything to the room as I had forgotten to bring my purse. I made a mental note to pay

Cole back for any extra charges. He may have brought me here but I sure as hell wasn't a freeloader.

I had planned to head back out for some sightseeing once I got back to the room and changed. The hotel had a botanical garden that rated high among previous guests. The minute I finally found the damn room, my mind was too fuzzy to drum up the motivation for anything more. Four too many piña coladas derailed my plans. I'm not a drinker. I'm a lightweight who feels the alcohol saturate my blood within a few sips. I flopped on the bed and passed out, face down.

My body began to hum as strong, muscular hands erotically massaged my calf muscles. I moaned in my sleepy state. Those skilled hands made gentle but firm strokes up my thighs. Lips replaced his fingers. He licked the valley where my ass and back met. My eyes remained closed even though I had become fully awake. I could hear his every intake of breath within the quiet confines of our room. All of my senses were on high alert. I could smell cigar smoke and bourbon mixed in with his woodsy scent. I wanted to turn over but he kept me pinned with his body.

Every touch sent ripples of desire straight to my throbbing core. He had my body on the verge of combusting. I withered beneath him. He answered my silent plea by placing his hands under my hips and pulling them up. I used my knees to steady myself.

"Harlow, you make a saint forget his pledge. You are so damn sexy. I'm sorry, baby, but I can't wait any longer."

"I need you, Cole. I'm begging you."

He hooked his fingers into my suit's bottom and

pushed them down my thighs. In a swift movement, he spread my legs wide and entered my wet opening. I tossed my head back in pleasure as he ravaged my body. Even in his haste, I felt worshiped. With every thrust, my heart sang out. Our tumultuous lovemaking entwined my soul to his. He took what he wanted and I willingly let him have it all.

That night we ventured out to the fountains. I leaned in to his strong chest as he circled his arms around my waist. The combination of the water and lights danced to the sweet classical melody. The complex choreography inspired romanticism from those of us watching the spectacular show.

When the show ended, disappointment hung heavily around me. Cole prodded me along toward the Venetian. He extended the romanticism by taking me on a gondola ride through the hotel. Our guide wore a straw gondolier hat with red ribbon tied around the brim. The classic loose-fitting, long-sleeved navy and white striped shirt allowed our guide to paddle freely through the water. If I closed my eyes, I could envision riding along the true Venetian canals instead of through the shopping center of the hotel.

The hotel was beautiful but not the classic beauty that the Bellagio emulated.

"You hungry?"

I smiled up at him, grateful to him for understanding that I eat real food and in regular intervals. He never made me feel uncomfortable about my larger hips and minor muffin top.

"Famished."

"Great. I know the best place to dine."

"Where might that be?" I cocked my head to the side.

A devilish grin radiated along his perfectly sculpted lips. "It's very private. I've already secured our reservation."

"Do I need to change first or can I wear this?" I swept my hands over my jeans and shirt.

"I was thinking less clothing and more whipped cream."

My eyelids popped open wide. "Where are you taking me? I don't think I can eat in a restaurant where half of my bits are hanging in my food."

He roared with laughter. "You are absolutely adorable."

He took my hand in his as we walked to our destination. I puzzled over our reservations the entire time. My nerves were frayed a little more with every step I took. He guided us down the path to our hotel and my tattered nerves repaired themselves enough so that I no longer felt like a donut junkie desperately needing a Krispy Kreme.

He led us back to our room. Once I crossed the threshold, I was almost back to normal. The door swung shut behind me. Cole wrapped his arms around my waist. He kissed along my neck, slowly working his magical lips along my collarbone. My body coiled tightly for entirely different reasons.

"You have far too many clothes on. Let's get you

naked and I can stare at your gorgeous body."

I hummed with pleasure as he undressed me. Our dinner reservations were completely forgotten. He maneuvered me toward the bed. He gently set me on top of the expensive thread. He hastily shed his clothes.

I scooted up the soft duvet until my back brushed against the coolness of the headboard. Goose bumps erupted all over my heated skin, pulling it taut. He climbed up the bed as though he were a wolf stalking its trapped prey. My muscles screamed for him to make his move. My heart raced as desire pumped through my bloodstream.

He pushed my legs apart as he moved between them. The breath in my lungs halted, keeping them full to the brim. He gently captured my mouth with his. I swear the minute our lips touched, a spark ignited. I opened up to him and sought out his tongue with mine. I exhaled and inhaled his scent. He invaded every one of my senses. My body hummed with each kiss and tender touch.

I wriggled my body and moaned as he licked his way down to my breasts. His tongue circled and pulled at the overly sensitive bud. My thighs tightened around his waist, caging him in place. The tip of his dick teased my opening. With every movement of his body, his dick rubbed up and down, causing the inferno to rage out of control.

I bit down on his shoulder as he grazed his teeth along my nipple. He growled with pleasure as he drove into my wet, pleading center.

I tossed my head back in pleasure. "More, Cole. I need so much more."

"Oh, God, baby. You feel so good. You can have it all." He thrust harder, filling me up.

I wrapped my legs around his waist to angle my hips upward. He plunged deeper. I moaned his name as I scraped my nails along his corded back. His cock jerked with each dig of my nail. The combination of his thrust and twitch triggered a potent orgasm. My head tossed languidly from side to side as pulse after pulse hit. My muscles clutched his cock, milking him until he cried out my name as his pleasure coated my inner walls.

Our earlier intentions of a meal were long forgotten. I curled into his side, placing my head on his firm chest. My body was thoroughly used and my eyelids closed with satiated heaviness.

CHAPTER 17

I snuggled deeper in the soft, feathery warmth, dreading reality. It was closing in on my blissfulness. Cole had one more meeting early this morning and planned to be back right after lunch. I took advantage of our big bed and lazily lounged.

I ordered myself a heaping pile of buttermilk pancakes. Lord, these pancakes were the right combination of fluffy with a slight crisp around the edges. Simply sinful. No one in a hundred-mile radius at home could cook this good of a pancake. This whole trip had ruined me but in all the right ways.

Dressed and ready in casual clothes for a mystery adventure that Cole had planned, I sat on pins and needles and wondered what it was. I bit on my second nail as Cole casually strolled through the door. I was merely seconds away from demanding to know where we were going.

He planted a searing kiss upon my lips, effectively shutting me up. "Are you all set?"

"Yep. Do you plan on telling me what we are doing?" I questioned nonchalantly.

"Nope. You'll figure it out once we get there."

I sighed with defeated exasperation. I should know

better; he liked to surprise me. I, on the other hand, disliked surprises.

We took a luxury town car to an airstrip. That was the only obvious clue to surface. He led me over and shook hands with a gentleman wearing a flight uniform. "John, it's great to meet you."

"Likewise, Mr. and Mrs. Devlin. Today is an excellent day for a helicopter ride."

I grinned like a fool when Cole didn't correct him. The stars dancing around my vision were bright enough to blind me. Then reality struck as "helicopter ride" sunk into my brain mass. *Oh, hell no!* I planted my feet to the hot asphalt when Cole tried to pull me along behind the pilot.

"You can't back out now. You'll like it, I swear." He pulled out the sexiest grin he owned.

It worked. I melted like ice in the Florida heat. I let him drag me to the waiting helicopter. My stomach only somersaulted a couple of times while I climbed in the back. *I hope this bird came equipped with an airsick bag.*

The pilot started up the blades and the loudest and most unnerving whooshing sound assaulted my ears. He pointed to his headphones and mic attached. We mimicked him and put ours on. Once the headphones were in place, I could clearly hear the pilot. He told us to sit back and enjoy the view. *Yeah, right!*

The higher we climbed, the queasier I got. I looked over at Cole and swallowed the bile that rose as fast as the helicopter did. He reminded me of a little girl receiving a pony. Yes, that's exactly what I thought. He was so giddy that all of the testosterone in his body turned immediately to estrogen.

I couldn't help but roar with laughter. He looked at me quizzically but I most certainly kept that vision to myself. It would be an awesome gem to pull out on a bad day. Focusing on him allowed me to forget about how high we were off the ground. My stomach settled and I was able to look out the window.

Holy cow! We flew right over the Hoover Dam. You could clearly see the white salt marks left on the rock from where the water level used to be. Lake Mead stood out of place with its crystal-blue water against the rugged reddish-brown desert terrain. I couldn't wrench my eyes away from the view. It all looked so small, like a blip on the radar.

The view of the Grand Canyon was like none that I have ever experienced. As the sun began its descent, the rock had turned a deep golden red. The river that had carved out this magnificent canyon seemed as wide as my finger.

The pilot came over the headset and informed us that we were going to land right there on a plateau in the canyon. Right about now, the nerves completely left and the geek in me bounced to an all-new high level. We stepped off the helicopter and roamed the desert basin. To be able to experience such a monumental landscape astounded me. Off to the edge ran the mighty Colorado River. What once looked as wide as my finger now raged fiercely and was miles wide.

Cole came up behind me and wrapped his arms around my waist. I leaned back into his strong chest, soaking up the wonderful memory. The pilot shouted for us to come over to a picnic bench underneath a canopy for some champagne.

We clinked glasses. "Thank you for the best day."

"My pleasure. Are you having a good time?"

"This has been absolutely mind-blowing. Actually, the whole weekend has been amazing. Thank you." I bent over the table and kissed his cheek.

I hated to leave but knew that the tour was winding down. I sighed thoughtfully over the last couple of days. Thirty-two years and this was the first time that I've experienced something bigger than Seattle. This vacation would be forever etched in my memory.

We sat on the balcony outside of our room. The fountain's spray could be heard splashing in tune with the music and lights.

I felt the need to say thank you again. "Cole, you have no idea how incredible this weekend has been for me. I have never been outside of Seattle. In the span of a couple of days, you've shown me so much. I'll never be able to return the favor or say thank-you enough."

He reached for my hand and rubbed his thumb along my knuckles. "There is no need for a return favor or a thank-you. Your happiness has been reward enough for me. You have made this trip special. If you hadn't come with me, I'd have gone to a meeting and returned home. There would have been no enjoyment." He brought my hand to his lips. "So, thank you for honoring me with your company. It is your presence that has made this trip worthwhile."

I got up from my lounge chair and straddled his hips.

I sunk down, aligning my hips just right so that I could feel his hardening length. God, the things that he did to my body and heart. I moved my hips back and forth, loving the close contact. Even though our clothing hindered what I really wanted, the friction felt incredible. His deep, throaty moan spurred me on. My hands flew to the bottom of his shirt. I worked the material up as my fingers grazed his tight abs and over his chiseled chest. I took my fingernails and grazed both of his nipples. He growled my name as his back came up off the chair. I took the opportunity to slip his shirt over his head.

He grinned sexily. "Your turn."

I lifted my arms above my head, allowing him to remove my top. He leaned up and placed his lips along my neck. I angled my head to give him more access. His mouth drove me wild. The way he used his teeth and tongue had my panties wet. My pussy clenched from the gentle nibbling. My body lit up as though it were the Fourth of July. Hot sparks ignited deep within my belly and spread throughout my blood, making it sizzle with desire. I licked my lips as his fingers swept underneath my bra straps, pulling them down my arms. I slipped my arms free as his wandered to the clips in the back. My bra fell freely, letting my breasts bounce slightly from being liberated from their constraints.

I moaned as his head dipped toward my rosy brown nipple. He lashed the tight bud with his tongue before he sucked it into his hot mouth as his fingers tweaked and lightly tugged the other nipple. He used his mouth and fingers to feast from my breasts. I gyrated my hips, needing to be closer, bare skin to bare skin. My thoughts jumbled the more he teased my body. I couldn't think over all of the sensations that pulled my skin taut. They drove me beyond the capacity to handle all of the stimulation. I was going to combust; the temperature of the inferno raged vehemently, turning against me.

He lifted me higher onto his chest so that he could work my pants and underwear down my thighs. His eyes locked onto mine as I shimmied out of them and worked on the button of his jeans. His normal chocolaty pools were now an intense mocha color. They locked me in place; the passion and a hint of possessiveness that lay underneath swirled and mixed together. They seared into my soul, anchoring apart of him to me. I was in deep and there was no coming back from this. Love for this man slammed into my body, shaking me to my core. The realization freed my inhibitions. I leaned down and molded my lips to his. My heart poured through me and I gave him everything that I had.

He lifted his lips and pulled his pants to his thighs, freeing his thick cock. It was gorged with blood, looking iron-hard and angry and so ready to plunge into my eager pussy. I rose up slowly and guided his swollen cock into my dripping center.

"Mmm. Feels so good." I sighed.

"So tight. Love fucking your pussy." His voice thickened with pleasure.

It was all so much. I could feel my orgasm coiling through my loins as I rode him. The closer my bliss came, the faster my hips pumped up and down. I teetered out of control when his fingertips spread my folds and encircled my clit. I tossed my head back as I cried out his name. My pussy tightened around his pulsating cock, drawing out his pleasure. Cole shuddered beneath me as he milked my womanhood.

***

I got up early the next morning, letting Cole sleep. It was our last full day together with no outside interruptions. I slipped on some shoes and headed down to the floor to get some coffee and a couple of muffins for breakfast. I placed a soft kiss on his forehead and whispered. *"I love you."*

The need to tell him consumed my thoughts. This feeling completely frightened me. I couldn't say it while he was awake. If I did, he might run for the hills. I wasn't ready for him to leave. Hopefully he never would. What I didn't see was Cole's stunned expression as the door clicked behind me.

I walked back to the room whistling. I had two of the biggest muffins ever in an overly pink decorated box in one hand. In the other, I held a drink carrier with a caramel latte and a black coffee. Damn, I hate when I don't think ahead. I hoped Cole was up because I couldn't reach my room key.

I used my foot to lightly kick at the door. "Housekeeping." I chuckled to myself at my own joke.

I pressed my ear to the door, listening for his footsteps. Silence greeted me back. I kicked the door harder this time. "Cole, it's me. Can you open up? My hands are full."

"Coming." He opened the door with only a towel wrapped around his waist. His body glistened from his recent shower. *Fuck the breakfast; I would lick him from head to toe!*

"Sorry. I was in the shower."

"I can see that. Why don't I set this down so I can get you dirty again?"

He winked at me cockily and twirled around, leaving my mouth hanging open in shock. "We don't have time this morning. As much as I would love to get you all sweaty, our flight leaves soon."

What the fuck was that fucking shit? That had to be the lamest excuse ever proclaimed. I don't know what the hell transpired to warrant that but I was going to find out. I knew for a fact we didn't need to leave until tomorrow morning. It wasn't as if it would take that long shit. Anything lasting longer than twenty minutes is no longer pleasurable.

I walked up behind him and wrapped my arms around his middle. I pushed my breasts into his naked chest. "We have plenty of time. A whole day and night, as a matter of fact. Are you sure I can't change your mind?"

He let out a frustrated sigh. He untangled my arms from around him. He continued to mess with his shaving kit as he spoke to my reflection in the mirror. "I got a call from work while you were gone. I have to be back sooner. So I changed our flight. We only have fifteen minutes before we meet the car downstairs." His tone was brisk and all business as though, he were talking to one of his subordinates. There was no mistaking otherwise.

I leaned up against the doorjamb and folded my arms across my chest. "Sure, Cole." I continued to bore holes in his back with my laser vision.

"Don't look at me like that, Harlow. We were leaving soon anyway. What does another day matter?"

The bite in his words cut me deep.

I cocked my head to the side. "A whole twenty-four fucking hours! How do you go from an awesome and attentive boyfriend to a cold-hearted prick with a flip of a switch?" My voice rose higher with each word.

He just stood there and stared at me with disinterested eyes and his hands stuffed into his pants pockets. He jammed his hand through his hair. "I don't have time to argue with your unfounded insecurities. We need to get moving. I will not miss this flight." He brushed past me to finish collecting his items.

I threw my hands up in the air, exasperated. I took the obvious hint that any further discussion on this topic had been closed indefinitely. *Oh my God*! *I am such a stupid idiot. This was his way of brushing me off.* The anger and sadness rolled into one massive ball. It swirled around in my chest cavity, knocking into everything that it could. My chest constricted at the onslaught of emotions. I would not give him the satisfaction of knowing he had hurt me. I took in a deep breath, grabbed my suitcase and threw my clothes in haphazardly. I didn't give a flying fucking monkey if my clothes were wrinkled. All I wanted to do was get the fuck out of his presence. If I had to look at his lying ass face much longer, I would throttle him.

The air inside the car filled with heated tension. My skin felt sticky as the humidity of our friction increased in the tight quarters. Not a muscle in my body moved. I wanted to yell at him until he broke down and told me the truth. My hand itched to slap the emotionless robot that had taken over this man.

I peeked over at him from out of the corner of my

eye. I noted his set face, his clamped mouth, and fixed eyes. He made no move to look at me. He blankly stared straight ahead. I huffed out a loud breath. I folded my arms across my chest and got lost in the blurry scenery whizzing past.

***

I clicked the seat belt around my hips. I leaned my heavy head against the thick plastic that framed the window. My limbs were heavy. It felt as though I had run a marathon while sick with pneumonia. I guess I did: one that had involved my heart. Cole hadn't spoken but a couple of words to me since the hotel. His abrupt change had my mind spinning in circles.

He placed a warm hand on my thigh, squeezing gently. "Are you feeling okay?"

Thousands of butterflies took flight inside my midsection. I hated that I still craved his touch. "Yes. I am feeling fine—just tired." Which was true. I was emotionally drained.

I couldn't help myself. I placed my hand on top of his. He intertwined our fingers together. I kept my body angled away from him even though I held his hand throughout the length of the flight. I couldn't bear it if he saw my heart placed upon my sleeve, right out in the open, for the taking.

Maybe I shouldn't assume that he would kick me to the curb. His demeanor could've been from having to go back early. Maybe he had a time of the month hormonal issue like most of us ladies do. Hell, this whole relationship was straight out of a dream. I never got this lucky in the guy department, especially the *GQ* model lottery. This might be what was wrong with him. He hadn't shown any other serious vices for me to pick apart. Whatever; I was sick of overanalyzing it to death. I had a great weekend and that was that.

He had the car pull up to the curb outside of my apartment and popped the trunk. The driver got out to get my suitcase.

I twisted my torso toward Cole. My eyes soaked up his entire body in the span of a second. "Thank you for a nice weekend. I enjoyed it immensely."

I waited for another second to see whether he would at least lean over and kiss me good-bye. No movement. He just stared at me with an opened mouth. *Okay, that's my cue to get the fuck out of the car.* I turned and put my hand over the handle, pulling it out toward me. It opened; I put one leg out of the car and onto the curb slowly.

Not even a peep from Cole. *R-I-G-H-T.* My heart seized and sunk into a painfully darkened pit. I pushed the rest of the way out of the car. The driver had met me on the curb and handed me my bag. "Thank you."

"My pleasure, ma'am."

I nodded as I snatched the bag from him and walked to the entrance of my complex. I wouldn't look back. That horse's ass didn't deserve the longing I held in my gaze. My hand landed on the handle of the door. I felt his hand pull my shoulder around.

I faced Cole. "Harlow?"

I remained silent. What else could I say? His body language told me all that I needed to hear. I stood statuesque, waiting for him to say or do something. He leaned into me, cupping his hands around my cheeks. He slammed his mouth against mine. He punished me with his ravaging lips. I eagerly returned his gusto.

His stubble scratched my chin as he assaulted my mouth. It became exquisite torture. I whimpered like a small child at the loss when he pulled away.

He slowly backed away from me. "I'll call you later."

I nodded and turned to go inside. I ran my fingertips along my swollen lips. The guy even knew how to blow your mind while he kissed you good-bye for the last time. He had poured everything he had into it and I took it.

CHAPTER 18

My heart had taken a severe beating. It lay in my chest cavity, swollen and battered. I took in deep gulps of much-needed oxygen and slammed the door behind me. I opened it again and slammed it shut once more, rattling the pictures that hung on my walls. To hell with my neighbors. For once, I didn't have the gumption to care what anyone else thought of my rude behavior. I collapsed to the floor and let the tears fall down my cheeks like petite rivers that soaked into my shirt.

I stood up sluggishly and lumbered to my bedroom after the last teardrop fell. My body had depleted its salty water source. I had no more to shed. With as much force as I could muster, I threw my suitcase into the closet. I took perverse pleasure as it thumped into the wall. I peeled my clothes off my body. I didn't want his scent that had lingered on the fabric wafting toward my nose. Petty and childish? Hell yes, it was.

I opened my dresser drawer and scoured through the shirts until I had found my favorite one. The collar had thinned with age. Minute holes robbed the firmness of the cotton over the years. It was ratty and had seen better days but it covered my body with its matured threadbare softness.

I opened the trunk at the end of my bed. I reached in and grabbed my grandmother's prized quilt. I draped the lovingly stitched squares around my shoulders and climbed into bed. I curled into a fetal position as I hugged my pillow. Salty droplets pooled along my lashes before they overflowed with heaviness. My pillow absorbed their sadness as I tumbled into a fragmented sleep. I awoke off and on from my tortured dreams. I had no desire to get up, so I lay there and wallowed in self-pity.

**

I sputtered and coughed as icy water traveled in my mouth and up my nose. I sprung up at the waist, wondering what happened. I used the back of my hands to wipe the excess water off my face. I squinted and peered at a blurry vision of my brother.

"Get the fuck up!" he shouted at me.

I shuddered at his uncharacteristic bark. Then, I sharpened my spine and prepared for battle.

"Are you fucking crazy?" I screamed at him as I jumped out of bed, dumping the drenched quilt to the floor in a soggy heap. I wrapped my arms around myself as I shivered from the cold. "Who gave you the right to come into my home and do something so asinine?"

"I did, little girl." His lips thinned with fury. "I've called you nonstop for two days. Everyone is flipping out because you haven't answered your phone. We didn't know if you had come back or were dead in some alley." He paced the room as though he were a lion trapped in a steel cage.

I had the good sense to look and feel ashamed at my behavior. *Two days?* "Cash, it's Sunday. What the hell are you talking about?" I huffed out. I was beyond annoyed with him. *I couldn't have missed two day. Or could I have?*

"Harlow, it's Wednesday morning." He sat on the edge of my bed with his shoulders slumped and his head buried in his hands, as though at his wits' end.

I pounded out of the room and grabbed my cell. I opened up the calendar app. *Fuck, he wasn't joking.* I had missed several phone calls from my mother, father, and Cash. *Shit!* Not a word from Cole. A searing pain shot through my heart. I turned back around when I heard his heavy footfalls.

"What happened? This is not like you at all. You really scared the hell out of me." He ran his hands through his hair.

"I don't want to talk about it. I'm fine. I'll come into work and you can take the rest of the week off. I'm sorry I worried you." I swiveled on my heel to go get ready.

He held his tree trunk of an arm out and blocked my path. "Look, I don't know what's going on exactly, but I have a pretty damn good idea. Tell me where he is and I will end his pathetic little life."

A genuine smile lit my face and I laughed for the first time since I came home. The chuckle sounded hoarse and unfamiliar. "Thanks, big brother, for having my back. I love you." I wrapped myself in his protective arms and pinched off some of his strength. I let it seep into my bones before I backed away. "It's not worth it. Let it go."

His scrutinizing gaze held me locked in place. Fury swirled in their depths. "I'll let it go for now. I make no promises as to what will happen if he shows his face."

I strode away from him and took my stinky self to the shower. I scrubbed every inch of my body, effectively eliminating all reminders of Cole. My skin turned slightly pink and tender from where I had overzealously rubbed the abrasive loofah. I pulled on my self-esteem boosting, butt-hugging jeans and most comfortable hoodie. I posed in front of the mirror. My outer appearance hadn't changed one bit, but on the inside, it looked as though I had tried to walk through a cheese grater. I squeezed my eyes shut and inhaled deeply. I exhaled slowly and regained some of my composure. I walked out of the bedroom and portrayed a more confident woman than when I had walked in.

I had assumed that Cash had left and went back to work. However, he sat on the couch and spoke in hushed tones into his cell phone. He ended his call right as my ass hit the cushion of the chair.

I raised my eyebrows. "Are you going into work or am I going in alone?"

His maniacal laughter made me shiver. "Nope. I just got off the phone with Peyton. She will man the store for us today. There are no appointments scheduled until Friday. She can handle any customers who come through the doors."

"So, what do you have planned? You are kind of freaking me out here."

"Get your range bag. We are going to go shoot the hell out of some targets. I called Marge and she reserved two lanes for us."

Tears rushed through their ducts and got trapped within the fine hairs woven in my lower eyelids. I couldn't stop the forward momentum of my body as my brother yanked me in to another bone-crushing hug.

He gently patted my back as though I were a child. "We all love you and hate to see you hurt." I nodded as he held me at arm's length. "Since you won't let me physically decapitate Cole, shooting is the next best thing. Come on, sis, let me take care of you for once."

Through my blurry vision, I saw sympathy churning in the depth of his soulful eyes. If it were pity, I would have run back to bed. Sympathy I could handle.

"Okay, Cash." I squared my shoulders and went to retrieve my bag.

As soon as I walked through the doors of the range, my shoulders relaxed and I was able to breathe. The range had become my home away from home. No other place could compare to the smell of hot gunpowder that filled the air. It was almost as sweet as my mom's baking.

I nodded to Marge as I walked past the counter. I donned my earplugs and pushed through the soundproof door. I marched to my reserved lane, ready to unleash my   gut-wrenching sadness. I lovingly placed my Sig on the waist-high shelf that blocked me from crossing the line into the live range. I unpacked two boxes of ammunition and placed it off to the right of my firearm.

My hand trembled as I placed each bullet in the empty clip. Adrenaline shot straight through my bloodstream. It pushed the sadness back to the dark recesses of my mind so that I could fully concentrate at the task at hand. After I loaded the gun, I   double-checked the safety, and then placed it on the shelf.

I turned around and walked to the rectangular table

pushed against the cold cinderblocks of the wall where I placed my range bag. I grabbed my favorite zombie target and walked back to my lane. I hooked the flimsy sheet of paper to the clip that dangled from the overhead wire. I flipped the switch to my right and watched the target zoom farther away from me.

I squared my shoulders and put my left leg slightly out to the front of me, with a marginal bend to my knee. My right hand closed firmly around the grip with my shooting finger on the outside of the trigger. I wrapped my left hand around my right, somewhat forward. I extended my arms out and took aim. I placed my finger over the trigger. I took a deep breath in and as I exhaled, my finger gently pulled back the trigger.

BOOM! Deep breath in, slow breath out. *BOOM!* I repeated the process until the clip emptied and the slide stayed open. It said, "Look at me, Harlow. I'm out of bullets; please reload me so that we can have more fun."

I set my favorite piece down and flipped the switch to bring back my target. As it flew toward me, I wondered whether Cole missed me as much as I missed him. Or was I just a fleeting notion of a good time? I scrubbed my face with my hand. I couldn't push him out of my thoughts no matter how hard I tried. The flying target stopped suddenly, sending a soft breeze across my flushed cheeks.

"Damn, Harlow. You splattered the zombie's brains all over the back of the lane. Nice grouping. Remind me to never piss you off." He stepped back into his own lane and loaded his 9mm.

My lips twitched as an involuntary grin strained to form. I stood behind and off to the left side as Cash took aim. The shells popped out of the barrel, pinging me with hot metal, after each feather-light squeeze of the trigger. I watched transfixed, by the beauty of the gun's mechanics. Put me in a room with old jukeboxes and firearms and the geek in me would burst through. We occupied those two lanes until all the boxes of ammunition were used. I sat in the passenger seat and enjoyed the way the buttery leather curled around my body. I rested my head on the back of the seat as though it were too heavy for my neck to hold up. My body had used up its last reserve of adrenaline. My eyes closed of their own volition.

"Harlow?"

"Hmm."

"Want to get Jets?"

My eyelids sprang open as though the pizza slice were right in front of me. My stomach growled like an angry beast that hadn't eaten in days. My mouth watered at the mere thought of the slice of heaven. I wanted to sink my teeth into the sweet-buttery and richly dense cheese. I could smell the spicy aroma of cooked pepperoni and oregano. We weren't even there but I had already transported my psyche to the pizzeria.

My leg bounced up and down the closer we got. I licked my lips with anticipation when the bright red neon light flashed in my view.

"Calm yourself down, sis. You can't go all Godzilla in Jets. You know they threatened to ban you for life the next time you entered while foaming at the mouth like a rabid dog."

I grabbed the handle of the door but before I could

exit the car, Cash stopped me with his commanding voice.

"Seriously, I got this. I'll just be a minute and then we will take it back to your place. I'll call Peyton and have her meet us there." He had effectively pinned me to my seat with his authoritative stare.

I pulled down the visor and checked my reflection in the mirror. *What an ass!* For a minute there, I seriously thought that I had drool hanging from the corners of my mouth. Cash was right. They did threaten to ban me. In my defense, there happened to be a torrential downpour. It poured from the heavens in buckets as I ran from my apartment building to my car. *Silly little Mother Nature!* How dare she think that a teeny bit of rain would stop me from my favorite, better-than-sex slice of cooked-to-perfection goodness?

I couldn't help it that it had quit raining by the time I parked and went to pick up the pizza. Between the hair product and the tidal wave of water, my hair had frizzed beyond what I thought was remotely possible. Think of Frankenstein's bride and Marge Simpson when she had a nervous breakdown. I may have unrepentantly scared some of their patrons and possibly sent the pimply teenage boy working the register to therapy for the rest of his life. *Good times!*

Cash gently placed the box on my lap. I greedily wrapped my hands around the sides. If Cash even thought about snatching the box back, I might growl and snap my canines at him. The rich fragrance wafted from the box, teasing my olfactory senses. I mentally urged Cash to push his foot down on the accelerator. There was comfort in the way that the familiar shaped box warmed my legs. A normal person would suggest that I had a problem. I refused to admit that I had one. Denial is best served warm and in a square cardboard box.

I carefully exited the car. I held my prized possession to my chest. If I dropped the pizza, I would not be opposed to invoke the five-second rule and go.

CHAPTER 19

I woke up the next morning feeling more rejuvenated than when I had drowned in my own self-pity. Which isn't saying all that much. However, today there seemed to be a sliver of light at the end of the tunnel. I owed a huge thanks to Cash for dispelling some of the rancid funk.

My brother could be a pain in the ass most days, but he could cheer me up in a way that no one else could. He had always been my champion. He fought alongside me, through every emotional battle that I had ever engaged in. He never once looked down at me nor ever judged. He was the master at making me forget my woes. He made sure that I continued to charge through my life, mostly by giving it to me straight and not coddling me. I appreciated that more than he ever knew.

Cole remained heavy on my mind. My fingers itched to call him but I had a little pride. I would not beg him to be with me, no matter how much my heart pleaded me to. It took me a long time to understand that you can't make someone love you when they don't. No matter how much you wished for it. On second thought, I could travel to New Orleans and find a voodoo doctor. All I needed was a lock of hair and maybe a small amount of Cole's blood to get the doc to mix me up a love potion. I shook my head. That shit isn't even real. At least, I don't think it is.

To get my head on straight, I treated myself to a large cappuccino on my way in to work. The first sip of warmth slid down my throat and heated my cold bones. I hoped it would be enough to get me through the day.

My brain switched over to autopilot as I completed the opening duties. It felt wonderful to have a moment where Cole hadn't entered my thoughts. The only messages my thinker sent were instructions to my extremities for carrying out the particular tasks. A shame, really, that it only lasted for ten minutes. But for those precious minutes it was glorious.

Cash texted me this morning and told me that he wouldn't be in today. This didn't surprise me. I expected it and thought that he deserved it. He would be in tomorrow because it was the day that High Society would grace us with her final presence. Giddiness bubbled up and out of my mouth at watching her backside leave our store for the final time. I hoped that she wouldn't need another collar for the rest of her life.

While the shop remained blessedly empty, I ran in to the back to see whether there were any projects on Cash's desk that I could tackle. My eyes twinkled as I spied an order that had more intricate designs on it than the last collars I'd helped Cash with. I looked forward to the challenge. It was sure to keep the gray matter busy for the next couple of days. I gathered some supplies and headed to the front counter. I placed a thick, black towel on the countertop to catch loose crystals. They were easier to spot against the thick black cloth. The dark material illuminated the crystal's color. Then, I systematically arranged all of the items around the vintage leathered collar. I reread the well-detailed description of the design that the customer wanted. The shrill of the phone through the quietness of the store startled me.

I placed my hand over my thumping heart as I answered.

"Thank you for calling Firedog Bling. This is Harlow. How can I help you?"

"Well, if it isn't my inconsiderate daughter," my mom seethed.

Shit on a stick! This conversation would not go well. I would have to open up my mouth wide and eat a big, fat, and hugely feathered crow. I sighed heavily. "Hello, Mom. I am terribly sorry for making you worry. As you can tell, I am fine and back to work. I will be at dinner this Sunday so you can see for yourself."

Okay, so I only stuffed half of the guilt-bearing bird in. I understood why she was upset with me. However, for shits and giggles, I was a grown woman and not one who had to check in with her any more. Haven't since I was seventeen and had a curfew.

The silence from her end meant that I would get a good ass tearing, of course, in a lady-like tone. She never yelled and never uttered a swear word. A true Southern Belle. Even though she had been born and raised right here in Seattle.

"Young lady, that was a feeble attempt at an apology. I will never forget this."

I rolled my eyes, knowing that she couldn't see me through the phone. Hell, she never forgot *any* of my indiscretions. She frequently brought up the one and only time I colored on the wall with permanent marker when I was two.

"Do not roll your eyes at me, Harlow Ann McCollum."

Uh-oh! She used my full name. Now, I had really pissed her off. I would forever be on her shit list for atrocious offenses. "Mom, I don't know what else to say, other than I am truly sorry to have worried you and Dad." I sighed heavily, not trusting my voice any longer. Tears burned the back of my throat as I tried to hold them back.

She must have caught the slight tremor in my voice because her previously stern voice gentled. "Sweetheart, we love you very much. If anything had happened to you, well, I don't know what I'd do with myself. It would be beyond unbearable."

I nodded my head in acknowledgment even though she couldn't see me.

"If you ever need to talk, I am always here to listen. I love you, baby girl. If nothing else, remember that. One more thing: I expect you at the house on Sunday and no excuses."

I didn't respond nor did I have to. She had hung up before I could utter another word. Our mother-daughter bonding moment abruptly ended. I sat on the stool, stunned, as I clung to the phone with a shaky hand. It wasn't until the incessant buzzing of the line having gone dead reached my brain that I snapped out of the fog. I slowly hung up the receiver. I managed to swallow the watermelon-sized lump that had lodged in my throat. I would not shed another tear, especially here. I sucked in a lungful and went back to the collar.

The design was supposed to encompass large and small rowels from Western spurs. I looked at my practice design and simply put, it was hideous. It resembled an oval-shaped antique mirror without the reflective glass and a clusterfuck of color. Man, I had my work cut out for me on this one. Thank goodness I had enough foresight to practice before I glued the stones. Moving them freely is ten times easier than trying not to fuck up the crystal after gluing it repeatedly. Not to mention, the ability to overturn the thick leather and dump the stones on to the thick material and start over.

That's exactly what I did. I turned the collar on its side and let the sparkling crystals land on the dark material. I laid the collar back down, grabbed my tweezers, and began anew. Smudged fingerprints dulled the stones' color, making it hard to visualize their former vibrancy. The collars were always cleaned in a painstaking manner before it reached the customer as a completed order. Being the obsessive person that I am, I enjoyed the symphony of rich color that the stones cast as I placed them. It was music for my eyes.

I may not be as creative or as talented as Cash, but I had a no-quit attitude. I would arrange and rearrange the stones until they were perfect. It felt as though I were in the passenger seat with my grandfather, taking a leisurely Sunday drive. Those drives were long and sometimes tedious, but when we pulled back in to the drive, I was able to forget all of that and bask in the happiness of having spent the time with him.

I mentally patted myself on the back for having the courage to start working on them. Instead of bringing in an apprentice, I figured that I could fill that role. I wouldn't want this part of the business all of the time, but I'd be ecstatic to learn more. I just finished placing a stone when the bell over the door chimed. I set my tweezers down and took off my latex gloves. I pushed the materials off to the side of the counter so that I could concentrate on the customer who just walked in.

"Good afternoon. I'll be right with you." I finally took my eyes away from the collar and looked up at the customer.

There he stood, right in front of me. The only thing between us was the counter. Which wasn't nearly enough space between us. My mouth went slack. My eyes bugged out in complete shock. I stared at the most beautiful milk-chocolate eyes. They reminded me of Willy Wonka's chocolate river, tranquil and sinfully smooth. I snapped my jaw shut hard enough to chip a tooth.

Really! I shouted in my head at the injustice of it all. I was not ready to face him yet. Maybe in say, oh, ten or fifteen years. Cole wore a grin on his face. It reminded me of the cat that ate the canary.

Play it cool, Harlow. "Hi, Cole. What brings you in today?" My voice sounded clear and unaffected. On the inside, I so was not. At any moment, my legs were going to give out. I locked my knees and stood a bit taller. My heart extended its claws and lunged at my mind. It wanted Cole desperately, but my brain would not allow any part of my wildly beating heart the satisfaction. *Way to hold strong, brain.*

"Good afternoon, Harlow."

He slowly elongated my name so that it sounded as though it had slipped through his mouth after an orgasm. My loins erupted with volcanic heat. My heart jumped in my throat as though it would fly out and pounce on Cole if I didn't do something soon.

I backed up an inch for every step he took around the counter. My back hit the door and it swung open. My hands flew out wildly, trying to grab hold of something to catch my impending fall. Literally, the devil's cohort yanked my body off balance. Otherwise known as gravity.

Cole and his cat-like reflexes saved me from bruising my tailbone. He hauled my body toward his chest as he continued to walk to the back. He wrapped his sinewy arms around my waist to imprison me. My legs betrayed me and allowed him to maneuver me where he wanted. My hands wanted to push him away so that I could clear my head. Once they touched his solid chest, they caved and fisted his shirt, holding on for dear life. Even my brain had a hard time making sense. He was too near. I couldn't breathe and my senses were dangerously close to short-circuiting.

My ass hit the back of Cash's desk, stopping our backward momentum. It was enough of a jolt to remove some of the lusty haze I was trapped in.

"Cole? I can't do this." My husky and breathless voice betrayed the words I just spewed. All lies and he knew it.

"I'm not giving you a choice. You are mine and I want you, Harlow. I thought I could stay away but I can't." He dipped his head and claimed my mouth.

I tried to resist, I really did, but it was futile. I had caved once his skilled tongue and lips had touched mine. He was my kryptonite. His growl vibrated through me as I returned the possessive kiss with equal ardor.

I lost all awareness to my surroundings. It was only Cole that I could see and feel. His hands slid underneath my shirt and plucked at my hardened nipples. Electricity zinged straight to my core. I pulsated with desire.

The continuous shrill of the telephone ringing brought me back to reality. *What the fuck was I thinking?* I pushed him away and took in a healthy gulp of oxygen.

"Cole! We have to stop. I'm at work and the only one here. You need to go." I turned away from him to grab the phone.

He wrapped his hand around my wrist, thwarting me from answering the phone. I looked over at him with large questioning eyes that looked down at where his hand gripped.

"Harlow," he said, with longing in his eyes.

The phone started up again. He released my hand, turned around and walked out. I'm not sure whether he left altogether or only to give me privacy to answer the phone. I didn't want him to leave but I didn't want him to stay either. *What the hell kind of game was he playing?* He had my emotions scattered all over the place. *Fuck the phone.* I couldn't drum up enough energy to care who kept calling. *Let the machine get it.*

I literally ran to the bathroom and splashed ice-cold water on my face. *Wow, that was fucking cold.* My face felt as cold as my brain does when I drink a blue raspberry Icee from the gas station too quickly. My eyes slammed shut and my hand went straight to rub my temples. I clenched the bathroom sink with an ironclad grip as I waited for the face-freeze to end its torture.

I wanted to run straight home and hide under the covers. Hiding in a dark world freed me from all the life and color around me. It numbed my heart. I didn't want to feel these crushing emotions. This wasn't me. My emotions were out of control and I was always in control. They were the only things in my life that did as I commanded. Cole had effectively ruined my carefully structured emotional state.

I bit the inside of my cheek hard enough to draw blood. The metallic taste immediately brought me back out of the black hole my mind generated. I double-checked my face just in case Cole had stuck around and headed to the front of the store.

CHAPTER 20

With each step that I took, the closer to the front I got. I became nervously excited, if that is such a thing, to see Cole and yet hoped he had left. He had me riding an emotional roller coaster. It was one of those that went fast through the dark and then suddenly stopped. Then, after a second's hesitation, it whipped you backward through the same but even scarier darkness. I loved and hated him at the moment. The ride in the beginning was exhilarating but halfway through, the mouth sweats started and I wanted to throw up my lunch.

I pushed through the door and scanned the silent area. A sigh of relief escaped. He was blessedly gone. I needed the time to gather my wits and get my head screwed on straight. I trudged toward the counter and sat my weary ass down. I wanted to shout as loud as I could, *what the fuck*, but what if a customer came in? Bad for business. So instead, I counted to ten in my head. It only worked to settle a nerve, not the damn bundle still bouncing around as though they were at a hard-metal concert, participating in a mosh pit.

I put my gloves on and got back to work on the collar. Nothing like an intricate, detailed design to get my focus straight and Cole out of my head. The bell above the door chimed and broke my concentration. I looked up warily. A genuine smile tugged at my lips.

"Hello, Sasha. Have you come to visit or schedule

an appointment with Cash?"

"Hello, dear. I have come to visit with you. That is, if you have time to chat with an old lady." The twinkle in her eye let me know that she didn't think of herself as old.

"Let me get you some tea. Please sit and I will join you in a minute."

I walked over to the coffee/tea pot. I can never remember its name but you put in one little cup and bam, you have it in less than a minute. Wonderful invention, if you ask me. I don't use it as much as my brother does. I like my coffee iced. He uses it for hot cocoa. He even puts miniature marshmallows in it. Watching a large and sometimes intimidating guy drink hot chocolate with marshmallows makes me giggle. After I watched the flavored water sputter through the tiny machine, I walked over to the table and sat down with Sasha.

"Where is Lady? You are never without her."

She smiled at me. "She is getting groomed. I did not want to wait so I thought I would come over."

"I am so glad that you did. How have you been?" I asked, sincerely interested in my favorite customer.

She patted my hand. "Wonderful, dear." She took a sip of her tea. "It seems as though my Peyton and Cash have been spending quite a bit of time together."

I smiled, pleased for Cash and Peyton. "Yes. They seem to be doing well. It has become serious pretty quickly. Cash isn't one to keep a girl around for long." I cringed at what had just popped out of my mouth. I had never meant to say that to her.

"To be young again. Honey, when the women aren't good enough, they never stick around for long. The same goes for men." She took on a glazed look and a tilt to her head.

I wondered what clip played in her mind. "I bet you were a minx when you were Peyton's age. Batting off the men like flies."

Her chuckle rang out from the pits of her stomach. Her laughter was infectious. Before I knew it, my sides hurt and my cheeks burned.

She playfully slapped my hand. "Oh my. Those days were something that I will cherish forever. I had the time of my life before I settled down with Michael."

We talked the day away. I had to remind myself that she was my mother's age and not closer to mine. She had fire and grit behind name-brand clothing and to die for jewelry. She easily painted the picture of a wild child: late nights and sexy men. I envied her ability to know what she wanted and the gumption to go and get it. I should take a page from her book. Easier said than done.

I went back to the collar but it no longer held my interest. I kept thinking about Cash and Peyton. *Were they serious about each other? How long before he popped the question?* I should start a pool when I go to my parents' for dinner on Sunday. My mom already had stars in her eyes of white lace. It wouldn't hurt to egg her on a little bit more. I put some music on as I cleaned up the shop and put my materials away. I stayed busy dusting and sweeping until closing time. I locked up and headed out to get some Chinese for dinner.

I sat on the floor with the food in front of me on the

coffee table. I put a movie in and enjoyed every minute of it. I paused the movie to go see what my fortune cookie had in store for me. I never ate them, just cracked it open and read the juicy tidbit nestled inside.

Try another cookie.

Are you fucking shitting me? I crumbled the cookie in my hand and threw it in the garbage. Half the crumbs bounced back out on to the floor. *Well, that about sums up my shitty life.* I'd boycott the damn place if their food wasn't so delicious. I grabbed a beer and flopped down on the couch and pressed play.

I jumped off the couch as my cell phone startled me awake. I had thought it was my alarm but when it didn't go off again, I picked it up to see what time it was. Only eleven o'clock. Not too shabby; I would get a good night's sleep in my bed then. I saw that I had a text, so I opened up the application. Of course it had to be from him. *Why, oh why, was he texting?* I guess if I read it, I would know.

Are you up?

Hmm. To respond or not, that is the question.

Yes. What's up?

He must have been staring at the screen because his response was immediate.

I'm in your parking lot. Can I come up?

God help me! Let's be real for a minute. I knew that this was nothing more than a booty call. Seriously, if he really cared, he would not have left me hanging after Vegas. Maybe I had things all wrong but my gut kept telling me that he was not the man to be in it for the long haul. *Did I want to entertain him for the evening?* The way that my underwear had already become saturated ratted out my body. It was my mind that I had to convince.

No more lying to myself. This would be for one night only. I'd get him out of my system once and for all. After tonight, unlike my Chinese food, I would boycott anything that had to do with Cole. I quickly typed in my response before I chickened out. Don't judge. I needed one last mind-blowing release to get me through another long dry spell after Cole left.

The door's open.

I went back to the couch and waited for him. My insides were at war. Desire coated my nether regions as sharp pains speared through my heart. I sat on my hands to try to quell their shaking. I was not cut out for mind games. I swung my head as the door opened and Cole strutted through, looking as though he hadn't a care in the world.

I soaked up his lean build covered in an expensive suit. He slipped out of his dress shoes. He laid his suit jacket on the back of the chair as though it rightly belonged there every night. He turned toward me. I sucked in a lusty breath. God had made the perfect specimen. I desperately tried to hate him.

The closer he came, the more my body betrayed me and reached out to him. I was a moth to his flame. I sat transfixed at the beauty before me. Describing Cole as pretty didn't do him justice but it was the only thing that came to mind at the moment. Getting naked quickly overshadowed every thought that I had.

He stood before me and offered me his hand. I easily slid my fingers over his larger palm. He threaded his fingers between mine as he guided me to the bedroom. I yearned to tell him how good he felt against my skin but my voice box chose to remain clamped shut. He flipped the bedroom light on. I blinked as the room flooded with bright light.

He led me toward the bed. He swiftly turned my body so that the back of my knees brushed the mattress. Tenderly, he urged me backward until I fell on to my back. I scooted up the bed to a more comfortable position. I lay in the middle of the bed watching and waiting for his next move.

He removed his clothing. I took my fill of the hard lines of his body as he stood before me. Anticipation pooled in my belly. My core overheated to the point of a near nuclear meltdown. He climbed on the bed and pushed my legs wide. He slid between my legs and nestled his hard cock up against my throbbing heat. My clothing made an obscene barrier. I had to get out of them. They were too restrictive and I needed to feel his gloriously naked skin against me.

His fingers reached for the hem of my shirt. With painstaking care, he shed me of my shirt. He bent down and placed his mouth over mine. The minute his tongue slipped between my lips, I moaned his name in ecstasy. I moved my hips, grinding into him with overwhelming desire and need. Unashamed of my wanton behavior, I continued to grind in to him, using his cock to bring me some minor relief, until he lost control and rid me of all of my clothing. I lay naked before him. I tried to read the thoughts swirling behind his lust-filled gaze. They remained a mystery. I couldn't read his mind as easily as I read his body.

"You are so fucking beautiful." He licked his lips as his gaze shifted to my breasts. My nipples hardened like diamonds. "You were made specifically for me and only me."

He dipped his head and suckled at the ridged peak. I thrust my chest forward, shoving my nipple farther in his teasing mouth.

"Please, Cole." I didn't dare say anything more. The urge for release consumed every thought that I had.

He plunged in to my boiling center as roughly as a caveman beat his chest in dominance. I submitted and rode the tidal waves of pleasure that crested from the tips of my toes to the strands of hair on the top of my head. I opened myself up and gave him everything that I had. He took it and then took some more. I chanted his name over and over again as my orgasm ripped through me. My vision clouded as the room spun. He growled my name as my core contracted around his length. Then he moaned my name as his face tensed with his own frenzied release.

My body shivered as he pulled out and flipped onto his back. I lay there next to him, dazed and trying to catch my breath. He hooked his arm underneath my neck and pulled me to his side. I cradled my head over his erratically beating heart. I sighed, fully satiated. I didn't want this night to end but my eyelids were too damned heavy to pry open.

CHAPTER 21

I rolled over and hit the snooze button. I languidly stretched my sore limbs. Soft snores greeted my ears. I smiled as I curled up against Cole. No sooner had I slipped into a light sleep than the damn alarm rang out again. I sat up and shut the annoying sound off. I twisted to take one last peek at Cole. In his sleep, he took on an almost boyish appearance. The sharp features slithered behind its daylight mask and revealed a man that I found more compelling.

The hardened lines of his face smoothed out and the lines around his eyes no longer crinkled around their edges. I sighed heavily, wishing that this were the part of himself that he would have shared with me. I quietly removed my covers and slid out of bed. A pang of regret settled cripplingly on my breastbone at the thought of him not trusting me enough to see this side of him.

I shook my head, fighting back the tears that threatened to spill down my cheeks. I knew what last night signified. I was no longer that naïve little girl with her head in the clouds. His body showed me more than what his words ever would and yet it wasn't enough. I wanted more and I don't believe he had it in him to give.

I had written him a note and left it taped to the bathroom mirror. It was simple and to the point: "Later." It was vague but I had hoped he'd read between the lines. *Thanks for a great night but I'm done with this back-and-forth shit.* He knew I wanted more. Hell, it was written all over my face whenever I looked at him. The elation I felt last night waned as I got ready for work. A dark cloud had settled over my head and followed me out the door.

I trudged through the parking lot toward the back entrance of the shop. Cash wouldn't be in this early, so I fished my keys out and unlocked the door. I stepped inside and from habit raised my arm toward the light switch and flipped it on. The room flooded in bright fluorescent lighting. Walking into the shop comforted me. Hopefully, I would be able to shut my mind down for the duration of work. I snatched the appointment book off Cash's desk and headed to the front.

I flipped on the coffee maker. Using one of Cash's hot cocoa mixes seemed logical. I preferred a nice sweet and cold latte but this morning, hot, smooth, chocolaty silkiness was what the doctor ordered. Plus, it was all that we had. It would do in a pinch. I flipped the closed sign to open, swiped my hot chocolate, and opened up the appointment book to see what was on the agenda.

No appointments until after lunch. I looked closer at my handwriting. "She-devil" was marked heavily in red ink. A lopsided grin formed. Today was the day that we signed off on Victoria's collar. I rolled my eyes to the ceiling and sent a silent thank-you to the big man upstairs. Some of the dark cloud that hovered over me broke away, taking some of the heaviness with it.

With my mood slightly elevated, I went to work on printing the online orders. I took the box that contained the rowels collar out and began the design once again. I had plenty of time before it needed to ship out. Cash thrived on last-minute completions. It brought out his creativity in droves. I, on the other hand, folded under extreme pressure. Working under the stress of last-minute conditions locked my brain on freeze mode. Nothing I did would make sense once that happened. I liked having the time to fiddle with the design until it flowed perfectly.

The shop remained relatively quiet throughout the morning. Cash showed up around eleven. He came whistling through the doors. I looked over at him, questioning his sanity.

"Don't look at me like that. Just because you woke up on the grumpy side of the bed doesn't mean that everyone else did too. So, check your attitude, take a sip of your sickeningly sweet latte, and get a grip on that death glare." He slammed the creamy mixture on the counter, jostling the stones that I had placed on the collar.

With his back to me, I squeezed one eye shut and I pinched his head between my pointer finger and thumb. Again, it was juvenile but warranted. Especially considering workplace violence was deemed socially unacceptable. However, I'm positive that any sane judge would agree with my side of things. He had the tendency to invoke insane behavior from me when he was around.

The first sip of deliciousness awakened my taste buds. Sugar and cream laced with the silky caramel drove my inner sweet tooth into a tornado that gobbled every saccharine morsel that poured in my mouth. I gulped half of the addictive brew in seconds. Once I gained control over the frenzied piranhas also known as my taste buds, I immediately forgave his last quip. Which happened to be pretty funny.

The coffee hit my bloodstream instantaneously. I used the extra jolt of energy to commence work on the collar. My hands fell into a fluid rhythm and my mind took a vacation to parts unknown. I attentively placed the last stone and called Cash to the front to check out my handiwork. I dug out my cellphone and took a quick picture of the design so that when I was ready to glue the stones I didn't have to conjure it up from memory. It would be as easy as painting by numbers. That was my theory anyway.

"What's up?"

"Check this out. What do you think?" My voice wavered just a bit.

I nervously stepped back while he dissected my work with his eyes. He was in tune with my idiosyncrasies so he was careful not to touch anything. I chewed anxiously on my thumbnail.

He swiveled his head toward me while he remained bent over the piece. His eyes swam with impressiveness. "Wow. You have outdone yourself with this one. I read over this job briefly. From what I skimmed, the client seemed very specific on what they wanted. Sis, you nailed it." He stood up and scratched his chin. "In all honesty, you went above that and created a one-of-a-kind piece that exceeds what the client described."

I gasped and placed my hand over my heart. I swayed backward a bit, astonished by his sincere compliment. "I hadn't expected all of that from you." I busted out laughing as joyful tears sprung down my cheeks.

A strange, twisted look came over his face. It was as though he contemplated bolting from my crazy emotions. *Fuck!* I was all over the place, like a ball in a pinball machine.

Instead, he wrapped me up in a big bear hug. "You have skills. Don't doubt yourself. You are smart, beautiful, and a pain in the ass. What's not to love?" He gently pushed me away.

He had an uncanny way of getting to the root of my emotional state without me having to say a word. Not to mention the ability to put a Band-Aid over the wound. The bell above the door rang out as Victoria swept through. She barely fit with all of the snobbery floating around her.

"Hello, Victoria," Cash and I said simultaneously.

I pinched him in the arm before he got me. This was our little game. Whenever we said something in unison, we would pinch each other. The first person to get in the tweak owed the other a beverage of their choice. Now, he owed me another coffee. *Score!* This day just kept getting better.

"Hello, Cash," she purred. Then her voice dripped with disdain and her eyebrows drew together as she spoke to me. "Harlow."

I couldn't understand why she hated me so much. I had been nothing but nice to her. Sure, I talked shit behind her back, but to her face, I was an angel. I know full well that I shouldn't say bad things behind her back but come on. She was a genuine bitch. She seemed to bring out my inner cattiness.

I gritted my teeth and spoke through thin lips. "Are you ready to see Fifi's collar?"

At the mention of her name she barked, enthusiastically.

"Yes, I am. However, I want to wait for my fiancé. He should be only a minute or two more." She placed her left hand on the counter. It was a classic move to show off her engagement ring.

Wow! The rock was the size of a small boulder. The beautiful monstrosity sat high in the setting. The ring itself was stunning but nondescript. The only thing that set the ring apart from a production line ring was the over-the-top size of the diamond. For all of its glitter and sparkle, it was quite bland, much like its owner. I'd rather have a smaller diamond with more character etched onto the band.

"Alrighty then. I'm going to go in the back and get the collar."

Before I could take a step toward the back, the bell jingled. I had to stay for the initial meeting of her fiancé. Curiosity about the man who chose to spend the rest of his life with this woman had my feet firmly rooted to the floor.

Victoria never took her eyes off Cash and me. "Ah. That must be him now."

"Sorry I'm late."

My eyes shot in the familiar voice's direction. I peered around Victoria. My hearing had to be playing tricks on me. As I got a good look at the man moving toward us, my stomach summersaulted. A healthy amount of bile shot up my throat. I coughed and sputtered from the acidic taste. Cash thumped me hard on the back. I swallowed the second round of bile.

Victoria slithered her snake-like hand through Cole's arm. He winked and smiled at me as he leaned down and placed a kiss upon her cheek. Victoria eyeballed me the entire time. Her sneer mocked me. I was told in clear enough body language that Cole was her man. She wore the engagement ring and I was the whore.

Another round of stomach juices threatened. I turned to Cash, trying to form enough words to let him know that I was hightailing my ass out of here. My lips opened and my jaw moved up and down but no sound came out. I squeezed his arm, pleading for him to understand.

"See you later, sis. Enjoy your weekend off." He practically shoved me through the back door.

I stumbled toward his desk. I took a second to regain my footing. I heard Cole shout my name. Cash's voice boomed and it sounded like he restrained Cole. *Oh, fuck, no!* Shaky legs or not, I had to get the hell out of here now. I ran out of the shop as though demons from hell had caught my scent.

I ran to my car and threw myself in the driver seat. I peeled out of the parking lot and headed straight to my mother. If I went back to my place, there was a high chance that Cole would come and try to explain his side of things. At this moment, I didn't want to hear a word from him.

Or maybe he wouldn't. He left me hanging after Vegas and now I knew why. *Fucking engaged to be married.* To Victoria, of all people. *More like a venomous snake lying in wait.* I knew he was too good to be true. I pounded the steering wheel at my stupidity. This had turned into a total cliché: a woman running away, tears streaming down her face, from a broken heart. I swiped at the tears angrily. I wanted the saltwater streams to stop but they wouldn't.

Through my blurred vision, bright blinding beams of light crossed in my lane. I swerved to miss the car headed right for me. The side of my car skidded along the guardrail. Sparks illuminated the side of my car as metal ground against metal. The tires squealed as I slammed on the brakes. Burnt rubber assaulted my nostrils. The deafening crunch was the last thing I heard as my world went dark.

CHAPTER 22

Incessant beeping noises buzzed around me like annoying mosquitoes on a humid summer night. I tried to shout for someone to shut the damn things off but no sound came out. I wished my hands to move to my ears and block out the sound but they wouldn't budge. *Everything is fine; don't panic.* I tried to wriggle my toes—nothing. *Okay, nothing is fine.* None of my extremities worked when I willed them to. All I could see was a dark void. Panic bubbled inside. *What the hell was wrong with me? Where was I?*

The rapid firing of the beeps increased the stronger my fear and anxiety grew. I recognized the richness of the deep male voice shouting for the doctor. *Cash,* I screamed until the voice in my mind could only vaguely whisper. I clawed my way through the darkness, reaching for somebody to rescue me. I made no headway, only floating around in my mind's vast void. My body served as a coffin that sealed my soul from the outside world.

The fire that entered my bloodstream coaxed a deep-seated desire for sleep. Finally, liquid gold hummed through my frozen limbs to calm my tired mind and inept shell of a body. For the first time since I awoke in this isolated murkiness, I felt weightless and no longer cared whether I woke again. There was peacefulness to relinquishing everything you cared about.

"The doctor said that her body would heal and that there was no brain trauma. All of her wounds were superficial. No broken bones and no deep lacerations. She didn't even need stiches. They don't know why she won't wake up. She was extremely lucky. Another foot to the right and the car would have careened off the cliff."

"Is she expected to make a full recovery?"

"The doctors seem to think so. It's up to her to wake up."

The irony was that I was awake. Just not in the sense that they wanted me to be. I could feel my mother run her fingers through my hair as her other hand held mine. I heard her conversation with Cash. Everything around me was crisp and clear. I fought and willed myself to move or make one muscle twitch. I failed at compelling my eyelids to open. It was as though someone had cemented them shut. They wouldn't budge. I was so tired. Sleeping sounded like a good plan.

I woke again to a heated argument. My curiosity would not let me fall back into the hollowness. There was absolutely nothing here. One would think that being trapped in your own mind would be entertaining. It wasn't, or at least mine remained hollow. *What did that say about me?*

"I have a right to see her."

"No. You really don't. If I recall, it is your fault that she is lying in this godforsaken hospital bed."

"Yes and for that, I will never forgive myself. However, I need her forgiveness. I owe her the truth, whether or not she can hear me."

"Not going to happen, Cole. You heard me the first time. I don't give a shit about you and your guilt. All I care about is that my sister is—and I hope to God she is—fighting for her life." He let out an angered sigh that I felt in my bones. "So help me, Cole, if you don't get out of here, you will wish that you had."

I felt the mattress move but couldn't tell what exactly was going on. *Cole.* That name sounded so familiar. That voice caressed my limp body. When he spoke, I felt a whisper of life radiate through this shit-hole that I had supposedly exiled myself to. For reasons still unknown to me. I wanted to yell at my brother to make him come back but I knew there was no use in trying. He wouldn't hear me. I curled up in the darkness once more and let it sweep me under.

I don't know how much time passed. Whether it was night or day. Had I been here overnight or months? Every day, I tried to entice myself back to the real world but it never happened. I couldn't even remember what brought me here in the first place. With all of the visits from my family, not one of them revealed the incident that placed me in the hospital and stuck in a place where my life halted. I knew the beginning. The middle was murky and I hoped that this wasn't the end.

I revered the one-sided conversations around me. I tried to imagine the workload that I forced on Cash—the tiredness that seeped into his voice when he talked—and the love that poured from Peyton and my parents but I couldn't help but feel that something was missing. That once, I had something wonderful. Their visits cheered me up but they still left me with a longing that I couldn't understand.

I didn't know what time it was but knew that it had

to be late in the night because there were long stretches of time where the only people who came were the staff. A screeching sound from the chair sliding toward my bed pulled me out of a silent sleep.

My hand lifted, not of my own accord, but from strong, masculine hands. They enveloped my hand and softly stroked my palm. Little zaps of electricity sparked up my arm and briefly lit the murky darkness that surrounded me. My pulse quickened at the new sensation. I marveled in the touch and strained to hear a sound. None came forward, only the gently stroking of my palm.

"Harlow?"

That one word sent my synapses firing. The person to whom the voice belonged seared my soul with its sadness. I felt every bit of its despair. I wanted desperately to comfort them, to take away such pain.

"I'm so sorry. Please come back to me. I love you."

He raised my hand and softly touched his lips to my palm. The minute those lips left my skin, the tears flowed freely. The longing that I had felt began to repair itself. Not enough to pull any color into my world but enough to need more and want more. His voice was achingly familiar and intimate. I grew angrier the more I tried to remember but it was too far out of reach. I sighed, knowing that I was my own prisoner.

***

"I am assigning a physical therapist for Harlow. It is imperative that she has the best possible chances for maximum recovery. For now, the therapist will work on preserving muscle tone and mobility. I will have her meet with all of you so that you are on the same page," the doctor pointedly stated.

"How long will the therapist work with her?" my mom questioned.

"For as long as she is here. When she awakens, we will do more testing as well as bring on any other therapists that might be deemed necessary."

"Dr. Marks, are you saying that when Harlow wakes up that she might not be the same? That there may be additional problems that we are unaware of?" My mom's voice trembled, on the verge of tears.

"I am not saying she will or she won't. I want you to be prepared for all of the possibilities that might occur once she does wake up. Our staff knows of Harlow's situation. We are ready and willing for when that day occurs."

"Yes, Doctor. I understand. Thank you for everything that you are doing for our daughter."

"She is in good hands. I'll be back to check on her later this evening."

As I listened to their conversation, my thoughts spiraled out of control. *What if I was stuck this way forever? Could my brain be damaged?* I cringed at the possibility of becoming a burden to my family. I'd rather stay in a coma and be bedridden than have my parents saddled with any potential physical or mental disabilities. It was terrible for me to think that way but I couldn't help it.

"Don't worry, sis. We will deal with it when it comes to pass. Your only focus right now is to wake up."

His faith in me helped lift some of the dark thoughts but I couldn't seem to shut them off entirely.

CHAPTER 23

I longed for the nights that my mystery visitor came. He would talk to me about his day and everything around him. Every time he spoke, I got lost in sensation. I didn't hear every word that flowed from him. I concentrated on the vibrations that drove awareness into my body. His visits pulsed life through my veins. With each one, my mind became brighter and more alive.

"I wish it were me lying in this bed and not you."

My pulse jumped at his statement. *No.* I wouldn't wish this existence even on my arch nemesis. I demanded movement from my finger. I wanted him to know that I was here and with him. I blew out a frustrated breath. He never stayed long and the time for him to leave again was drawing near. I concentrated so hard that I thought I would die of an aneurism.

Yes! I shouted in my head. *Finally! Fucking movement.* My pointer finger twitched with life under his hand. I had wanted to point my finger in his face, demanding him to take that statement back. Even if I couldn't remember my time with him, I cherished what he gave to me now.

His hand stilled and then brushed over mine again. I'm not sure he received the message. I hoped that he believed it to be real and not his imagination. I needed him here as sure as the air that I breathed. He never uttered another word. However, this time he gently placed his lips over mine. I inhaled his scent deeply, letting it pervade and awaken me further. He whispered his love and left me reeling.

My mind buzzed with awareness. Those lips tortured my sleep. I could feel them all over my body, as though he were physically touching me. I may not remember his name but flashes of his fingers and mouth pleasuring me unfolded all around me. Colorful images radiated through my dream state for the first time.

***

"Wake up, Harlow," Cash all but roared in my ear.

I swear I could feel the vibration of his frustration through my bones.

"You've had your vacation. It's time to get back to the real world. I need your help. The shop is going to hell in a handbasket. I'm seriously thinking about firing Peyton. She is not you. I need my sister back working with me. I'm not getting anything accomplished and my designs are pure shit."

I could picture my brother running his hands through his hair, thinking of anything to get me to open up my eyes. I wanted to shout at him, telling him that I tried and that I was still here. He couldn't give up on me yet.

"Seriously, Harlow. Please wake up. I'm thinking of proposing to Peyton and that scares the shit out of me. You know I need you to help me pick out this ring. I don't know shit about girl stuff." He trampled through the room. His heavy footfalls echoed off the walls with every stomp. "I swear to all that is holy that if you don't wake up right now, I'll break things off with Peyton and start whoring around again."

What? He better not do a stupid thing like that. Without much coaxing, I pointed my finger—at what, who knows. The point is that I did and with very little effort.

"Holy shit. Did you just point your finger at me?"

Well, aren't you bright, brother. For good measure, I did it again.

"That's it, Harlow. Now open up your fucking eyes."

I tried. I really did but they were still sealed shut.

"Come on, sis. Give me something more."

That little movement drained me. I couldn't respond to him no matter how badly I wanted to.

"Fuck." He breathed heavily and walked away.

I wanted him to come back but knew that he wouldn't, at least not today.

***

The chair slid across the floor. It was music to my ears. I knew who it was before he took my hand in his. He did this every visit. At first, his visits were few and far in between. They came more frequently now.

"I couldn't concentrate all day. My mind kept flying back here. Your family doesn't want me here and I honestly don't blame them but I can't stay away." He brought my hand to his mouth. His lips heated my cold skin.

"I'm not sure what's going on in your pretty mind. I wish I knew. I'm lost without you." A chuckle escaped. "I think I'm going mad. Every street grate I pass makes me pause. I stand there, looking for answers for which there never are."

I could hear him situate his body more comfortably in the chair. I hoped that tonight he would stay longer. I needed him. He made me stronger.

"I heard you that morning you told me you loved me. I pretended to be asleep so that you'd think that I didn't. I ran from you in that moment. I pushed you away and made you believe that you meant nothing. The truth was that I freaked out. I didn't know how to handle your feelings because I didn't understand my own." He brought my hand to his cheek and leaned in. "All my running did was cause a world of hurt. It made you believe that I wasn't who I had said I was. The look on your face when you saw me step in to the shop will haunt me forever."

I squeezed his hand. I wanted him to continue. His voice lured me slowly from the darkness. The murkiness faded with each plea.

"Can you hear me, Harlow?"

I applied faint pressure to his hand again, wanting him to continue his story.

"I knew you wouldn't make it easy on me." His deep chuckle reverberated through me. He sucked in a deep breath. "Do you remember me telling you that I had a sister? Squeeze my hand if you do."

I gave him nothing because it only sounded familiar. I wanted to remember so badly that I could be only wishing that I had.

He continued, unfazed. "She had overheard me talking to my mom after our trip to Vegas and decided that she wanted the details. So I told her about you. At the time, I dismissed the look of hate that poured off her face when I said your name. I should have known something wasn't right but I was so confused that I ignored it."

I scraped my fingers along his palm, willing him to continue.

His intake of breath was sharp. He dropped my hand. Loneliness immediately blasted through the light, whisking away the array of colors. I heard the clicking and movement of the bed but couldn't figure out what it was. I waited for it to reveal itself. I felt the bed dip at the weight of his body moving alongside me. I don't know how he was able to contort his body but he managed it so skillfully that my slack body slid into his side.

He cradled me as he spoke. "After I left Mom's house. I needed to see you. You took me in and loved me as though I hadn't been a super ass to you. I left your house the next morning on a high. So, when my sister called and asked me to meet her at the shop and take a look at Cash's design, I jumped at the chance because I would get to see you again." His breath whispered along my cheek.

The intimacy of our position had my limbs tingling as the numbness began to clear. With every breath that fanned my skin, my mind brightened and the fog lifted. I was within reach of opening up my eyes. *Needed to fight harder.*

"When I had walked in the store and Victoria had linked her arm through mine, I hadn't realized that she had led you to believe that I was her fiancé. I ran after you to explain but Cash had made it his mission to block me. It wasn't until I had calmed down and took in Victoria's gleeful sneer that I realized what you had thought you saw. You had no idea that she was my sister and that her real fiancé stepped through the door minutes after you had left." He placed a kiss where his breath had warmed my skin. "I have not spoken to Victoria since that day and I don't plan to. She hurt you out of pure spite and jealousy. I am so sorry. Please forgive me."

His kiss sent me in a tailspin of remembrance. The first day I met him flew past on a huge projection screen. The ice cream shop and the way he wrapped his arms around my waist. The love I had professed to him in Vegas. The pain of believing that I was a whore, my heart breaking into a million pieces, running to my car. *Oh God, the sickening crunch of metal.* The images flew past in a violent storm.

As the torrential storm of memories collided with one another, his apology put them in a momentary freeze. It was as though I were looking through the pictures on my phone. I could use my finger to swipe through the screen. I let each memory rush over my body and fill the holes that had been missing.

My soul soon filled to the brim and burst with light and energy. The tingling sensation started at my head and slowly built to a crescendo that pulsed life through my limbs. Bright, natural light burst through the darkness, breaking it apart like dynamite blows up a hillside. The most beautiful chocolaty pools surrounded my vision. I drank my fill. I raised my hand to the hard lines of his chin. I ran fingers over the bristling stubble.

My lips formed a toothy grin. "Apology accepted." My voice was scratchy from lack of use.

Cole threw his head back and roared with anxious laughter. "You've been in a coma for a month and the minute I say sorry, you wake up. If that was all it took, I would have done it days ago." He bent his head and claimed my mouth. "Harlow, I am truly sorry that you believed I was married."

I put a finger to his lips, effectively shutting him up, "No more apologies. Just love me."

"I do. More than you will ever know. I have a lot to make up for and I will prove to you everyday that you are mine and only mine." His chin quivered as he spoke. "Promise me that you'll never leave me again."

Tears slid down my cheeks as I looked at him through blurry eyes. "That is a promise that I can keep."

A nurse cleared her throat. "I hate to break up this reunion but our patient here needs to be checked over. I'll get her vitals and then I'm going to call the doctor to let him know that she is awake." She swung her steely gaze to Cole. "I trust you to keep her calm and under no stress."

Cole nodded his head in confirmation. He moved his lean body back to the chair but held fast to my hand as though I might slip away.

CHAPTER 24

My mom hustled into the room with my dad close on her heels. She bum-rushed the bed in hysterics. I hugged her tight and whispered in her ear that I was okay. She pulled away and soaked me up. Tears streamed down my face. I had missed my mom terribly. Cole stood off to the side, watching the interaction with a bright smile on his face.

"I love you, Mom." I sniffed and wiped away the wetness on my face.

"Oh, sweetheart. I didn't think you were ever going to wake up." She slumped in the chair, blowing her nose in a tissue that my dad had magically supplied. "Such a stubborn child."

My dad bent over at the waist and placed a gentle kiss on my forehead. Immediately I was transported back to my bedroom as a little girl. He'd read to me at night. When the book was through, he'd tuck me in and place a gentle kiss upon my forehead. The tenderness brought another round of fresh tears.

"Don't cry, baby girl. All is right in the world now." His lips pursed. "Don't you ever do that to me again, you hear?" he growled at me in overprotective bear mode.

I smiled. "Yes, sir."

"I love you, baby girl." His lip trembled. He quickly moved to the side to compose himself.

Like a bad host, I forgot that Cole had molded himself in the corner, letting our reunion play out. Mom spotted him before I could introduce him to my parents. *What a way to meet for the first time!*

My mother turned toward Cole. "And you are?"

A smile formed on her face so big that I thought it would stay there permanently. *Forever looking to marry her daughter off.* He chuckled as he moved toward my parents with his hand extended. He shook my dad's first and then placed a kiss on my mother's cheek. I'm pretty sure she swooned as much as I did.

"It's nice to finally meet you both. I'm sorry that it's not the ideal situation to be meeting you." He angled his head toward me and mouthed *you owe me* before he turned his attention back to my parents. "I've been dating your daughter for quite some time now."

"Why haven't you been to the hospital until now?" my dad interrupted accusingly.

"I've been by Harlow's side every night for the past month, sir."

"Why only at night?"

"Sir, if I may, Cash and I do not get along and I didn't want to cause the family any unnecessary anguish. Nor did I want to put Harlow through any more trauma."

Speak of the devil and he appears.

"What the fuck are you doing here? Haven't you

done enough damage?" Cash roared, lunging for Cole.

Dad put his hand on Cash's shoulder to hold him at bay. "That's enough. We will not bring this drama here. Let Harlow get her rest and be with Cole. It is not our decision if he should be here or not. That is up to your sister," his deep guttural voice boomed, effectively ending the argument. Dad pointedly looked over at me and I nodded my head to confirm that I wanted Cole here.

Cash turned his anger on me. "You and I have a lot to talk about. This is not the end of the discussion by a long shot." He stormed out of the room, leaving me to stew in my retort.

My parents left shortly after Cash stormed out with dramatic flair. I hung my head to my chest, ashamed that Cole had to witness that.

Cole lifted my chin with his finger. "Look at me."

I shook my head as tears pooled on my lids and threatened to spill over.

"Baby, please look at me," he pleaded.

When his voice broke, I had to look up.

"Never be ashamed of your family and how they react. That is on them, never on you. Do you hear me?" His eyes examined mine, desperate for me to heed his words.

I nodded my head, clinging to him as though he were my lifeline. In many ways, he was. He saved me from my self-inflicted dark exile. It wasn't my family who managed that. I loved them fiercely but I breathed for Cole. I shuddered at the thought of the misunderstanding that drove a wedge between us. I loathed Victoria but for him I would push those feelings aside and deal with them later.

He kissed my hairline. He kissed my nose. Finally he brought his sweet lips to mine. He tasted minty with a hint of sin. He cupped the back of my head and deepened the kiss. Our tongues danced, moving to lust-filled music. My body rode the crescendo. I burned from his touch. My clit pulsated with need. I craved him. I wanted him inside me. I needed him to fill me up. He broke from the kiss and I whimpered from the loss.

I gazed into his lust-filled depths. "I can't wait to get home so you can fuck me."

"No, baby." His breathless chuckle vibrated right to my pleasure zone, letting me know that he was just as affected. "I'm going to love you. As soon as the doctor releases you, I will take you home and show you how much."

I loved when he called me baby. No one had ever given me a simple yet special nickname. *God, I needed out of here.*

"Why don't you rest? Morning will be here soon enough. You're going to need it for what I have planned for you."

I smiled and kissed the palm of his hand, dashing my tongue out to lick the tender skin.

"You're killing me."

"Now we are even." I snickered at him. Then I got serious. "Please stay with me until I fall asleep."

"I'll stay all night if you want me to. I'm not willing to let you out of my sight. Not when I just got you back."

I closed my eyes and listened to his even breathing. He rubbed his fingers along the tops of my knuckles, lulling me to sleep.

The next morning, the doctor came in and smiled when he saw that I was awake. "Good morning, Miss McCollum. How are you feeling?"

"Good enough to want to get the hell out of here, Dr. Marks." I laughed.

His eyebrow lifted in surprise. I'd like to believe that it was from my use of his name. He had not introduced himself nor did my family or Cole tell me.

"I'm sure you are. I've read over your chart and there is nothing holding you here. You are in good health and all of the wounds that you sustained in the accident have healed some time ago. We will have to do some more testing before you will be released. I've ordered a cranial CT scan for this morning. Once the results are in, we will proceed from there."

I nodded my head as he patted my shoulder before he walked out of the room. Cole remained silent next to me.

"Do you think that they will find anything wrong?" I turned a worried gaze toward Cole, allowing doubts to overshadow what I felt.

"No, baby. I don't think that they will. If they do, we will deal with it as it comes." He placed a gentle kiss to the back of my hand.

We remained silent, lost in our own thoughts for what lie ahead. I felt fine. My body was weak from lack of use. My brain seemed to be functioning properly. My speech hadn't changed. I prayed that my self-analysis was accurate. Not long after Dr. Marks had left, a nurse came in and helped me into a wheelchair.

It was slow going. I hadn't used my limbs in a month and they felt sluggish and unsteady.

"I'll be right here when you are through." He smiled reassuringly.

The nurse wheeled me back to my room and as promised, Cole was waiting for me. My smile grew exponentially at the sight of him. My soul could feed off him for the rest of my life. I would do everything necessary to ensure that I walked out of here with a clean bill of health.

Cole helped guide my tired body back to the bed. I sighed heavily. Completing simple tasks exhausted my body quicker than I liked. I wasn't giving up but I did have to be smart not to overtax myself. Otherwise, it would take me that much longer to heal.

He smoothed the hair from my face. His fingertips whispered along my skin. I murmured my appreciation and slipped into sleep.

"Harlow, baby. It's time to wake up. Dr. Marks is here and would like to go over the results of your scan." His voice was a soothing salve to my weary state.

My eyes blinked repeatedly until they adjusted to the fluorescent lights that hung above me. "I'm ready, Doc. Hit me with it."

He chuckled. "You don't beat around the bush, do you?"

I grinned. "Nope. I'd rather you give it to me straight."

"Very logical. I reviewed the scan and I found nothing that indicated future complications nor could I find any reason for you to have slipped into a coma. You my dear are a medical conundrum."

I gripped Cole's arm tightly. "That's great news. So what happens now?"

"I'd like to keep you an extra couple of days." My eyes widened and my mouth opened, about to decline the offer, but he continued before I could get a word in. "I want the physical therapist to work with you twice a day for the next three days. As long as I see improvement and you promise to continue therapy on your own, I will release you to go home."

"I can help her with her therapy. The therapist showed me what to do while she was in the coma and I worked with her every night. I can do the same with her when we get home," Cole responded with finality.

The doctor nodded his head and walked out of my room. I turned toward Cole. "That's what I felt. It was your hands that took away the numbness while I was sleeping." Tears slipped down my cheeks as the love I had felt blossomed into a nontangible entity.

He sealed his lips over mine. "And I'll continue when we get you home."

The next few days were chaotic and long. My desire to get the hell out of here overrode my innate yearning to quit physical therapy. I pushed myself past any limit I had thought possible. Every night, I would pass out after all of the work that I had put in. My parents and Cole were there to help push me through it. My only wish was that Cash would have been here too. Fighting the exhaustion was the worst. My arms and legs would fatigue quickly. I wouldn't be able to walk more than thirty steps before I wanted to cry with frustration. Looking back on it, I'm thankful that I pushed myself. Dr. Marks was due in and one way or another, I was leaving this hospital.

***

The doctor strolled in the room with his nose plastered to my chart. Nervous energy rolled through my entire body, making it difficult to remain in the bed quietly.

He finally brought his eyes up to meet mine. The smile that softened his features immediately doused the nervous energy. "Everything looks wonderful. I spoke with the therapist and she assured me that you passed all of their tests. I'm happy to tell you that you are cleared to go home. I will complete the paperwork and get you on your way. Do you have someone who will be picking you up?"

At that moment, Cole strode out of the bathroom. He shook hands with the doctor. "I will be taking her home."

The doctor nodded his head. "Very well. Make sure she rests up and takes it easy until she regains her full strength. Other than that, she has no limitations." He turned to leave but halted. "I'm glad to see you awake. Take good care of yourself." Then he left the room after he issued his final instructions.

The nurse came in and took out the IV and unhooked the monitors. She set my bag of clothing on the bed and let me get dressed. I took out the clothes and cringed. They were the same ones that I had on the night of the accident. Bloodstains coated my shirt.

Cole grabbed the pile of sullied clothes and threw them in the wastebasket. "You are not wearing any of that home. Give me a minute. I'm going to run down to the gift shop and see if they have something better for you to wear."

I kissed him and sat back on the bed. I looked around at the stark white walls and sterile atmosphere. It suddenly hit me that I'd been living my life the same way. Devoid of the more colorful aspects of life. I realized that I had used the business to erect a wall around me. I allowed it to run interference between good friendships and my family. I even called upon it to shut Cole out when I felt that I wasn't good enough for him. I no longer wanted to live that way. I wanted more meaningful relationships with everyone around me.

Cole rushed in the room with some clothes hanging from his arm. "They are not the best and probably too big but who cares. We can trash them when we get you home."

He held them out to me and I slammed my body into his chest, seeking his warmth. I looked up at him. "I love you."

He kissed my lips as softly as a butterfly's wings. "I love you more."

He lovingly helped me pull the sweatpants and

hoodie on. They were much too large but felt comfortable against my skin. Not long after that, the nurse came in with the paperwork and wheelchair. Cole got the car as she wheeled me out of the hospital. I could've walked and pleaded to do so but it fell on deaf ears.

I thanked the nurse as I settled down in the lush leather seat of Cole's car. I sighed as the seat molded around my ass like a feathery pillow.

"You ready?"

"More than." I turned toward him and smiled.

I don't live that far from the hospital, so I wondered where he was taking me. After trying to figure it out, I finally asked him, "Where are we going? I thought you were taking me home," I said, a little more than confused.

He quickly took his eyes off the road and glanced at me. The sexy grin that rooted over his face turned my vagina into a volcano about to erupt. "You'll see. Be patient; it's not that much farther."

I sat up straighter in my seat and looked out the window as Seattle's skyline disappeared from my view. We were headed north of the city. *Where was he taking me?* He pulled off the highway toward Lake Union. I bit my lower lip with nervous anticipation. Lake Union was a beautiful area and it cost a pretty penny to live here.

We wound around so many homes that I had completely lost my sense of direction. He pulled his sleek car into a designated spot and killed the engine. He quickly got out of the car and ran to my side of the door. He took my hand and helped me out. I looked all around me. We were surrounded by water. His home looked like a Southern plantation nestled on the water.

I sucked in a breath. "This is where you live?" I said with pure amazement.

He stuck out his chest proudly. "Yes. This is where we live."

I spun around, somewhat confused. "What? Who else do you live with?"

He nervously chuckled. "Only you. That is, if you want to. I hoped you would."

I squinted and placed my hands on my hips. "And when were you going to   ask—or were you going to just move all my shit in for me?"

I was only slightly angry and a whole lot thrilled that he wanted me to move in with him. Before, I couldn't get him to commit and now he had us living together. He grabbed me around the waist and clung to me as though he were starving for my touch.

"I've had a lot of time to think. About us and about what I was running from." He kissed my lips. "In my mind, we had already made this decision. I don't want to miss out on any more time with you. I've lost enough and so have you."

He pulled me along and up the narrow walkway to his home. I hadn't quite decided whether this is where I would permanently lay my head. Maybe one day. It was moving so fast that I had a hard time catching my breath.

He opened the door, picked me up and carried me over the threshold. "Welcome home, baby."

He gently set me down and I spun in a slow circle, taking in the beautiful home. The only way it could be described was as though it were a home made up in your mind. What I didn't realize until I walked through the upscale kitchen and out onto the porch was that he lived in a floating house and it was spacious. Right here on Lake Union with a gorgeous view of the city's skyline off his deck.

"Holy cow, Cole. This is gorgeous." The awe was evident in my voice.

His sexy mouth formed a grin. "You haven't seen the best part yet."

He placed my hand in his and led me inside and up the stairs. We walked through the spacious bedroom and my jaw hit the floor. A large king-sized bed sat in the middle of the room. A nautical theme splashed across the pieces of furniture in the room. Cole pressed a button and the wall slid up on tracks, much like a garage door. The view that presented itself stole my breath.

You could see across the expansive lake. His home was the last on the lot and there were no neighbors in front of him. I strolled out onto the upper deck and scanned the horizon. I could see the Space Needle jutting out in the bright blue sky. The soft laps of water hit the cement foundation, calming every single nerve.

Cole wrapped his arms around me and tucked his chin in the crook of my neck. His breath sent goose bumps scattering all over my heated skin. I leaned back, absorbing his strength. His tongue snaked out and traced a languid path from my collarbone up to my earlobe. He nibbled at the sensitive flesh as I moaned my pleasure. He licked the skin where his teeth had previously tasted.

I squirmed in his arms as his tongue danced along my flesh. Just when I thought I couldn't take any more teasing, he twirled me around and his lips captured mine in a searing kiss. His tongue coaxed mine into an intricate tango. He picked me up and laid me on top of the bed gently, as though I might break. It was endearing but that's not what I wanted right now. Later, yes. Now I needed to be fucked hard.

I wriggled out of his grasp and knelt on the bed, shucking my clothes as fast as I possibly could. His heated gaze traveled along every inch of my flesh. Wetness pooled between my legs, making my pussy glisten with arousal.

"Come here," I commanded.

He shed his clothing and climbed up on the bed. He cupped the back of my head and traced his mouth and tongue down my throat. His stubble tickled as it sensuously aroused the sensitive skin.

I hummed. "I love the way your mouth and tongue tease my skin. It makes me think of another place where they are in desperate need."

His throaty growl vibrated down my body, heading straight for my clit. "Is that what you want? You want me to taste you? Tell me that's what you want."

I tightened my thighs around him to mitigate the pressure as he continued his assault on my breasts. "Oh, God, yes."

"Yes, what?"

"Please, Cole. I want you to lick and suck on my clit until I come apart in your mouth," I replied breathlessly.

"Fuck, Harlow. You are so sexy," he rumbled.

He continued his agonizingly slow descent with his mouth, making sure he covered every inch of my bare skin. My whole being came alive and hummed with desire. My breath came in pants as I squirmed and wriggled underneath his touch. My body was on fire and only he could douse the flames. He spread my legs wide, opening me up to him completely. Hot air from his mouth fanned the flames, making me push up closer to his mouth.

"I'm going to fuck you with my mouth, sweet Harlow."

I cried out as his tongue leisurely traveled its way from my wet opening to my hard bud.

"You taste so sweet. I could dine from you all day." His voice vibrated through my already sensitive lips.

He continued his lavish licking and sucking as I bucked up into his mouth. I dug my fingers through his hair, keeping his face right where I wanted him. He drove two fingers inside. He curled them in a come-hither motion and hit my g-spot. His tongue swirled around my bundle of nerves once and then twice; my orgasm shot through my body. I wriggled and squirmed as my body trembled as though I had stuck my finger in a socket. I screamed his name as his unrelenting tongue lazily flicked my oversensitive clit. My body shuddered each time he came in contact with the delicate button. He removed his fingers and wiped his mouth on the back of his hand. He worked his teeth and lips up my body, igniting another fire.

"I'm not done with you, sweet Harlow," he growled as he slithered up my body and claimed my mouth.

His tongue languidly swiped mine much the same way he lavished my pussy. The thought had my clit pulsating once more. The need for him to be inside me consumed every inch of me. "Fuck me, Cole. I want to feel you inside me, filling me up."

With one last lingering kiss, he gradually inched his thick cock inside. My inner muscles grabbed at his cock, pulling him deeper and deeper. My body quivered as his massive girth pillaged my soft inner walls.

"You feel so good. I can't go slow. Need to fuck you hard." His muscles constricted and trembled as he tried to be gentle.

I didn't want gentle—I needed him to make me feel alive again. I wasn't going to break. "Harder," I cried out to him.

He thrust his hips and slammed against me. His balls slapped against my ass with every thrust. The harder he drove, the wetter I became. I could smell my desire when he pulled out, making his manhood glisten. The sweet mix of my essence and the soothing sounds of the water made me feel light and heady with arousal. My body hummed and then took off like a rocket as he placed his thumb and circled my sensitive flesh. I tilted my hips up to allow him to fill me to the hilt.

"Jesus, Cole. I'm going to come," I hissed out between my teeth.

"That's it, Harlow. Come with me now." His command plowed through my blood, setting my orgasm free.

I cried out as I dropped off the ledge and fell out of control as my orgasm tore through my body. The weight of his body grounded me as the last of the pleasure seeped out through my heavy limbs. He rolled to his back, bringing me with him. I lay my head on his chest, listening to the steady beats of his heart.

"I'm never letting you go," he breathed softly, ruffling my hair and tickling my scalp.

"I hope not. The sex is phenomenal." I bit my lip to contain my laughter.

He tickled my rib cage. Giggles erupted as I squirmed, trying to get away. His firm hands kept me secured in place with nowhere to go.

"Is that all I am to you? A piece of meat?" He tried for irritation but failed miserably.

"Yep, pretty much." I breathed through each giggle.

"Good to know where I stand."

I tipped my chin up. "You are so much more."

He placed his lips upon my forehead. I closed my eyes from the tenderness and fell asleep in his cradling arms.

CHAPTER 25

I rolled to the middle of the bed and stretched my pleasantly sore muscles. The sheets on his bed alone were absolutely sinful. The Egyptian cotton felt like tiny whispers of silk along my skin. I couldn't help but rub my naked body all over them, almost as though I were marking Cole's bed with my scent. Maybe I was.

"You're the only woman that I've ever brought home and to my bed," he crowed from the doorframe.

I stopped rubbing myself on his sheets and looked over at him with a sheepish smile. "Was I that obvious?"

He chuckled. "No, but I wanted you to know that you're the only woman I have fallen asleep to and made love to in that bed."

I grinned cheekily at him. "Well, you're the only man I've fallen asleep to and made love to in this bed."

He inched closer. "And I better be the only one."

"Silly boy. From the moment I laid my eyes on you, I knew you were going to be the last man I ever saw. Whether you knew that or not!"

Guilt flashed so quickly beneath his brown depths that I thought I had imagined it. Nope, he was hiding something. "What was that look for and what do you have in your hands that you feel the need to hide behind your back?" I questioned with a sharp tongue.

He looked sheepish as he swung his arm from behind his back.

"My cell phone?" Now I was really confused.

"Please listen before you automatically spout a no at me." He sat next to me on the bed.

"Alright, you have the floor."

Queasiness settled low in my belly. I didn't want to hear what he had to say because I had a screaming notion that it was about my brother. I had yet to talk to him since the day he stormed out of the hospital room. On the one hand, I loathed myself for picking Cole over my brother. On the other hand, Cole was my future and he made me happier than I could ever recall. Blood was thicker than water but in this instance they needed to mix and thin out so that I could have them both.

"Why do I have to call him? Can't he grovel for once?" I whined.

Cole's deep chuckle eased the anxiety that had burrowed deep in my bones. "Because, sweetheart, he is hurting, too, and you have to be the bigger person and squash all of this turmoil. If you let it fester for too long, your close relationship will drift farther and farther apart." He sighed and ran his fingers nervously through his hair. "You don't want your relationship to turn out like mine and Victoria's. I miss the old her but I don't much care for the new her either. I envy your relationship with your brother. I hope that one day he and I will overcome our issues and become friends."

Fuck. At the mere mention of her name, I saw red. I

didn't want to but I couldn't help the instantaneous anger that blasted into my heart cavity. *Damn her!* She was a succubus. She not only managed to create gaping holes in her family, she almost tore our lives to shreds. *Did she even care?* I doubted it even crossed her mind that she was in the wrong. She was that heartless. Cole was better off without her but I could understand the need for her to be in his life too. I would not be the one to draw that line. If he wanted her to remain in his life, I would find a way to deal with her.

I cupped my hand along his strong jawline and rubbed my thumb across his scratchy stubble. God, he was perfect for me in every way, flaws and all.

"I love you and I will not fault you for keeping Victoria in your life. I will find a way to get past my hatred toward her." I wasn't going to sugarcoat it for him. That was the honest truth. I did hate her but she was his family.

"I don't deserve you." He gently sealed our lips with a tender kiss. "Now call your brother. When you are done, come on downstairs and I will make you breakfast." He silently left the bedroom.

I held my phone in my hands, staring at the screen as though it would magically dial the numbers for me. My finger shook as I pulled up my favorites list. There was his ugly mug looking back at me. He had such a goofy grin on his face when I had snapped that picture. I don't even remember now what transpired when I took it but it made me laugh as tears rained down my cheeks. He was my best friend and I couldn't imagine another second going by without him in it.

I pushed on the contact and held the phone up to my

ear as I held my breath. It rang and rang. Disappointment speared through me. He wasn't going to pick up. When I thought that it would go right to voicemail, I heard his deep baritone voice.

"Sis."

That one word said it all. There was no need for apologies. He had managed to string that one syllable together with a whole lot of guilt and regret. It broke my heart to know that we were both in the same place, hurting each other.

"Hey, big brother. I miss your ugly mug." I forced my voice to stay strong.

"I'm so sorry, Harlow. I am being a big horse's ass."

I promptly interrupted him; hearing him grovel would not accomplish anything. "You are forgiven."

"What?"

"You heard me. I don't need an apology. All I want is for you and Cole to get along in some capacity."

"Unacceptable," he growled at me.

"So you are not even going to try to get along with Cole?" I asked, flabbergasted.

"No. I mean, yes. What I meant to say was that you deserve an apology from me. I am so sorry about the way that I acted. I was beyond scared that you were never going to wake up. Then all of a sudden you do and all you want is Cole. Who had a hand in what happened. I wanted to kill him. He didn't protect you from that bitch." I heard the intake of his breath. "I did an obscene amount of thinking since you woke up and I've come to the conclusion that it was Cole who had you wanting to live again. It hurt because it felt like I was losing my best friend, so I lashed out at you. It was unfair and I'm an ungrateful ass."

"Yes, you definitely are an ass. You had a part in my recovery too. I heard you talking even when you thought that I didn't. My accident was nobody's fault. There were just many steps that led to it. I can think all day about the what-ifs but it won't change anything. I love Cole. Can you just be happy for me and put the other bullshit aside?"

Asking my brother to forgive was a hefty request. From the silence on the other end, he agreed. I continued to stay silent while he mulled over a decision.

"Yeah, I can let the other stuff go. I want you to be happy, sis."

I smiled with glee. "Good. Now, on to the good stuff. When are you going to propose to Peyton?"

He sighed deeply. "I honestly don't know. We haven't dated that long and well, I know that she is the one I want to be with but I'm not ready to buy the ring just yet."

"What's holding you back?"

"Can't say. Don't really know. It's hard to explain when I'm not sure even I know."

I could feel his uncertainty through the phone as it punched me in the gut and stole my air. I had faith that he'd figure it out but I still hurt when he hurt. I had to change the subject and quickly.

"Are you ready for me to come back to work yet?"

"Does a bear shit in the woods?"

"I'll be back first thing Monday." I laughed at his joke.

"Go and get some rest and let Cole wait on you hand and foot. Love ya—bye."

"Love ya—bye."

I pressed End and exhaled with relief. We were going to be just fine. Water under the bridge and all of that. Time would tell how he treated Cole but I will be there to slap him upside the head when he acted like a gigantic dick. I jumped off the bed and went downstairs to find my incredibly sexy and thoughtful man.

Enticing smells generated a loud, protesting rumble deep within my stomach. I was a tad scared at the thought that my stomach might revolt if I didn't hurry up and shovel in the delicious food. I jovially skipped to the kitchen and plopped down in the chair, resting my chin in my hands. Cole, in front of the stove, cooking French toast, was about the sexiest thing my eyes had the pleasure of viewing. He turned around with the spatula still in his raised hand and smiled at me as though I were the most precious gem in the world. The love that shimmered off him radiated throughout my body, warming up every facet.

He gingerly walked toward me. He planted the sweetest kiss upon my lips. "Everything okay with your brother?"

"Yep. Thank you for forcing me to make that call. It was long overdue. I feel as though a huge weight has been lifted off my chest."

"Good. Are you hungry?"

"Starving." I would've told him about our conversation if he had asked but I also felt an insane amount of relief that he easily let it go.

I got up from the chair and rummaged through his cupboards, looking for plates and utensils. I set the table and then sat back down and waited to be served. He was relaxed in his own environment. It was a side of him that I hadn't had the chance to experience before the accident. We had plenty of time to get to know each other.

I bit into the piece of syrupy bread and thought I would die. The sugar and cinnamon danced along my tongue. "Wow. I'm impressed. Your culinary skills are exceptional."

"I can cook some things well and others that are not even edible but I am glad that you like it," He beamed at me.

"I'll be the judge of that." After taking in my last tasty morsel, my belly was completely satisfied. "What's on the agenda for today?"

"Well, I was thinking that we could go meet my mom and then see where the rest of the day took us." He looked a little nervous and yet hopeful.

My insides bounced around as though they were at a jump zone, jumping from one trampoline to the next. This was a major step for him. He cherished his mother and for him to want me to meet her had me smiling with excitement. "Would love to."

***

She lived in a beautiful sprawling neighborhood. You could tell that the community took pride in their homes and the aesthetics surrounding them. The lots ranged from one to two acres. The area was gorgeous. Cole knocked on the heavy oak door to announce our arrival. He didn't wait for her to answer; he simply opened it up and ushered us through. Her home was spacious and tastefully decorated. The one thing that stood out was that it was lived in. Family pictures decorated the walls. Rich hues and thick carpeting made you feel right at home. She rushed from the kitchen, drying her hands on the apron around her petite midsection.

With her arms raised out to the sides, she practically ran to Cole and enveloped him in a tight hug. She held him at arm's length, smiling with so much adoration that my eyes had misted. "My baby is home!" she cried. She looked over Cole's shoulder. Her warm eyes so, much like Cole's, welcomed me into the mix. She semi-pushed Cole out of the way and barreled straight for me. I braced myself for the contact. She wrapped her arms around me just as she had Cole. There was no reservation. Pure, unadulterated love poured from her body, making me feel as though I were already a part of the family. "You must be Harlow. It is such a pleasure to meet the young woman who has captured my son's heart."

I looked away, a little sheepish and yet comfortable at the same time around her. "Yep, I sure did. It's mine forever but I will share him with you." I chuckled. "It's a pleasure meeting you, Ms. Devlin."

She laughed heartily. "I'm glad to hear that. While

we are at it, you are practically family—please call me Eve."

She ushered the both of us into the kitchen, where she had made us a hearty lunch. I smelled meatloaf and my salivary glands drooled from the delicious meat-spiced aroma that saturated the air. I couldn't wait to dig in.

"Why don't you guys set the table and I'll bring the food out. Oh, and put two extra settings for your sister and her fiancé." The look that she tossed at Cole held no room for an argument.

I knew that look well. I'm pretty sure that all mothers had that look and it was best to heed their wishes. No one wanted to deal with the consequences of going against their commands. I sucked in a breath from being blindsided. Once we were in the dining room, Cole leaned into my side and spoke softly. "I had no idea that she was coming. If I had, we wouldn't be here now. I'm not going to let her hurt you again. If it gets to be too much, we will leave and I'll explain things to my mother later on." He nipped along my earlobe and down my neck, effectively thwarting my panic attack.

Once my heartrate increased from arousal instead of fear, he gently kissed my lips and resumed setting the table. *Flipping tease.* But in that moment, I loved him more than I thought possible. He read me like a book and easily knew exactly what I needed in any given moment. The door opened with a whoosh and loud voices carried through the house. I straightened my spine and held my chin high. I would not give her the satisfaction of tearing me down.

Eve had hollered from the kitchen for Victoria and

Jackson to hang up their coats and head into the dining room. There was no warm welcome or the excitement toward her daughter the way that she had with Cole. I wondered what that was all about. She seemed like the type of mother who loved and treated her children equally. The devil and her fiancé strolled through the archway of the dining room as though they were above their surroundings. Which baffled me, considering as this home was twice the size of my parents' house. This was no cardboard box squatting along the riverbank.

Before I had the chance to glance up and say hello to the devil's right-hand lady, my skin prickled under her scrutiny. I could feel her judging me as inadequate on all levels. I shivered from the cold glare that radiated from her perfectly coiffed face.

Time to grow some lady balls. "Hello, Victoria. It's a pleasure seeing you again." I practically grounded my molars down to nubs.

"I wouldn't say that it is a pleasure but I'm glad that you are out of the hospital," she smarmily quipped.

Oh, I bet my next twelve paychecks that she was supremely disappointed that I had lived. She would have taken great pleasure to watch me be buried six feet under. I shook off her condescension as I stuck out my hand toward her fiancé. "Hello, I'm Harlow. We have not been formally introduced."

He looked down at my hand and turned up his nose. *Well, well, well. They were like two peas in a stuck-up pod. Screw them and their hoity-toity attitude.* Cole emitted a low guttural growl that had Jackson backing up. The only reason I knew his name was because Eve had shouted it from the kitchen. I really didn't care one way or another; he was a pretentious dick and perfect for Victoria. They would live happily miserable for the rest of their godforsaken lives. It was the perfect revenge.

Eve walked in, carrying a tray full of dishes. *Gosh, that had to weigh a ton; there was so much food.* I quickly took two of them and placed them in the middle of the table. "Thank you."

"It's the least I could do. That tray looked heavy."

She winked at me as she set the rest of the dishes down. Cole took the tray and set it in the corner of the room on top of the server. We each took turns dishing up our plates. I loaded mine to the brim of delicious comfort food.

"Careful, Harlow. Too much of that and you'll add more to your already curvy waistline," Victoria snipped.

"Watch your mouth, young lady. You will not disrespect Harlow in this house. Is that clear." Eve chided her, as though she were a mere toddler.

I sat stunned from the moment her comment left her surgically enhanced lips. I had dealt with some pretty callous people along the way but never anyone so malicious and intent on hurting me. Cole sat beside me, fuming. I could feel the heat of his anger when he placed his hand upon my thigh.

I picked up my fork and plopped a heaping pile of meatloaf and mashed potatoes in my mouth. I hummed silently in my head as the combination of flavors exploded on my tongue. I picked up my glass and washed the remnants of food down my throat. "Better to be curvy and have something to hold onto and keep you warm at night than a cold heart and bones poking into your side." I looked pointedly over at Eve. "I apologize to you for my retort."

She winked and dug in herself. Jackson smirked at my comeback, Cole laughed, and Victoria glared at me. I didn't care. She had already done enough damage. I was done letting her get to me. The rest of the meal was relatively quiet. The bottom-feeder didn't quit with her snide comments but I didn't fan the flames nor did I allow Cole to say anything either. I kept my hand on his muscular thigh and pinched him anytime he so much as moved a muscle. I appreciated and loved him for wanting to stick up for me. However, I was a big girl and could handle myself. He didn't need to fight my battles for me. After Victoria and Jackson finished their meal, they quickly made their excuses and hightailed it out of there as though any more time spent would seriously hinder their societal status. She made sure to hiss that I'd never be good enough for Cole as she brushed past me on her way out the door.

Eve wrapped up some leftovers for us to take home. She handed them to Cole as she fiercely hugged me. I tightened my arms around her, basking in her love.

"Victoria is an unhappy spoiled little girl. I'm not sure where I went wrong with her. I'm sorry if she made you feel uncomfortable. You are always welcome in my home and I hope that you come to visit me, even if Cole is not with you." She kissed my cheek.

"Thank you for a wonderful meal and welcoming me into your home. Cole is lucky to have such a wonderful and doting mother. I will most definitely be back. There is no need for you to ever apologize for her behavior. It had nothing to do with you. It's her issue to work out and I don't much care to give her a second thought." I hugged her one more time and walked out the door behind Cole.

Cole took my hand and kissed the knuckles as we sat in the car with the engine idling. "You are the most beautiful, most bravest, and most sincere person I've had the pleasure of falling in love with. You take my breath away."

I cupped his cheek as I placed my lips over his. I poured all of the love that I had for him in that kiss, completely besotted by his declaration.

He moaned. "Did I mention the most sexiest too?"

I grinned. "Nope. But you can show me just how sexy you think I am when we get home."

"Oh, I will. You can bet on that." He put the car in reverse and gunned it the rest of the way home.

CHAPTER 26

The minute I walked in the door behind him, he pushed me up against the wall, pinning my body between him and the wall. My chest heaved with surprise and desire. In an instant, my body hummed as though it were a high-voltage electrical line. A rush of desire slid from my center and drenched my underwear. I cried out as he snared my bottom lip with his teeth and sucked it between his lips, all the while running his silky tongue along the pink flesh. I hadn't experienced the possessive side of him and by God, it turned me the fuck on. My body squirmed under him, desperately seeking his touch. He continued his greedy attack on my mouth as his fingers unbuttoned my pants and with one quick movement, he had pushed my pants and underwear down to my calves.

I pulled on the material with my feet until I could step out of the confines of the material. He nipped and lapped his way down my neck. I stood, unable to move from his carnal onslaught. He bunched the hem of my top with his fists and wrenched it off. Bringing his fingers to the front clasp of my bra, he deftly unhooked it and freed my heavy breasts.

"So beautiful and all mine. Tell me this sweet body is mine to worship," he growled before sinking my taut nipple between his lips.

His ravenous mouth had me seconds from coming.

The way that he worshiped my breasts alone had my clit pulsating and my core tightening. His pushed his clothed erection against my pussy and my knees buckled. He easily caught me and held me upright, never missing a beat. The rough fabric created the perfect storm against my inflamed flesh. I moaned my answer, not able to formulate any coherent syllables.

His mouth roamed to the other breast, paying equal attention to the tight bud. I arched my back as the heady sensation tore through my body. I needed him to fill me up and feed the hunger that he had built. His fingers fanned along my heated skin, skimming lower until he inserted two of his fingers.

"Ah," I cried out as his fingers delved in and out of my slick center.

He crooked the pads of his fingers so that they rubbed my g-spot. "Say it, Harlow. I won't let you come until you tell me that you are mine."

Fuck, his commands drove me wild. I panted, trying to formulate the tiny sentence. I licked my lips. "I belong only to you, Cole. I am completely yours."

My chest heaved as his mouth traced along my overly heated skin. His fingers played my center, bringing me to the brink and then backing off. I gyrated my hips, seeking my release. Each time I did, he slowed his teasing, building an intense pleasure. His mouth grazed down my quivering stomach, inching lower and lower. My thighs trembled, my blood boiled, and my moans increased in pitch. His satiny tongue swiped over my mound, gingerly making its way toward my needy clit. He spread my outer lips and exposed the bundle of nerves. The warm air from his breath had my hips bucking involuntarily. I no longer had control over my body. It was a machine built of raw nerves programmed to relentlessly pursue until it had found its zenith.

Deliberately, he took his time twirling his tongue until my eyes crossed. He lightly grazed his teeth against my clit and stars exploded behind my eyelids. I cried out as my orgasm blazed through my body, as though it were an out-of-control wildfire. He stood up, shucking his jeans along the way. His strong hands grabbed my thighs, lifted them around his waist and he plunged his thick cock into my contracting center. His engorged cock reignited the dying embers. I wrapped my arms around his neck, holding on for dear life as he brought us both higher than ever before.

While still sheathed inside me, he walked us toward the couch. The back of his knees hit the cushion and he plopped down, taking me with him. He twisted our bodies so that my back faced the end of the couch. He gently laid us down, easing his cock from its warm cocoon. He maneuvered between my legs until his head rested upon my breast, directly over my heart. I ran my fingers through his hair and along his scalp, enjoying the intimate moment. It wouldn't be long and our little world would become filled with outside obligations.

With his voice low and sleepy, he asked, "Have you thought anymore about moving in?"

My heartbeat increased with minor anxiety. I didn't want to hurt him but I hadn't made my decision yet. "I haven't come to a decision yet."

"Mmm, 'k. I don't want you to feel rushed. The offer is permanently on the table for when you are ready."

His breathing evened out, signaling that he had passed out. I glorified myself in that moment as a complete and utterly fabulous sex machine. I continued to run my fingers through his hair; it was just as soothing to me as it was to him. While he slept, I let my mind imagine what it would be like to wake up and fall asleep next to this wonderful man. I couldn't rationalize any reason why living in my apartment alone would be anything other than miserable. Only seeing Cole occasionally literally hurt my heart. A grin spread from ear to ear at having made up my mind. I immediately felt the anxiety leave my body. I felt as though I had finally come home.

I woke up feeling refreshed and stronger than I did that morning. Whatever Cole was making for dinner smelled delicious. I got up from the couch and tiptoed to the kitchen. I wanted to take a moment and watch my man cooking. There was something so sexy about a guy making dinner. The fluidity of his movement was seamless, almost as though it were choreographed. He dipped his finger in the saucepan. He brought it to his mouth, sticking his sexy tongue out and swiping the sauce off his finger. A shiver of desire ran through my body, heating the blood in my veins. I hoped to the heavens above that I would always be slightly obsessed with this man.

I stepped into the kitchen and silently walked around the marble island separating us. I lovingly wrapped my arms around his waist. I rose up on my toes and placed a gentle kiss on the back of his neck.

"Mmm. Did you sleep well?"

"Yes. I'm feeling fairly energized at the moment."

He chuckled. "Good. Let's fill you up with some carbs and then we can burn it all off between the sheets or any surface that you'd like."

"Sounds like an excellent plan." I kissed him one more time along his neck before I walked away to set the table. "By the way, we are invited over to my parents' tomorrow for dinner." I kept my head down, fearing his reaction. The last time I asked him to my parents' it hadn't gone over that well.

"Um."

My head snapped up, sensing déjà vu. I tried not to glare but I knew I was burrowing holes in the back of his head.

He turned around with a boyish glint and loudly laughed at my expression. "Would love to come with you to your parents'."

He drew near and I smacked his arm for giving me a mini heart attack. "Not nice, not nice at all."

His lips assaulted mine, effectively shutting me up.

CHAPTER 27

The warm rays of the sun peeked in the room, warming up my exposed skin. I must have tossed my covers sometime during the night. I rolled to my other side, wondering whether Cole was already up. I chuckled to myself. Snoring lightly was the blanket thief. I could only see the crown of his head poking out from the top of the comforter. He had wrapped himself up like a burrito. I argued with myself for about five minutes about whether or not I should wake him. He had been running himself ragged, taking care of me. With my decision made, I silently slipped from the bed and tiptoed down the stairs.

Once my foot landed on the last step, my phone vibrated with Jason Aldean crooned about dirt roads. It was still pretty early and hearing my brother's ringtone made me a little uneasy. I ran to the phone and answered it before it went to voicemail.

"What's up? Everything all right?" I asked, a little leery of the answer.

"Nope. Shit's about to get real," he smarted back.

"What are you talking about? Is Peyton okay?" Now I was getting nervous.

"Oh, yeah. She is fine. I'm the one freaking out here."

"Okay. So spill it. What's got you all bent out of shape? You know I suck at the guessing game, so spell it out for me." I wanted to laugh at his theatrics but I bit my cheek and kept myself in check.

He huffed, already irritated with me. "I'm going to propose to Peyton tonight at the 'rents house and what I failed to realize is that a ring doesn't just buy itself."

This time I actually busted out laughing, with huge ugly snorts and all.

"Shut up. It's not that funny," he literally whined.

"Yes, it most certainly is. Look at it from my side. You figured out either last night or this morning that you couldn't live without her and you needed to put a ring on it, like now. Have I got this down so far?"

"Look, there is no reason to patronize me. Will you go with me or not?"

"Don't you think that maybe you should wait to propose until you have the ring in your hand? I mean, what if you don't find what you are looking for?"

"I haven't really thought all of this out. We will find one today. I just know it."

"Alright there, Casanova. Come and pick me up in thirty."

"I can be there in ten. See ya."

"Wait!" I shouted.

"What?"

"I'm at Cole's. I'll text you the address; it's just

outside of the city. It will take you at least twenty from your place."

"Fine. Text it to me." He hung up.

I shook my head. Typical male, waiting until the very last minute to figure out all the details and then scrambling to tidy it all up. Tonight was going to be legendary. I rubbed my hands together. I couldn't wait to watch Cash propose, giving up his proclaimed bachelorhood status. Mom was going to go bat-shit crazy with happiness. She loved Peyton and couldn't wait for Cash to settle down. His plan would also help make Cole more comfortable, taking the spotlight from him so that there wouldn't be the standard inquisition.

I took the stairs two at a time and dashed into our room, shedding Cole's tee shirt as I went. I stopped dead in my tracks. *Shit!* I didn't have any clothes except for the ones that Cole had purchased from the hospital. I'd just wear those and have Cash stop at the apartment so that I could do a quick change. I'd figure the rest out later. Cole stirred in his sleep as I maneuvered around the bed. I quietly went into the bathroom, making sure that I didn't disturb him. I quickly threw the sweats and sweatshirt on and walked over to Cole. I carefully slid the cover down from over his face. I bit my bottom lip, stifling a moan. He was sinfully sexy even while he slept. I gently placed a kiss on his cheek. He stirred and wrapped his arms around me, pulling me on top of him.

He smiled at me as though I was the sexiest woman alive and he'd die if he couldn't have a taste. "Morning, love."

"Good morning to you too." I pecked him on the lips. I knew if I gave in to the desire I would never make it out the door. "Cash is on his way to pick me up and go ring shopping. He is going to propose to Peyton tonight."

I was so excited for him that I could hardly stand myself at the moment.

"Really? Good for him. Tonight should be interesting then, huh?"

"Yep. And you know what that means?" I smiled wickedly at him.

"Not a clue."

"That means we can duck out early without being noticed and all of the attention will be on them. No inquisitions about my baby maker and all the cobwebs surrounding it." I laughed at the absurdity of it all.

"And this is a good thing, right?"

I laughed and kissed him again. He was absolutely adorable. "Yes, it is. I'm going to go wait downstairs. Oh, do you mind if I pack a bag and stay the night?"

"Why don't you pack for about a week and use the time to contemplate moving in permanently?" He kissed my nose.

"Okay, I will. Love you."

"Love you more," he shouted as I descended the stairs as quick as my feet would carry me.

I couldn't wait to get to hang out with Cash. It had been a long time since we had hung out, just the two of us, and I missed him.

His blacked-out truck pulled in behind Cole's luxury car. I ran to the passenger side and hopped in.

"Hey, fuckface. Good to see you." His grin stretched from ear to ear.

"Let's pump the tunes and go find your woman a ring." I smiled back giddily.

He turned up the stereo and we thumped along to the music until we hit downtown. Right in the heart of the city was the perfect jewelry store. Seattle's Fine Jewelry was located in a chic brick building with the classic black-colored awnings. If you wanted a beautiful—mind you, expensive—engagement ring, this was the place to be. There wasn't a ring there that didn't cost at least a year of my salary. We stepped out of the truck and headed into the swank store.

I looked around the interior of the brightly lit store. Three counters displayed all of the jewelry. My eyes enlarged at all of the exquisite pieces, gleaming in my eyes. I immediately left my brother's side and walked down, looking into the glass counters. I briefly glanced back to make sure Cash hadn't passed out from the overwhelming task ahead of him. He was chatting up with one of the customer representatives so I went back to perusing.

"Can I help you with anything?"

I looked up into the smiling face of a woman around our mother's age. When she smiled, her whole face lit up. I smiled back. "No, thank you. I am here with my brother, helping him pick out a ring for his girlfriend." She nodded her head and walked away.

This brought me back around to the reason that I was

here. It wasn't so that I could gawk at all the pretty parcels but to help him find the perfect ring for Peyton. I turned back around and headed back to where my brother was. *Oh my, would you look at that!* I stopped in my tracks as the perfect ring winked at me. I walked gingerly up to the glass, put the heels of my hands tenderly on the edge of the glass and peered over the top. Then I bent down and looked through the side of the glass to get another view of the ring. It actually stole my breath away. This was the one for Peyton. *Pure perfection.*

"Hey, Cash. Come over here and check this one out. I think it's absolutely perfect for Peyton." I shouted to him from across the room. *How uncouth is that?* Heck, I didn't really care; I was that excited about it.

"Whatcha find?"

The sales associate followed behind Cash. Once she took her place behind the glass counter, I pointed to the ring that I wanted her to pull out.

She set the ring on top of the counter. "It's a four-stone emerald-cut diamond set in platinum. It's a little over two carats." She handed Cash a little magnifying glass. "Look through the lens while holding up the diamond to check the clarity."

Cash did what she said but I could tell that he was just as clueless as I was. We didn't know shit about clarity. All I knew was that this ring was elegance defined and it fit Peyton to a tee. She radiated elegance without the snobbery, quite similar to this very ring. If Cash didn't purchase this ring right now, I would be reduced to smacking him upside the head. As far as I was concerned, we were done browsing. *Shit just got real.*

He turned and faced me. "Are you thinking what I'm thinking?"

I smiled genuinely, excited for him. "I believe so, brother. Bag her up and let's go get lunch."

I love when a plan comes together this quickly. We walked out of the store feeling as though we had conquered the world. We headed to my apartment before we grabbed a quick bite to eat. Cash was too impatient to let me change before we headed to the jewelry store. He said I looked fine the way I was. *Men—they didn't get us at all.* I had rolled my eyes at him, crossed my arms over my chest, and said fine.

As I walked through the door of the apartment, I immediately felt as though I no longer belonged here. Everything was still in its respective place and yet it felt empty. It was as though I had walked into a strange apartment even though I was surrounded by all of my things.

"Is it weird being here?"

I hadn't realized that Cash was right behind me. I let out a heavy breath that I hadn't realized that I had been holding in. "Yeah, it is. It doesn't feel like anything in here belongs to me. Does that make any sense?"

He laid a hand on my shoulder. "Yeah, it does. Think about it. Cole is your home. It doesn't matter where you live as long as he is by your side." He wrapped his tree trunk arms around me and squeezed. "Pack what you need for the week and next weekend we will get you moved out and into Cole's."

I nodded, not quite ready to verbally solidify anything yet. It didn't feel right being here and yet it was hard to completely say good-bye to it. I had only stayed with Cole a couple of days but it felt right. I quickly packed everything that I needed.

"Hey, what do you say to Jets?" I asked, lugging the suitcase behind me.

He rubbed his hands together. "Best idea all day. Think we can chance eating there or will you get us kicked out again?"

I laughed menacingly. "Guess we will find out."

As soon as we stepped through the doors of Jets, I about lost my cool. The smell of garlic and baked bread had saliva pooling in my mouth. My eyes glazed over. This place was utopia. If Cole and I didn't work out, I'd move into the apartment above. It would be the only way to survive the breakup. Cash maneuvered me away from the counter and into a booth. More like shoved but from the way that I had started psychotically staring at the girl behind the counter, it was for the best. I swear, the pizza was laced with crack. I turned into a cat that had its first taste of catnip. My synapses quit firing and my body turned ravenous. I couldn't believe that Cash let me come inside. Either he was crazy or sadistically enjoyed watching a potential freak show.

Cash plopped onto the bench seat and let out a heavy breath.

"What's up? Are you worried about tonight?" I asked, concerned about him.

"Nah. It feels right. The ring is perfect. You managed to pick out a ring that was exactly like Peyton, classic and elegant. I know that she will love it. Thanks for going with me today."

"Welcome but you still didn't answer my question." I stared him down.

"Are you sure about Cole?"

I ran my fingers through my hair with frustration. "Yes. I am one hundred percent sure about Cole. And you know what? I don't care if I'm wrong because being without him hurts worse than the fear of him growing tired of me." I looked up at him and smiled. "He threw me a bone and I snatched it up. And I won't ever look back."

He held his stomach as he laughed. "Only you would describe it that way. I'm happy for you then. However, if he hurts you again, I will kill him," he wheezed out, barely holding onto his laughter.

My laughter died down. "It won't be Cole who hurts me. It will be Victoria. She is evil, Cash, and she hates my guts. I can't figure out why, either. I have never said anything to deliberately piss her off. Once she found out that I was dating Cole, it escalated." I shook my head with disbelief. "She came over for lunch when we visited his mother. She never apologized for what she had done and she called me fat on top of that." I placed my head in my hands. "I don't know if I can stomach her for the rest of my life. As long as I am with Cole, I will have to deal with her."

He fumed. "Did Cole stick up for you or did he just let her lash out at you?"

"Oh my goodness. He was seething. His mother laid into her but it didn't stop her. That's okay because I got a good dig in on her being boney and that no man wants to be poked by a rib."

He coughed into his hand he laughed so hard. "I don't think you have to worry about her much. Sounds like you put her in her place. But I'm not afraid to hit a bitch."

My mouth hung open in shock. "No, you wouldn't."

"No, but I'd definitely hold her down while you kicked her ass."

"Thanks, big brother."

"Welcome. Now let's eat."

The same girl behind the counter delivered our slices and quickly retreated back to the safety of the kitchen. She was probably afraid that I would bite her hand if she stayed any longer.

Come to momma! I bit into the glutinous slice and moaned at the richness of flavors tantalizing my taste buds.

With my mouth full, I managed to sputter, "Best pizza ever."

My brother and I laughed until my sides hurt. Today reminded me of old times when we could simply hang out and talk. He was my best friend in every way. I didn't have any girlfriends I could turn to. Cash had always been my go-to and that would never change.

CHAPTER 28

I walked in the front door with my suitcase trailing behind me. I left it in the small foyer and searched for Cole. I found him in his mahogany recliner, kicked back and watching television. He looked damn sexy with bare feet, ratty jeans, and a white V-neck shirt that stretched across his cut chest. A wave of desire struck my midsection. His eyes met mine. The chocolate swirl turned black with lust. His chest heaved as he took a deep breath. A smoldering grin transformed his chiseled face into more of a fierce predator. The possessive monster spouted *all mine.*

I strutted over to him and straddled his lap. "Looking mighty fine, relaxing in your chair, Mr. Devlin." I pushed up his shirt, exposing his defined torso. I raked my fingernails down his quivering abs.

"It's all yours to do what you please." He licked his lips.

I found myself craving the taste of his mouth. I bent my face over his, inching my lips close to his but not touching. I could feel the warmth of his breath caress my lips. My tongue darted out and licked the seam until he opened for me. He gently pulled my bottom lip into his mouth and nibbled erotically until I moaned with ecstasy. I could dine on his kisses for days.

His hands roamed down my back, finding the hem

of my shirt and tugging it off. He tossed it to the floor carelessly.

While he unclasped my bra, his mouth rained smoldering kisses along my hypersensitive neck. "You are so beautiful."

I ran my fingers through his hair, grabbing a fistful as his mouth trailed down to my breasts. He licked the valley between my breasts before selecting one of my hardened nipples, grazing his teeth over the sensitive peak. I arched my back, jutting my breasts out for him to tease. I ground my hips over his swollen cock, pressing him to my moistened center. The need for him to be inside me drove me to the point of insanity. His fingers skillfully unbuttoned my jeans and pulled the zipper down, all while never taking his mouth off my breast. He switched to the other breast and swirled his tongue over the taut bud as his fingers slid underneath the thin lace of my panties. I tossed my head back as fingers slipped through my slick folds.

"Already soaking wet for me, love," he growled.

I moaned his name as he pushed two fingers inside my aching center. I ground my pussy shamelessly as his fingers fucked me. I cursed out when his thumb circled my clit. Breathing heavily, I murmured incoherently as I chased my euphoria. He gently bit down on my hardened peak. I cried out from the onslaught of sensations. My orgasm spread through my body like wildfire. My muscles clenched around his fingers as I rode wave after wave. He eased his fingers out of my pussy and drew them to his mouth. He sucked my essence off as though he were savoring his favorite dessert.

"You taste so sweet. Next time I'll be fucking you

with my tongue instead of my fingers."

My breath hitched at his erotic words, turning me on even more. His hands cupped underneath my ass as he rocked us out of the chair. He gently slid my body down his until I stood in front of him. Hooking my fingers in the waist of his pants, I pulled them down as I kneeled in front of him. His engorged cock burst free from the confines of his jeans. *Sweet Jesus, he wasn't wearing any underwear.*

He moaned and threaded his fingers through my hair as I licked my lips with anticipation. I hadn't even touched him yet and the ability to affect him like this made me greedy with power. I wrapped my hand around the base of his shaft and applied a little pressure as my mouth pulled him in. He thrust his hips the farther I drew him in. I used my tongue to swipe up and down as I sucked him in and out of my mouth. My hand followed my mouth, twisting slightly up and down. I placed my other hand underneath his balls and gently rolled them around my palm. As I sucked him harder, I felt his muscles begin to contract. He tightened his hold on my hair and he thrust into my mouth as he chased his own release.

"Fuck," he growled as his seed squirted into my mouth.

I milked his cock until every last drop of his semen filled my mouth. I swallowed it down as though it were the very thing I needed to survive. I slowly slid his cock from my mouth, licking the head one last time. His body twitched from overstimulation. I glanced up as he looked down and I smiled mischievously at him.

"You are one wicked woman. I am going to enjoy

watching you squirm, begging for me to fuck you." He playfully swatted my ass.

I yipped from the slight sting and yet was secretly turned on. *Might have to put that into play tonight!* I headed upstairs to grab a shower and get ready for dinner. Tonight would be epic. I couldn't wait to see Peyton's surprise when Cash proposed. My mother might have a coronary from all the excitement. My dad would be happy for him. I could see him slapping his back with congratulations and probably saying something along the lines of *it's about damn time you got your head out of your ass.* I chuckled to myself as I stepped into the steam that hung heavily in the shower. I stepped underneath the spray, almost scalding my skin.

I took the bar of soap and worked up the perfect lather. I bent over, soaping up my legs. I jolted, surprised by the growl that emitted from Cole. I hadn't even realized that he stood on the other side of the glass, watching me. He opened up the door, placing the front of his body to my backside. His thick erection grazed the crack of my ass. A raging heat slammed directly into my clit. I moaned from the contact of his body.

His husky voice seared a path of goose bumps along my skin. "Hand me the soap, Harlow."

I twisted and slipped him the bar of soap. He produced his own lather, running his hands up and down my body. He torturously skipped my heavy breasts. His hands soaped up my arms and legs with rapt attention. I pushed my ass into his cock, reminding him of what I needed. He chuckled devilishly as he continued his path over my shoulders and down my back. He inched his way to my ass and I squirmed with anticipation. He placed his hands around my waist and walked us forward until we stood in front of the shower tiles.

"Place your hands on the wall, baby, and spread your legs."

I loved when he commanded me and took control. I placed my forearms on the slick tiles in front of me, making sure to spread my legs wide enough to allow him the perfect access to my most sensitive and aching parts. I pushed my ass out and angled my head down as his hands trailed from my hips and cupped my ass. His palms circled my flesh, driving my desire to an all-time high. His fingers followed the seam of my ass down to my inner thighs and back up again. I was so ready for him to take me that my legs began to shake.

"Cole." I pleaded for him to touch me and fill me up.

"What do you need, baby?" He moved his body closer, hovering over my back.

"I need you to fuck me, Cole. God help me, I need it so badly."

With a moan he moaned and brought his teeth to the top of my shoulder and bit down as he inserted two of his fingers into my wet pussy. I cried out from the sensual sting of his bite and the pleasure of his fingers fucking me. His other hand massaged my heavy breasts. I felt the pull of my orgasm build. I wouldn't last much longer.

"You don't get to come yet. This is just the beginning." His voice dipped lower.

"Please," I begged him shamelessly.

I whimpered as he abruptly pulled his fingers out of

my aching center. I whimpered. I tried to twist around but he held me firmly in place with his hard body. He gently placed his hand on my back and bent me lower, causing my ass to push out further.

"So fucking beautiful."

I bit my lip, waiting for his next move. I was so turned on that my body froze in place, allowing him to manipulate me the way that he wanted. The same hand that had maneuvered me lower skimmed down my back and over each of my ass cheeks, massaging the tender flesh. His other hand cupped my mound, sending bolts of pleasure to my core. I immediately clenched my muscles, wishing that they were wrapped around his hard cock. His fingers slid through my slick folds, lubricating them as they continued their path past my taint to my asshole. I squirmed at the foreign sensation as he circled the rosette. Gently he inserted a finger, pushing in and out slowly. I tossed my head back and moaned at the pleasurable invasion. His other hand moved to my clit, circling the bundle of nerves.

"Cole, fuck—that feels so good. Don't stop," I cried out.

"Are you ready for me, baby? I'm going to fuck your perfect hole."

Oh, fuck yes! He pulled his finger out and replaced it with the tip of his dick. *Holy shit!* Inch by inch, he slid his thick cock inside my ass. I hissed as he stretched me. The sting lessened once he buried himself deep.

"Relax, baby. I got you."

He held still, allowing me to adjust to him. I sighed, relaxing my muscles, letting his cock invade my virgin hole. He continued to circle my clit, driving me to a whole new level of pleasure. He slowly pumped in and out of me, increasing the slow burn of desire to lick along my body.

"Fuck, Harlow. You are so fucking sexy. I'm not going to last long." His growl vibrated along my back, making me shiver.

He increased the pressure along my clit as he drove in and out of me. My chest heaved as the sweetest of pleasures built. I moaned as my pussy clenched and my sphincter muscle tightened around his pulsating cock.

"Ah," I cried out as my orgasm ripped through my body.

"Fuck," he growled as my body clamped down on his cock.

He thrust into me one last time as he grunted with his release. I rode wave after wave as his fingers continued their onslaught over my clit. The pads of his fingers caressed my body lovingly as he pulled out of me. He turned me around and attacked my lips with his teeth and tongue. I matched his fervor with my own.

He pulled back slightly. "God, I love you."

I gazed up at him through hooded eyes, fully satiated and my body feeling thoroughly used. I reeled from the effects of my orgasm, remaining speechless. He had driven my body to places that I never had known existed. He placed a kiss to my forehead and then washed my body all over again. I sighed, so in love with this man.

***

Cole parked behind my brother's truck. He ran to my door before I could step out. He held the door open for me. I smiled up at him and placed a loving kiss along his sexy mouth.

"You ready?" I looked up into his chocolate pools.

"Let's do this."

I chuckled and kissed him one more time for good measure. We headed up the pathway that led to the house.

"Mom. Dad," I hollered, announcing our arrival.

"In the kitchen, dear," my mom shouted back.

I squeezed his hand for comfort.

He laughed. "Don't worry, baby. I'm fine. They don't scare me."

They may not scare him but they sure as hell did me. This was the first time I had brought any man home. My body was coiled with nervous anxiety. Before we got back to the kitchen, he halted our movement. He hauled me back to his chest and wrapped his arms around my waist.

He enveloped me with his warmth and whispered into my ear, "I love you. I'm not going anywhere."

My body immediately relaxed. I released a breath that I hadn't realized I had been holding in. "Love you more." I marveled at his uncanny ability to immediately know what I needed to calm my anxiety.

As soon as we walked into the kitchen, my mother pulled me into her arms and hugged me as though she hadn't seen me in years. She kissed my cheek and smiled lovingly at me. Then her gaze sought out Cole. She gently pushed me aside and embraced him in the same tight hug.

She kissed both of his cheeks. "Thank you for bringing our daughter back." Her eyes glistened with tears, as did my own. He looked down, obviously uncomfortable with the praise.

My dad slapped Cole on the back. "Come on, Maggie. Let the poor man breathe."

"Oh, I'm sorry. Yes, of course, dear." She dabbed at her eyes with the pads of her fingers.

Cole nodded at my dad for the reprieve.

The door opened and I could hear Cash and Peyton come into the house. They were about as quiet as a herd of elephants. Peyton rushed through the kitchen and threw herself upon me, knocking the wind out of me. I laughed at her and hugged her back.

"It's so good to see you again. You look positively radiant," she gushed, looking between Cole and me. "And I can see why you are." She giggled as though she revealed some big secret. I couldn't help but laugh along with her. She was a fantastic woman and I couldn't be happier to have her become apart of our family. Well, that is, if she said yes tonight.

"I could say the same for you. You must've dumped my brother." We both laughed like hyenas.

He came up behind her and pinched her ass. She squealed, twisting around, and thumped him on the shoulder. He never flinched, hauling her lithe body against his and kissed her as though she were his favorite flavor. My cheeks inflamed, feeling a bit uncomfortable with their display. It was totally hot and yet vomit-inducing at the same time.

"Cash, my goodness! Save it for your own home," my mom admonished as her own cheeks held a twinge of pink.

My dad just shook his head and chuckled. "Reminds me of us, Maggie, when we didn't have any children. We couldn't keep our hands off each other."

I covered my ears and yelled for my dad to stop. My mom simply giggled, turning a shade of red that I had never seen before. Cole pulled my back up against his chest and placed a teasing kiss along my neck. I shivered as desire drenched my core. I pushed my ass in to his hips, loving the feel of his cock swell.

"Mmm. You'll pay for that, love," he growled along my ear as he nipped along my earlobe.

I squirmed, trying to ease my throbbing clit. "I hope so."

My mom clapped her hands, getting everyone's attention. "Alright, let's move this to the dining room and eat. I don't know about you all but I am famished."

I laughed as I left the warmth of Cole's arms to help my mom distribute the dishes around the table.

I had lifted my first bite of chicken to my mouth when my mother cleared her throat. *Oh shit!* I looked up, praying that she had latched her sights on Cole. *Fuck!* She had the dangerous twinkle in her eyes and the *trust me* grin busted out. I had no clue what crazy thoughts were racing through her brain at the moment but I knew it would totally embarrass me. I couldn't think of anything fast enough to catch her attention.

"Cole, dear," she began.

I would so get a load of shit for doing this but I had to stop her whole "intentions" conversation before it started. I knew exactly what that sly devil was up to. I plucked the piece of chicken off my fork. I held it steady between my fingertips. I took my aim and hurled the chunk toward my mother's plate. Unfortunately, my aim sucks as bad as my throw did. It hit her square in the chin, leaving an oily, Italian seasoned, wet mark. She looked over at me in utter shock. I couldn't contain my laughter bubbling up to the surface. The stunned expression on her face was completely hysterical. My whole body vibrated with laughter. After my mother sputtered incoherently, the rest of the family released their mirth. I reveled in my spontaneity. I had never in my entire life acted out. In my defense, I had to save Cole from the barrage of questioning that my mother was about to unleash.

"Damn it, Harlow. What the hell has gotten into you?" my mother boomed.

Holy cow, old Maggie had actually used a swear word and more than one in the same sentence. I have never heard her cuss. This made me laugh even harder as her face turned a shade of red that I had only seen once and then it was directed at Cash. He had decided to take the car for a joyride around the block when he was fifteen. I looked up at my dad apologetically, feeling a smidge of guilt.

Cole placed a hand on the inside of my thigh and

rubbed his thumb in small, delectable circles. Every so often, he inched his way higher, effectively shutting down my laughter. And so the punishment began.

I looked over at my mom. "I'm so sorry, Mom. It slipped from my fingers," I barely sputtered out.

My breathing had increased dramatically, making it difficult to act normal. His thumb abruptly ceased but he kept his warm hand placed on my thigh. I sucked in a deep breath as his knuckles rested against my panty-soaked mound. I was on the verge of combusting in my seat when his knuckles whispered along my covered folds. Thankfully everyone else around the table seemed too engrossed in their food to notice the way that I was acting. Even Cole had maintained his nonchalance by eating his dinner while maintaining my punishment.

"Is everything all right, Harlow? You are looking a little flushed and you have barely touched your dinner," my dad questioned.

"Yep. Everything is fine." I jumped up from the table. "Gonna go use the restroom. My stomach is a little off."

I hurried off to the bathroom. I shut the door and gripped the sides of the sink, trying to slow my breathing. Cole had really worked me up. *Maybe if I rub one out, I could go back to the table under control.* I seriously contemplated getting myself off in my parents' bathroom while everyone sat at the dinner table. I pictured the satisfied smirk on Cole's kissable mouth. I flinched from the muted knock on the door.

"You better not be touching yourself, Harlow. That's mine. Open the door." His gruff command spiked my arousal.

I hurried to unlock the door. My breath caught in my throat at his domineering stance. He stalked toward me until my ass banged against the counter of the sink. He twisted around and shut the door. The audible click of the lock engaging amplified my hunger.

"Hop on the counter and spread your legs. I want to see how soaked you are."

His command sent a current of electricity sparking across my clit. My center clenched with need as I hopped on top of the counter. He roughly bunched my skirt around my waist, exposing my black lacey thong. I sucked in a ragged breath, silently begging him to tear them off and fuck me hard.

"You won't be needing these anymore."

He grabbed the thin material that barely covered my slick folds and tore them from my body. I moaned in pleasure. He shoved them in his pocket. "That was fucking hot. Give me what I need."

"What do you need, love? Tell me and I will make it happen," he growled, reining in his own needs.

"I need you to fuck me hard and fast." My rapid heartbeat made me breathless.

"Fuck, love. You are trying to kill me, aren't you?"

I bit the bottom of my lip, waiting for him to shut up and thrust his thick cock inside. His fingers attacked his zipper, pulling his pants and boxers past his hips until his cock sprang free. He grabbed my waist, scooting me closer to the edge of the counter, and plunged his hard cock inside my throbbing sex. I tossed my head back, hitting the cupboard. I didn't care. The pleasure his cock elicited surpassed any pain that radiated from my head. He plunged in and out of my pussy as though I would disappear. Pleasure coiled tightly, signaling my impending release.

"That's it, love. I can feel you tightening around me. Take your pleasure. I'm not far behind you." His voice was laden with carnality.

"Ah, Cole," I hissed, biting down on my lip to remain as quiet as I could.

His mouth slammed over mine to swallow my moans as I rode out my orgasm. My inner muscles continued to milk him as he thrust one last time. He placed his forehead over mine. We stayed like that until our breathing went back to normal. He placed a gentle kiss along my lips, covering my whimper when he pulled himself out of my warm cocoon.

"Mmm, I could happily stay inside your tight pussy all day long but if we stay in here any longer, your mother will be tapping on the door, demanding us to open the door."

I giggled. "You're right. And for the record, I would love having you fill me up every minute of the day."

He winked as he plucked me off the counter and helped me right myself. We walked back to the dining room, looking exactly like the part we played in the restroom.

"Feeling better?" Cash sarcastically asked.

"Much. Thank you for your concern."

"Shall I grab dessert?" my mom interrupted before

Cash and I could start an argument.

"I'll help." Cash rushed out of the room.

I reached over and clasped Cole's hand, smiling like a fool. I was bouncing off the walls with excitement. I couldn't wait to see Peyton's reaction. They walked back and forth from the kitchen to the dining room, doling out a slice of cherry cheesecake to each of us. It was my favorite dessert that my mom made. The cherry sauce oozed off the sides of the slice, pooling into puddles of goodness on the plate. My mom sat in her chair with her plate. Cash served Peyton last.

"This looks scrumptious, Mom. I can't wait to dig in." I cooed.

We all gawped at Peyton, not wanting to miss her surprise. She didn't disappoint either. Her hands shook as she covered her mouth. Silent tears slid down her cheeks as my brother dropped to one knee. I coughed into my hand to stifle the giggle from watching him transform from a cocky bastard into a nervous wreck. My heart tugged in my chest when he spoke.

"Peyton, I don't deserve your love. I am a selfish bastard but I thank God everyday for sending you my way. It is your confidence and love for me that make me a better man, one that might one day be worthy enough for you. I promise to never take your love for granted for as long as I draw a breath. You have made my life meaningful and I want to spend the rest of my life with you wrapped in my arms. Will you marry me?"

She slipped from the chair and clung to him as she nodded her head yes. She cried softly as he put the ring on her finger. Her eyes twinkled with happiness when she spread out her fingers and looked down at her hand.

She tilted her chin up and touched her lips to his. She whispered a *yes* when he kissed the tip of her nose. He gathered her into his arms and pulled her up as he stood. We hooted and hollered when she turned toward us and squealed.

I pushed out of my chair and ran over to give her a congratulatory hug. "Welcome to the family. I am excited to finally have a sister."

She squeezed back. "Me too. I love you all so much."

"We love you too." I moved out of the way so that my mom could lavish her with her giddiness. I moved to Cash and hugged him tightly. "Congratulations, big brother. You picked a good one. I'm glad you finally got your head out of your ass and realized what a catch you have."

"Thanks, sis. I am one lucky son of a bitch."

I couldn't have agreed more.

EPILOGUE

ONE YEAR LATER

I found it hilarious to watch Cash slowly become unglued, waiting for his bride to walk down the aisle. I had just left her dressing room and made my way to stand next to my dad and the rest of the groomsmen. Thank God, Cash didn't make good on his threat and make me wear a tux. My outfit was the same coal-black as their tuxedos but that was where the similarities ended. The way Cole's intense gaze heated my body pretty much confirmed that I had chosen the perfect dress. The satin caressed my skin with every movement, reminding me of the way Cole touched my body. What was only hours ago seemed like days. I slid my gaze off Cole and peeked over at Cash.

I chuckled to myself as he switched from foot to foot. Then he would clasp his hands together and then unclasp them. Sweat beaded along his forehead. I felt a smidge of pity watching gleefully at his nervous state. I'm not sure whether he feared Peyton might change her mind at the last minute or the fact that he was getting married and in a church no less. His wing-tipped shoes hadn't caught fire yet. I'm pretty sure that the big man upstairs took pity on him today.

My dad leaned over and whispered, "So, when are you and Cole going to tie the knot?"

I tossed my head back and laughed uproariously, causing some stares but I didn't care. I looked over at

Cole and winked as I answered my dad. "Not sure. We are in no rush."

"Well, when you all figure it out, make damn sure I don't have to wear one of these penguin suits. They are uncomfortable as hell." He gently kissed my cheek and stood tall as the organ began to play.

One by one, the bridesmaids walked down the aisle in perfect formation and exactly ten-Mississippi counts in my head. They were an assortment of friends and family. What I adored the most was that she had asked her Aunt Sasha to be her matron of honor. Sasha brought up the rear and positively glowed. Between her and my mother, their excitement for the wedding and babies could generate enough energy to light up a small country. They had become quick friends throughout the wedding planning. Which turned out to be great for me because they never once harped on Cole and me to set a date.

***

Cole proposed a month after I had moved in and I greedily accepted. How could I possibly say no when he had gotten down on one knee while we were at the range? We had finished obliterating our targets and packed up our gear. Before I could grab the gear, he took my hand and bent at the knee.

"Harlow, you had stolen my heart from the moment I laid eyes on you, even though I didn't quite realize it at the time. You saw the real me when no one else did, including myself. I don't want to go another day without knowing that you belong to me in every way. Marry me and I promise to spend the rest of my days showing you how much you are loved." He looked up at me with a vulnerability that I hadn't seen since my car accident.

My heart bled for this silly man who thought that there was a chance that I would say no to him. A tear slipped down my cheek as I tried to form the words that I wanted to say but was having one hell of a time spitting out. I could only nod my head yes for my answer. He stood, reached into his pocket and pulled out the tiny black box. My heartrate accelerated to the point where I thought that I would pass out. He gingerly opened up the box. Before I could get a solid look at the ring, he pulled it out and slid it on my finger. I kept my fingers splayed and stared at the most gorgeous pear-cut emerald surrounded by diamonds set into a beautiful platinum ring. I couldn't even begin to fathom what this cost him. More tears trailed down my cheeks. It was more extravagant than I could have ever imagined and the best part was it was unique as I was.

I wrapped my arms around his neck and clung to him for dear life. This man was far too good to me. "Yes. Yes, I'll marry you," I exclaimed through my tears of joy.

***

I snapped out of my daydream when I heard Cash suck in a noisy breath. I looked up and watched Peyton begin her walk down the aisle. Her dad walked next to her, smiling proudly. She was the epitome of beauty and grace in one awesome package. Cash couldn't have handpicked a better woman to stand by his side. I envied her dress; it was absolutely stunning. She had picked out a vintage-style ball gown with a lace overlay. The pearl buttons that started between her shoulder blades and went down to her hips would be a headache for Cash later. I chuckled at the thought of his mammoth fingers trying to undo all of those little buttons. *Poor bastard!*

I looked over at Cash as he gawked at his beautiful bride. His mouth quirked into a boyish grin the closer she came. The adoration that shone in his eyes made me tear up a little bit. After her father had given her away to Cash, the ceremony proceeded rather quickly. Thank goodness, because all I wanted to do was eat some cake and tease my man. I loved to get him all hot and bothered, provoking him to threaten me with punishment. I loved every sentence he delivered. I highly benefited from getting him all worked up in public.

I zoned back in when the preacher announced, "You may kiss your bride."

I clapped along with the rest of the guests as Cash mauled Peyton. I couldn't help but turn my gaze in the direction of Cole. My face lit up like a Christmas tree when my eyes connected with his chocolaty pools. Desire punched me straight in the solar plexus. I was in church, so I sent a prayer up, begging God to never allow him to tire of me. I also thanked the smug bastard who knocked me onto that grate. Otherwise, I'd be here praying for something else entirely. While cat hair bonded to my rocking dress and my vagina resembled a dusty old attic.

We filed out of the church and loaded the bus that would take us to the reception. My brother made it very clear that it was for the wedding party only. Cole followed behind us. I pushed my way to the front to get to Cole quicker. I hopped off the last step and sashayed to my man.

I jumped into his outstretched arms. It was my

favorite thing to do. I loved when he caught me. I wrapped my legs around his waist, covering his lips with mine. His skilled tongue had me wishing that we could duck out of the reception right this moment.

"You in a hurry to leave?" He cocked his head to the side, mocking my enthusiasm for wanting to go home.

"Yes. I want you all to myself, preferably naked. Can we go now?" I puckered my lips in a pout.

He teasingly swatted my ass and slid me along his body until my toes hit the pavement. "Be a good girl, love, and maybe I can whisk you away early."

I sighed heavily when he placed his hand in mine, interlocking our fingers and walking me back to the wedding party. I would have preferred to walk in with Cole but I had duties to perform. I pasted on my best smile and looped my arm through my dad's and waited for us to be announced.

It's customary to stay seated at the wedding party table but I shimmied my way toward Cole and my mother after the toasts were given. I scooted out the empty chair between him and my mom. I leaned over and kissed my mom's cheek before I pecked Cole on the lips.

"The ceremony was beautiful. I'm so happy that your brother finally settled down." She dabbed at her leaking eyes.

"It was wonderful. I liked the short part the best. Peyton is good for him. They will be happy." I patted her back, offering her more assurance.

"When are you two going to get married?" She dug

her nagging claws in.

Cole and I exchanged a secretive look before we both busted out laughing. I shook my head at her silliness. We sat in the midst of a wedding and she still managed to harp on me for being unwed.

Cole nodded at me.

"I'm just going to come out and say this." I inhaled deeply, gathering up all the strength I could. After I said my piece, all hell would break loose. Now was probably not the time to divulge our little secret but what the hell. A little drama on my brother's perfect day never hurt anyone. At least I hoped not.

Cole placed his hand along my thigh, supporting my decision to share our secret. I smiled at him lovingly. With my head held high and my eyes shining with happiness, I turned and faced my mother. "Cole and I are already married."

Her eyebrows shot up to her hairline. Both of her palms instantly covered her mouth as she gasped. She sat there, stunned, much longer than I had anticipated. Maybe I downplayed her disappointment. My leg bounced up and down as I waited for her to say something. Hell, at this point, I'd take a slap in the face from her.

She burst out laughing as tears streaked down her beautiful face. She leaned over and enveloped me in her arms. Her whole body vibrated along mine as she continued her laughter. Anxiety from her reaction crept along my skin. *Was she having a nervous breakdown?* This was so out of character for her. She pulled away as images of padded rooms and straitjackets flooded my mind.

Her strong hands cupped my cheeks. She placed a hard smacking kiss to my forehead. She looked over her shoulder and shouted to my father. "Steve, we are going to Alaska!"

I was stuck in the twilight zone. *What did Alaska have anything to do with eloping?* My confusion only made her laugh harder. My dad walked toward us at a snail's pace. His grin was unmistakably mischievous.

My head whipped from one parent to the other. "What the hell is going on? What am I missing?"

Mom patted my knee. "Your father and I made a bet after you and Cole announced your engagement."

"What kind of bet?" I questioned, still in a stupor over what was happening.

"Baby girl, you fail to realize that I know you better than you know yourself. Once Cole had popped the question, I made a bet with your father that you would run off and get married to avoid a traditional wedding. You are terrible with making decisions and with certain things, everything has to be perfect. Planning a wedding would have made you absolutely miserable."

"If you won, the trip to Alaska." I tilted my head up to address my dad. "What was your prize if I had gone through with a big wedding?" I asked with genuine curiosity.

He chuckled and winked at me. My mouth formed an *O* shape when it dawned on me. "Eww, gross." I shook my head, trying to rid the nasty vision. When I had gained control of myself, I asked uncertainly, "You guys aren't mad?"

"No, sweetie; not at all. It was the best decision for you. I am a little sad that I wasn't there to see you in your dress. I bet you were exquisite." She sighed wistfully.

"I had it videotaped. I will give you a copy," Cole piped in.

I turned around to face him. "You did?"

"Yep. I figured you might feel a little guilty that your mom wasn't there. I also made a copy for my mother as well. She didn't take the news of our elopement as well as your parents."

I threw my arms around his neck, placing kisses all over his face. "I love you."

"And I love you more."

ABOUT THE AUTHOR

Jenni Bradley lives in Indiana, with her husband, three daughters, four dogs, two cats, and four horses: pretty much a small, funny farm where there is never a dull day. She enjoys riding most days. The other days are usually met with hard dirt and a happy horse.

You can find Jenni online at jennibradley.com to find out more, plus news on upcoming books.

You can also find Jenni on Facebook at https://www.facebook.com/Jenni-Bradley-1453178658324928/

Goodreads at https://www.goodreads.com/author/show/14237910.Jenni_Bradley

OTHER BOOKS BY JENNI

The Midwest Series

Release Me: Book 1

Seduce Me: Book 2

Jenni Bradley

Jenni Bradley

Made in the USA
Charleston, SC
10 May 2016